*Couple Mechanics*

# COUPLE
# MECHANICS

*Nelly Alard*

**TRANSLATED FROM THE FRENCH BY**
Adriana Hunter

**OTHER PRESS**
**NEW YORK**

Copyright © Éditions Gallimard, 2013
First published in French as *Moment d'un couple*
by Éditions Gallimard, Paris, in 2013.
Translation © Adriana Hunter, 2016

Production editor: Yvonne E. Cárdenas
Text designer: Julie Fry
This book was set in Bembo with DIN by Alpha Design &
Composition of Pittsfield, NH.

10 9 8 7 6 5 4 3 2 1

Library of Congress Cataloging-in-Publication Data

Alard, Nelly.
    [Moment d'un couple. English]
    Couple mechanics / Nelly Alard ; translated by Adriana Hunter.
        pages cm
    ISBN 978-1-59051-731-4 (pbk. original) — ISBN 978-1-59051-732-1
(e-book)   1. Spouses—Fiction.   2. Adultery—Fiction.   3. Paris
(France)—Fiction.   4. Domestic fiction.   I. Hunter, Adriana, translator.
II. Title.
    PQ2701.L3M6513 2016
    843'.92—dc23

                                                           2015008473

All men are liars, fickle, false, blabbermouths, hypocrites, proud and cowardly, contemptible and sensual; all women are deceitful, artificial, vain, inquisitive and depraved; the world is nothing but a bottomless sewer where hideous shapeless sea creatures crawl and squirm over mountains of mire; but there is one sacred and sublime thing in this world and that is the union of two of these monstrous, imperfect creatures.

*On ne badine pas avec l'amour*
**ALFRED DE MUSSET (1810–1857)**

**COUPLE**, in mechanics, pair of equal parallel forces that are opposite in direction. The only effect of a couple is to produce or prevent the turning of a body.

*—Encyclopaedia Britannica online*

# PART ONE

# 1

It was Thursday, May 29, 2003, late in the afternoon. Ascension Day. Still springtime, then, but already very hot. The lawns in the park at Buttes-Chaumont weren't blackened by the crowds but brightly colored, exuberant with noisy, active families. There were balls, beach towels, squeals, laughter, little panties drying on the grass, children running around naked or in their underwear; there was something Popular Front about it, the first paid vacations.

Juliette had arrived early. She was sitting next to her friend Florence in one of the most sought-after places, a wide sloping lawn with the river below. They both were watching their children paddling with other kids in the stream when Juliette's cell phone rang.

Juliette had just called out to Johann, her four-year-old son, to keep his sandals on when he walked in the water. Not only because of the pebbles that carpeted the riverbed, which could be sharp or slippery, but also, more importantly, because there could easily have been broken glass, used condoms, or beer cans. There could easily have been pretty much anything, in fact, even though the park was shut at night and watchmen made regular rounds.

Emma found a ski pole at the bottom the other day. Can you believe it? Who would do that, throw a ski pole in the river at Buttes-Chaumont?

Juliette still had a smile on her lips as she picked up the phone.

It was her husband, Olivier. His voice sounded strange, as if he were breathless, or choking.

Where are you? —At Buttes. —Are you alone? —No, I'm with Flo and the kids. —Can you go somewhere else? I have something to tell you.

Juliette's smile had vanished. She glanced at Florence, stood up, and walked some thirty feet up the slope. Olivier seemed to be sobbing on the other end. What's going on? she asked. Before hearing the reply, she felt a kind of biting sensation in the pit of her stomach. She thought maybe Maria was dead.

Okay, so. I'm seeing a girl, she's a Socialist politician, it's been going on for three weeks, and now she wants me to leave you. We were just on the phone, and when I told her I was going to the movies with you, she had an epileptic fit. She's dropped the phone, she's screaming, I don't know what's wrong with her, I don't know what to do, I have to go see her.

He caught his breath, added:
I won't make it to the movies.

Juliette listened, motionless. From where she was now, high up, she could see the gazebo and the suspension bridge, a couple kissing. The sun was starting to go down over the trees. Apart from the nasty little critter doing its thing in the pit of her stomach, everything felt familiar, normal.

Where does she live?
Pantin.
Well, go then.

A pause. He didn't answer. He hadn't hung up, though.
This irritated her. Go then, she said again, and Hello several times, her voice increasingly loud and exasperated. Then she hung up and came slowly back to sit down beside Florence, who was eyeing her inquisitively.

What's going on?

She shrugged, shook her head. Flo didn't push it. Anyway, it was time to go home. They called the children, dressed them, then walked along the avenue Secrétan in silence, holding their younger children by the hand while the older two ran ahead boisterously.

When they reached the crossroads with the rue Baste where Florence lived, they parted. Juliette kept walking, looking at the road ahead as she waved an absentminded good-bye. She could feel the weight of her friend's puzzled expression but didn't let it bother her. Later she'd explain things to her. Later, when she'd recovered the power of speech, when this still unintelligible event had reached a competent area of her brain. Florence, as usual, would understand.

Florence understood everything.

Juliette had known her since they were teenagers, since Sainte-Euverte school. They'd ended up as neighbors in the late nineties, when quite independently and with their respective partners, they'd each decided to buy an apartment here. The explosion in Parisian real estate prices had made the Nineteenth Arrondissement the only neighborhood in central Paris still accessible to the thirtysomething first-time-buyers they were at the time. Sure, the proximity of the place Stalingrad with its drug dealers, the virtual ghetto sprawling around the rue du Maroc, the density and sheer size of the public housing tower blocks on the boulevard de la Villette, not to mention the bad reputation of local schools, were massively off-putting factors for potential buyers, particularly in the case of couples thinking of starting a family, which they were. Confronted with this situation, the group of friends they had at the time—comprising a high proportion of journalists and underemployed performers of various descriptions—had fallen into two camps. Some had chosen the suburbs, mostly to the east, and congratulated themselves on this decision. For the others—a group that included Juliette and Florence, and that was mostly originally from the provinces—moving outside the beltway would have been worse than repudiation, a sort of condemnation. This schism between the neosuburbanites and the Parisians-at-any-cost was the subject of impassioned discussion for months. From then on, every invitation to dinner from one camp or the other sparked off the debate again, with everyone standing their ground, the suburbanites proudly showing off their seedy scraps of garden on summer evenings, while the Parisians politely went into raptures but secretly pitied them, delighted they themselves had chosen the convenience of public transport and the cafés along the Saint-Martin Canal over the illusory peace and quiet and graffiti-covered warehouses of Montreuil.

In fact the neighborhood was very pleasant. The market on the avenue Secrétan was bustling, the Butte Bergeyre dripping with flowers, the attacks at knifepoint barely more frequent than anywhere else in Paris, and the whole earnestly left-wing gang sang the praises of the social mix that was imposed by economic constraints but that, when you got to know it, turned out to be a valuable asset, an indisputable factor in their children's development. The fact that the National Front had reached the second round of the previous year's presidential elections, on April 21, 2002, had been a major wake-up call for them all. Having voted for the Socialist Jospin from the start, Juliette herself had a clear conscience. But those, like Olivier, who'd allowed themselves to be tempted by the Green Party or the far left were now struggling to atone for their sins by signing up for the Socialist Party and getting involved in the fight for the homeless or schemes to tackle illiteracy.

Of course they weren't naively optimistic; circumstances in the neighborhood were far from rosy. One time a group of frantic mothers had gathered outside the day-care center.

A caretaker had found a kid in the schoolyard playing with a syringe that had been thrown over the wall by a junkie. Miraculously, the swiftly performed HIV test proved negative. As far as schooling was concerned, things were even more complicated for those who lived on the far side of the place Stalingrad, toward the rue du Maroc and the rue de Tanger. Several of them had caved when they found their little darling was the only child of European origin in the class. They'd decided to forgo the spacious apartments complete with terraces overlooking the canal that the Paris council rented to them at favorable prices, and withdraw to minute square-footages in the bosom of less working-class districts. It was their most fundamental right. The others bemoaned their leaving but never actually criticized them. After all, no one could say what the future held. They couldn't exclude the possibility that once their own children were old enough for junior high, their legitimate parental concerns might end up toppling their political convictions. They couldn't exclude the possibility that some might prove willing to commit the basest acts to outwit the school allocation system. That others might go the private route. But at the point when this story takes place, this was all far from their thoughts because Emma and Jeanne, Juliette's and Florence's older children, were still only six.

Once home Juliette hovered, undecided. She didn't feel like going to the movies anymore. But she'd arranged for a new babysitter to come over this evening. It would be awkward, not to say impolite, to cancel someone she didn't know at the last minute. The front doorbell put an end to her dilemma. It was a young Senegalese girl who seemed gentle and kind. Juliette concentrated on the instructions she needed to give, the recommendations she should make, then kissed the children and left. When she was out on the place Stalingrad, the bustle did her good. She walked to the Quai de Seine movie theater down by the river and looked at the posters. She and Olivier had been planning to see *Un homme, un vrai*; the critics were saying all sorts of good things about it. "The convoluted life of a man and woman," according to the synopsis. No, thank you, she thought. The screen next door was showing François Ozon's *Swimming Pool*: "A suspense in suspense, an anxiety waiting to happen, a permanent danger," according to *Télérama*. She bought her ticket and went into the auditorium.

Toward the end of the movie, not once but twice, her cell phone, which she'd made a point of putting on silent, started vibrating, making a plaintive growling sound like a muzzled dog tugging at its chain. Oooooh ooh. Oooooh ooh. She huddled down in her seat and checked who the calls were from, without throwing too much light on the people near her, to reassure herself it wasn't the babysitter trying to get hold of her. The calls were from Olivier's cell. She shuffled deeper into her seat. A few seconds later she heard the small, stifled yapping sound indicating she had a message. Ten minutes after that, it happened again. And then again five minutes later. In the end she gave her purse a good kick. Up on the screen Ludivine Sagnier was naked and Charlotte Rampling was crying, then it was the other way around, dead leaves floating on a swimming pool, Ludivine Sagnier killing Charlotte Rampling. Or the other way around. She didn't try to understand. Before the end of the film she disturbed everyone in her row to go to the restroom, taking the opportunity to listen to the three messages Olivier had left for her. He was outside the movie theater, looking for her. She returned to the auditorium and stood at the back to watch the last few minutes until the credits. She was the first to head for the exit.

# 2

In a girl's life, it's the father who establishes the pattern.

Juliette's father had left her mother when she was five years old.

Of course, she convinced herself it was her fault.

*He's gone.*
*Her mother's crying.*
*She's frightened.*

That's her first memory.

After a lot of crying, her mother threw herself into sleeping. Juliette's father had made a new life for himself a long, long way away. Juliette didn't really see him again until she reached adulthood. Her mother spent long bouts in rest homes and entrusted Juliette's care to her grandparents until their declining health meant they could no longer take the responsibility.

Walled up in her depression, Juliette's mother was incapable of looking after her daughter. And so she made the obvious decision.

She decided to wall Juliette up too.

She signed her up as a boarder at Sainte-Euverte.
Sainte-Euverte was an excellent boarding school for Roman Catholic girls. It was by far the best establishment in the Limoges area. Juliette's entire education from sixth grade to twelfth grade was spent there.

Sadly, she did not find faith there.

Sadly. Because only a divine love could have filled the immeasurable need for tenderness Juliette accumulated deep inside herself during her teenage years.

Tenderness was an unknown commodity to the Dominican sisters.

At Saint-Euverte the girls were guided with a hand of iron inside a horsehair glove.

At Saint-Euverte Juliette developed an acute sense of survival in hostile environments.
It was there that she had her apprenticeship in injustice, humiliation, and duplicity.

From a strictly academic point of view, Sainte-Euverte's reputation for excellence was in little danger, and Juliette was a brilliant pupil.

For other issues, everything probably depended on the initial terrain.

On well-tended plots, which should be construed as the filthy rich, reactionary Catholic families who constituted the bread and butter of the school's clientele, Sainte-Euverte knew how best to cultivate the young seedlings entrusted to its care and took pride in its ability to turn out perfect future wives and future mothers, destined to become the cream of the crop of Limoges high society.

On the soil of a disintegrating family like the one that produced Juliette, it was a whole other story. So when she left at the end of twelfth grade with her final exams and excellent grades under her belt, it was perhaps inevitable that despite the sisters' efforts, they'd only succeeded in developing her into a pretty head brimming with ideas and absolutely on fire, desperate for freedom, for revolt; a weather vane ready to swivel in line with whatever iconoclastic winds were blowing at the time. And those winds would converge in a paroxysm of enthusiasm at the place de la Bastille one evening in May 1981 with the election of a left-wing president.

But more than anything else, she was impatient to set out on a discovery of the male continent, having only the vaguest of notions of what that was, and it seemed all the more exciting because she knew pretty much nothing about it.

At night Sainte-Euverte's dormitories had been the scene of intense experimentations. Books and seventies feminist magazines in which sapphic practices were pretty much openly encouraged were circulated in secret. The Sainte-Euverte girls didn't take much persuading. On those Sainte-Euverte nights Juliette was an adventurer setting out to discover her own body and the cloying softness of another girl's, the moist warmth of a woman's core. Beneath the sheets she plied herself with different-shaped objects, trying to illuminate the mysteries of pleasure and penetration. But despite the nefarious arousal these episodes afforded, she was well aware that she was only acclimatizing herself by default to this too-wet, too-sweet tropical dampness and that in order to attain the giddying summits of pleasure, this whole performance was lacking the main ingredient. And when, barely a month after she had left Saint-Euverte, in the confines of her twin bed she discovered the stiffness of a man's erect penis, grasping it with her hand, soft and hard as a well-polished wooden stick, she knew that she'd found her calling and that the love of a man would be what her life would revolve around.

# 3

How's the epileptic? Juliette said lightly as she sat down.

When she'd come out of the movie theater, she'd immediately spotted Olivier standing with his back to her by the la

Villette waterway. He was looking at the far bank. It was dark, the lights in the windows of buildings opposite were coming on one by one. Since this movie theater had opened in a former warehouse soon after they moved to the area, the face of the place Stalingrad had changed a lot. Cafés and restaurants had appeared, and across the water, the quai de la Loire embankment had been prettified as a promenade. Juliette had walked along there for hours on end, pushing first Emma and then Johann in the same baby carriage. Later, when they'd started walking, she often used to load the stroller onto the ferry to the park, to take them to play in the Jardin des vents.

Despite the darkness, she'd recognized him, his tall silhouette, the way he carried himself, with his hands crossed behind his back, his chin tilted up slightly. She went over to him, stopped about three feet away. He turned around, smiled apparently casually, and asked whether she'd liked the movie. She didn't answer but gestured to the nearby brasserie.

All around them the embankment was seething with happy crowds making the most of the warm evening. People were clustered around the entrances to the movies, standing in line for ten o'clock screenings, while others emerged from the previous movie in compact groups. The lights were reflected in the water, a boat passed; there was a holiday mood in the air. There were no seats free on the terrace of the nearby café, so they took a small table inside.

How's the epileptic? she asked again.
Olivier's face clouded.
It's not funny.

He made his voice darker still and added, It's actually pretty tragic.

Oh, she said.

Apparently she's really sick. I didn't know, I just found out. One of her friends was already there when I arrived. He explained. Something about a past rape, if I understood it right.

Stop, she said. I don't give a damn.

Which might seem harsh but is more easily understandable if you know that Juliette too had been raped and that Olivier was of course meant to know this. Unless he'd forgotten—he was sometimes prone to peculiar bouts of amnesia. Or conversely, unless he thought that discovering this additional common ground would fill Juliette with instant compassion for the woman who was sleeping with her husband. If this was the case, it was a gigantic error in judgment. Raped or not, the potential for empathy in Juliette toward this person whose existence she'd only just learned about was minimal—in fact it was pretty close to zero.

Which is why she said, Stop, I don't give a damn. There are only two things I care about: One, do you want to leave us, leave me and the kids?

No, he replied immediately, without any perceptible hesitation. No, that's not what I want.

She didn't try to disguise her relief.

Good. Two, are you in love?

He hesitated. Stammered something that was neither yes nor no but that ended with: It's powerful, yes.

Oh, shit, shit, shit! Juliette sighed.

She put her face in her hands, covered her eyes, murmured: I really don't want to go through this.

Don't want, don't want. It's so banal. So mediocre. I feel I've been through it a thousand times, in books, through other people, by proxy. Not us, not to us. So sure it would never happen to us, to the two of us, you and me.

Meanwhile he was trying to make her understand that actually there was something exceptional about this, it wasn't banal at all, not banal, not for him anyway, exceptional actually.

But it always feels exceptional to the people experiencing it, she interrupted him, devastated, dropping her hands and looking him in the eye, you know that, that's exactly what makes it banal.

So what do you want to do?

Olivier let himself slump against the back of his chair, hesitated a moment, sighed.

I'm going to have to extricate myself from this, I guess. But it'll take a bit of time.

Juliette turned away, waved an arm in the air as if she were drowning, tried to attract the attention of a waitress. She needed a scotch. But the place was packed, smoky, all the staff were frantic. No one took any notice of her.

You have to realize I didn't want this to happen, Olivier was saying. He sat up tall and tried to catch her eye. It happened to me, that's all, and at the time I thought it wouldn't change anything between us. I even thought it wouldn't matter much to you, I have to say. But to explain, I'd have to tell you everything from the beginning. How it happened.

Surely not, she said, turning toward him and lowering her arm, tired of waiting. I don't want to know a thing. Not where or when or how. I don't even want to know her name.

Olivier looked disappointed. He really would have liked to tell her, clearly.

We'll get to it one day, we're bound to, he insisted. Right from the start, in the back of my mind I've thought that I'd be able to talk to you about it later. I still think one day that'll be possible.

No way, she said. Not now or later. Why did you tell me, anyway?

I couldn't help it, I had to explain. I couldn't make it to the movies.

She shrugged. Bad excuse, she thought. He could have kept lying. Invented some problem with a deadline, a piece that needed finishing urgently. She was so trusting, never asked any questions, it wasn't difficult.

Maybe, he said. But it's a relief too. I feel better now.

She nodded.

Good for you. Because I personally feel like shit.

They still hadn't been served, and now Olivier was the one getting frustrated. It was always like this here. You had to beg to get some overworked waiter to deign to take your order, which then took hours to arrive or, 50 percent of the time, never showed up.

This place really is crazy, he said.

In the end he got up and went over to the bar. When someone finally brought their drinks, she took her glass of scotch and immediately ordered another, defying her husband's obvious disapproval. Right now she didn't give a fuck.

Maybe if it were a fun thing at least. But this is already so over the top, isn't it, the Nervous Breakdown, the Psychodrama...If she gets in this kind of state just because we're going to the movies together, believe me, I know that sort of girl, in ten days we'll be calling one-one-two.

He laughed. That's really not her style. Really not. I can't explain because you don't want me to talk about her, but she's been elected to local government, and she even went to the École Normale Supérieure.

Juliette sniggered softly. Am I supposed to be impressed?

It might be interesting to note that later, when the two of them went over this conversation, Olivier flatly denied saying the words "she even went to the École Normale Supérieure." He said they were the sorts of words his father would have said, and in those circumstances it would have been pathetic to have talked like his father.

And yet he did say them, those words, Juliette is convinced. But never mind.

The alcohol is beginning to have an effect; she's not used to drinking two whiskeys in quick succession like that. She's gradually relaxing, everything's becoming unreal. There's her husband, sitting facing her, nothing's changed between them, nothing need change, he agrees, soon this will all be in the past. Unless. Except if.

She's thinking out loud, looks at him attentively.

Do you want to carry on with this relationship and also stay with me? I haven't said I was prepared to accept that, and on this first evidence, neither is she, but if it was possible, is that what you'd want in your heart of hearts?

No. So long as you didn't know, possibly, but now that you know, no.

Good. End of story then, Juliette thinks, but the discomfort is still there. A strange sensation like a film where the resolution comes before the intrigue, where the reels have been switched around.

They finish their drinks in silence. It's time to go home. They walk across the place Stalingrad side by side, a little way apart, not running any risk of touching, even by accident.

In her relationship with Olivier, Juliette often had the feeling the reels had been mixed up. Their story hadn't made any sense right from the start.

There was their first kiss and, two weeks later, their first night together.

Between these two events, Olivier had met Maria and had already been unfaithful to Juliette.

As a result of that they split up, then three years later they met again and got married almost immediately.
Only then, a month later, did they move in together and introduce each other to their families.

Meeting then Betrayal then Love then Breakup then Marriage then Living Together.

What the hell.

Since their children came along, things seemed to have settled into a normal pattern at last.

But it seems the projectionist was still hitting the bottle and getting the reels wrong.

Back at the apartment, they paid the babysitter, then headed for the bedroom. She asked him what time he'd be leaving for Rome the following Saturday.

I don't think I'll be going.

Oh yes you will! she exclaimed. I want you to go, it'll do me good not having you around for a few days.

She stroked his cheek. It'll do you good to go too. It'll change your headspace.

Olivier didn't answer.

Just one thing, she added. If you have to leave me, leave me now. Not when I'm fifty. That's really disgusting.
He smiled.
I agree. I get it. It's okay.

Alone in the bathroom, she rummaged around in a box and found a strip of sleeping pills only just past their expiration date. She took one, went and lay down next to Olivier, and fell into a deep sleep, with her back to him.

Two hours later she woke with her heart hammering, bathed in sweat. Johann, her little boy, was sleeping right up against her. She hadn't heard him come in and slip into their bed. Shoehorned between him and his father, she was now dying of the heat and couldn't get back to sleep. She got up carefully and picked up her son, making every effort not to wake him. She took him back to his own bed, then returned to her bedroom and unceremoniously woke Olivier. She was crying. Groggy, disoriented, and tousled, all he could manage was to keep saying: Go back to sleep, please, try to rest. Don't cry. We'll get through this.

I just need a bit of time.

# 4

It was an enchanted interlude.
It wouldn't last long.

In 1975, amid booing, the French parliament voted in Veil's law legalizing abortion for a probationary period of five years.
In 1979 a new law established the legislation definitively.

As for the contraceptive pill, it had been available and reimbursed by social services, including for minors, since 1974.

The sky was bright, and the way ahead looked clear.

It wouldn't last, but no one realized that yet. By the mid-eighties AIDS would be casting its shadow, weighing on the shoulders of the young. But in the meantime, right at the end of the seventies, when Juliette left Sainte-Euverte, moved into university digs in Limoges, and pursued her studies in the sciences, the world was her oyster, and freedom welcomed her with open arms. Despite a few reservations—inevitable after several years spent in a girls' boarding school—about the Intrinsically Good Nature of Women, she had joined a "women's group" and subscribed to a feminist review crammed with capital letters emphasizing well-chosen words ("Paternalistic Press," "Pharaohs of Power, Pharaohs of Powers") and littered with puns on words such as "man-datory."

Juliette rarely managed to read an issue all the way through but let herself be lulled by the "multiplicity of letters in words," which were like "so many women bound together and safe in their womanhood: warm and straightforward, rich and concise, eloquent and sincere." A sort of decompression chamber after Sainte-Euverte, so to speak.

Was it in *Women in Movement* that Juliette first read about lunaception? No, most likely not, because it was too serious a magazine to promote such a whimsical method. What is for sure, though, is that the contraceptive pill had a bad reputation in *Women in Movement*. A chemical product that altered a Woman's Ovarian Cycle could only be viewed with suspicion. So Juliette used a diaphragm and spermicidal cream as her method of contraception, a system whose effectiveness had been tested and measured to be 97 percent.

Before each sexual encounter she slipped away by herself for a moment to take the thing out of its case, open the tube of spermicide, and deposit a thread of cream around the circular rubber edge. She finished by putting a large hazelnut-size blob in the cupped membrane. Then, pressing the circle into a flattened oval between two fingers, she eased the contraption into position and checked it was sealed over the neck of her uterus, before going back and throwing herself into the arms of her lover for the day. Granted, in the heat of the action it wasn't always easy to discipline herself to do this, but she stuck to it all the same. Still a student, on the brink of what she imagined would be a brilliant career, there was no way she could allow herself to get pregnant, and she was sufficiently responsible to envisage abortion only as a last resort. As for condoms, she'd never seen one. They seemed to belong to a barbaric age now long gone, and if a man had offered to use one, she was unlikely to have consented because she felt so strongly that contraception was exclusively the preserve of the Woman. My Body Is Mine and my responsibility alone; she'd learned that lesson well.

To be even more sure, she added a pinch of lunaception to the diaphragm method, bathing her naked body in moonbeams every time the opportunity arose (which sadly meant not very frequently) in order to synchronize her cycle with the Female Heavenly Body. She conscientiously avoided making love when the moon's quarters weren't favorable. By doing this, she thought she would reduce her likelihood of contraceptive failure from 3 to 1 or 2 percent, but she probably hadn't exposed her body to the moon enough, or the statistics must have underestimated the fertility of girls her age, or both. In any event, Juliette became pregnant when she was just eighteen years old.

# 5

People were "bridging" Ascension Day with the weekend and taking the Friday off. Neither Juliette nor Olivier was working. And the children didn't have school either. Juliette looked at the sky and thought they could have gone to the country. But three weeks earlier Olivier had decided that he would spend a couple of days in Rome this very Saturday. Three weeks earlier. As they were finishing lunch, she sent the children to play in their bedrooms and, without really thinking, just to be sure, she said:

Put my mind at rest, this weekend in Rome, it doesn't have anything to do with all this, does it?

He shrugged.

I've been talking about it for months.

You've been talking about it for months but you made up your mind three weeks ago. And yesterday you told me this had been going on for, yes, three weeks. His eyes were evasive. She looked at him incredulously.

So you were planning to go to Rome with her?

I'm going to cancel it, he muttered. I told you that yesterday, I'm not going.

You were planning to go to Rome with her, she said again.

She suddenly felt overwhelmed. It was in Rome that her relationship with Olivier had started. She pictured him taking the plane the next day with this other woman, the phone calls over the next few days, her thinking about them together there in the sunshine, wandering through the streets, chatting on café terraces. Impossible.

Where were you planning to stay with her? At Maria's apartment?

A few months earlier Olivier's ex-girlfriend had found out she had breast cancer. It was even one of the reasons that had allegedly helped Olivier make up his mind to visit her.

The tone of his reply to Juliette was clearly intended to point out her heartlessness:
Maria has better things to worry about. I didn't want to mix her up in our problems.

After a pause he added, But Katarina's in the know. She's just had an affair herself. It ended badly, actually. She confided in me one time when she was in Paris. I talked about my situation too, and she said we could stay with her. She's the only person who knows.

That sucked. That really sucked. Katarina had come to visit the year before with her husband and their little girl. Now she was going to have Olivier over with his "mistress," as they say in trashy stage plays. Juliette could feel her hands getting clammy.

I don't see what difference it makes, Olivier was saying stubbornly. Would you rather I'd spend money on a hotel?

Juliette shrugged.

Either way, it's a no. If you go to Rome with her, I warn you, when you get back you'll find your suitcases outside the door.

I'm going to cancel, he said.

A moment later he added: I bought a nonrefundable ticket. It's money down the drain, but hey.

Juliette didn't reply, but her thoughts must have been written all over her face because he didn't press the point.

I'd better go let her know, he said. She's already packed. I'll go right away.

Call her, she said.
I can't tell her on the phone, he retorted. That would be cowardly.

Juliette laughed quietly.

Whereas calling your wife on her cell phone to tell her you're cheating on her and leaving her to get her shit together with the children while you go off to comfort your girlfriend, you didn't have any issues with that?

He had his impenetrable look on his face.

I can't, he said again. I really have to go.

Okay, she said with a vague impression she was reenacting an already familiar scene. Go then.

When Olivier closed the door behind him, it was two in the afternoon.

Juliette cleared the table and sat down for a while to think. Although she was off work that day, she'd asked Yolande, their Caribbean nanny, to come look after the children at the usual time so she could go to the hairdresser. She was a regular at a ridiculously expensive salon near her office in the Eighth Arrondissement; it was one of the few luxuries she allowed herself. Olivier had tried to persuade her of the merits of their local hairdressers, but she had stood her ground as much out of vanity as a need to demonstrate her independence. This particular day she felt less inclined than ever to make concessions to her husband's economizing. After all, she earned more than he did, was financially autonomous, and wasn't accountable to anyone.

Sitting in her robe by the bay window with a pile of women's magazines before her while she waited for Fabrice to attend to her, she tried to take her mind off things by watching the entrance, the flurry of drivers dropping off customers, smiling receptionists in the lobby, manicurists offering their services. Close to her a very elegant brunette was describing her latest trip to Saint-Barth in a high-pitched voice. That was the sort of woman the word "adultery" had been invented for, thought Juliette. All at once she was crushed by sadness again, and she gazed at her reflection in the mirror.

Like all women of her generation, or nearly, she thought she didn't look her age, and like all women of her generation, or nearly, she was right, although "looking her age" was a difficult concept to define accurately. In its rather muddleheaded way, what it meant to Juliette and to most people was that she looked much younger than her mother had at the same age. This objective and indisputable fact was not due only to the illness and abuse of medications that had prematurely worn her mother down. Juliette's generation had seen women so radically emancipated that they seemed to have conquered a good ten extra years of youth as a sort of bonus. They were now deemed entitled to powers of seduction and an active sex life pretty much up to menopause, and notwithstanding plain arithmetic, Juliette had only a very abstract notion of passing time and felt much closer to her childhood than to that particular phase. She felt very close collectively to all the Juliettes she had been, and maintained constant, affectionate conversations with these former versions of herself that constituted who she was, with the significant exception of the few years following her rape, years that were like a black hole in which Juliette had lost track of herself; the person she was then had been wiped from her internal radar screen.

Right now it was the fifteen-year-old Juliette looking at herself in the mirror, trying to make her reflection coincide with the image she had always had of a betrayed woman.

She couldn't.
*It was impossible.*

She couldn't accept that this was happening to her now. To her. Adultery. The very word conjured bourgeois dramas or fusty vaudeville acts. Inside the word "adultery" was the word "adult," that couldn't be coincidence. She felt as if Olivier's confession had propelled her violently into a new stage of her life. It was the end of dreams, youth, ideals. His way of telling her she was just a little woman like all the rest. The previous day he'd looked amazed that she wasn't persuaded by his argument that he felt he was somehow allowed to betray her because "everyone was doing it." He seemed to think it was a solid argument, a really good one that couldn't be countered in any way. That was probably what she resented him for most, for seeing theirs as an ordinary sort of love, a banal love, there wasn't far to travel between banal and mediocre. The celebrity magazines she started leafing through to clear her thoughts had headlines about people she'd never heard of. She was barely past forty, and all of a sudden she felt old.

Seized by a blast of inspiration when the hairdresser asked her what she wanted, she asked him to cut it. Short. She'd had long or mid-length hair since she was a little girl and had never had the nerve to go shorter than a chin-length bob. It was now or never: Olivier was cheating on her. A page had been turned. This was one way of registering that fact.

Next she went to see the doctor, having managed to secure an appointment that morning. The doctor's office was in the Eighth Arrondissement too, a short hop from Juliette's work, which made it easy for her to drop in when she had a cold or sore throat without eating into her workday. There were actually two doctors, sisters, one called Haddou and the other Haddou-Duval, and Juliette never knew which one she was talking to until she was handed her prescription and one of the names had been crossed out. Most likely identical twins. She went straight into the large waiting room, which was stuffy and completely deserted, there was no reception area. The place was old-fashioned, and its cleanliness dubious, fairly surprising in a neighborhood like this. After a long fifteen minutes she spent gazing, motionless, at the stains on the carpet, the doctor's door opened. A slightly chubby, plain-looking middle-aged woman in a white tunic said Juliette's name before standing aside to let her in.

What can I do for you? she asked.

Juliette claimed she had a backache and allowed herself to be examined swiftly. She waited until the doctor was sitting at her desk and had started writing out a prescription before adding nonchalantly, as she got dressed:

And I'd be grateful if you could prescribe me some Bromazepam.

Dr. Haddou (Duval?) raised an eyebrow as she looked up.

Is there something you're worrying about?

My husband's just told me he was having an affair, Juliette heard herself saying with masochistic jubilance.

The doctor nodded, not showing any surprise or compassion or any particular interest. She went back to her prescription and, still scribbling, asked: Will one box be enough, or would you like two?

Perhaps this was routine for a doctor in the Eighth Arrondissement, Juliette thought as she left the office. Perhaps in this very bourgeois neighborhood Dr. Haddou (Duval?) spent most of her time prescribing tranquilizers and antidepressants to ultrarich, idle, cheated-on wives. She looked at the prescription in her hand. Duval.

On her way back to the subway station she walked with her head tilted up toward the Haussmann-style buildings on the boulevard Malesherbes, trying to imagine the apartments behind their tall windows. Given the price per square meter in the neighborhood, they'd be worth a fortune. So who could afford to have an apartment like that in this day and age? No one she knew, anyway. Who were these mysterious inhabitants of the Eighth Arrondissement whom she never met anywhere, not at work or on vacation or in any of the places where her social life took place? Even in their working-class neighborhood, she and Olivier wouldn't have been able to afford buying a place now. Prices had nearly doubled in seven years. Those of their friends who'd missed the boat at the time were forced to continue renting, probably for life, and even paying rent was becoming more and more difficult. It suddenly occurred to her that Paris must be populated by millionaires or wealthy heirs, people she came across in the street without even realizing it, or she could only guess they were there, lurking in their cars with tinted windows, because it seemed unlikely people like that would ever take the subway. She was surprised to find herself daydreaming about this world she had glimpsed at the hairdresser's, where women wearing designer clothes and expensive jewelry sipped cocktails as they confided their marital woes to each other before amusing themselves with draining their husbands' astronomical bank accounts. Which must be quite a consolation, whatever anyone says.

She went home, gave the children their supper, put them to bed, and then started watching a documentary on the arts channel. At ten o'clock she looked at her watch. It was eight hours since Olivier had left.

She picked up the phone.

He answered immediately. He was coming out of the subway, walking quickly, short of breath. I'm on my way, he said.

He's back. Lets himself drop into a chair, looking exhausted. Looks at her.
You had your hair cut, he says.

An observation that requires no commentary.

So? Juliette asks.
So I told her. It was awful. She unpacked her bags. She screamed. She cried.
For eight hours?

He looks surprised.

Eight hours?

That's how long you've been gone. I don't mean to be petty, but I'm struck by a certain lack of proportion: five minutes on the phone to tell the woman you've been living with for ten years that you're having an affair with someone else, eight hours to tell the girl you've known for three weeks that you're not going away for the weekend with her.

Silence.

Let's drop it, she says. And now?

What, now?

What did you say to each other about what happens next?

I told her I needed to think, that I didn't want us to see each other or talk for ten days. Anyway, I have some paid leave to use up before the middle of June, I thought I could go to Aubigny with the children. Use the time to think things through.

Juliette looks at him, totally incredulous.

You didn't tell her it was over?

No, I told her we're not going to Rome, I didn't tell her it was over. I didn't say I would do that, Olivier retorts warily.

I must have misunderstood, Juliette murmurs.

She smiles feebly. If it takes you eight hours just to cancel a weekend, set aside a good week to tell her it's finished.

He softens slightly. You need to give me some time, Juliette. I need to go about this gently. Believe me, it's not easy.

# 6

It was her fault.

He'd made that perfectly clear.

*Her fault, her fault, her fault.*

And he was right, you really did have to be very stupid, all that stuff about lunaception, everyone had told her.

In her defense, she did also use a diaphragm, 97 percent, let me reiterate.

Diaphragm or not, her fault anyway, stupid, stupid, stupid.

The doctor, a man of about fifty, made sure she was well aware it was her fault, then was so sweet. She'd asked him what to do—luckily she was an adult, only just—where and how to make an appointment, which hospital, how the whole thing worked. He'd put his hand on her shoulder, really sweet.

Are you sure you don't want to keep it?

Oh God, was she sure, übersure. She had exams to take, and the father, the father-to-be, well, the ex-father-to-be, the soon ex-father-to-be, okay, the boy, didn't even know about it.

You're three weeks pregnant, no more, I can do it here.

She opened her eyes wide, amazed.

When?

Right away, if you like.

It was too beautiful to be true. She would have kissed him if she'd dared.

This guy was so sweet, really.

An hour later she'd left his office bent double, in tears, the fucking bastard, that knitting needle he'd driven into her—you have to know what you want, young lady—like in the days of backstreet abortionists, her with her feet in stirrups, shrieking at such pain, indescribable, pure torture, end of story, and the bastard went on talking, talking while he rummaged around in there, come on, come on, it doesn't hurt that much, try to relax, you should have thought first, only just stopping short of calling her a pathetic little whore, what do you mean, stop? But I haven't finished yet, be a shame for you to leave now, you'd still be pregnant, well, whatever you want, but now I'd really recommend you go have an abortion unless you want to give birth to a monster, ha-ha-ha, because I must have messed it up a bit already, your little ectoplasm, ha-ha-ha, that'll be one hundred twenty francs. The sadistic bastard probably enjoyed making her scream, poor stupid, poor stupid, poor stupid little bitch.

A fortnight later, Juliette had had an abortion in the hospital under a local anesthetic while the nurses, they were so sweet too, joked among themselves and chatted about their weekends, nothing to complain about here, not that it was anything to laugh about, but she didn't feel a thing, that was all that mattered.

She came out of there with a prescription for the pill. Which one should I give you? the doctor had asked, a woman this time, they make minidose versions, even microdoses

now, it's better for you, you know, at your age, no, thank you, not the mini or the micro, thank you, I'd rather have the normal one, Juliette said, I know the risks but I don't give a shit if I get cancer later, I want the highest dosage, I want the megadose, I don't want
Ever
To go through this again.

# 7

Hey, weren't you meant to be going to Rome? Stéphane asked.

This Ascension weekend was going on forever. On Saturday morning they'd met up with a whole group of friends for a picnic at Buttes-Chaumont. Olivier was standing next to Stéphane joking, making expressive gestures as he talked, sandwich in hand. Sitting a little way away next to Sylvia on a checkered tablecloth on the grass, Juliette watched him.

Since April there had been a succession of strikes in the national education system. In their children's school a lot of teachers had joined the strikes. Parents had to juggle between emergency nannies, their own paid leaves, and fellow moms who took turns taking a day off and running a day-care center at home.

But the day before, it had been announced that the strikes might spread to transport services.

In the circumstances, Olivier couldn't leave Juliette alone with the children, he explained, not to mention running the risk of ending up stuck in Rome for an indeterminate period.

Stéphane, Paul, and the other men in the group nodded understandingly.

Two-faced asshole, thought Juliette.

To think she'd always thought Olivier was a bad liar.

The next day they had lunch with friends in the country, not far from Paris. Olivier was going to drive on to Normandy afterward. He'd insisted on taking the children to Aubigny, but Juliette had refused to let Emma, who was in first grade, miss any more school. So he would take just Johann, and she would catch the train back to Paris with their daughter.

Shortly before sitting down for lunch, she took him off to a corner of the garden.

Just one thing. You didn't sleep with her, did you, yesterday?

That evasive look again. Again Juliette felt her stomach knotting.

I thought you realized that, he replied.

No, she said. No, it may seem incredible, but I hadn't even thought of it.

She looked at him coldly, like a stranger, with the beginnings of disgust.

Be careful. I do hope you understand that soon the problem won't be breaking up with her, it'll be not losing me.

Emma appeared at the open window. She was watching them.

Mommy, why are you mad at Daddy?

Juliette sighed. I'm not mad at him, honey. We're just talking.
She waited till their daughter had gone back to her games before continuing.

And Aubigny? You're not going with her, by any chance?

He shot her a hostile, offended look.

I've told you, I'm going there to think. *And* with Johann there. What do you take me for?
I don't know, Juliette replied. I don't know anymore.

She went back to help in the kitchen and made it her job to cut up the melon. After Olivier and Johann had left, her friend took her and Emma to the station at Mantes-la-Jolie.

Juliette loathed commuter trains. This one had two-story carriages. She asked Emma whether she'd rather sit upstairs or downstairs.

Upstairs, Emma said.
Up we go then, said Juliette.
But halfway up the stairs, she noticed that there was one solitary male passenger in the upper compartment and was gripped by a familiar terror.

*Never take commuter trains, particularly on Sundays or in the evening.*
*Quiet times are the worst.*
*Never take the high-speed subway either, particularly the C line, midafternoon.*

But you can't say the normal subway is safe either.
Nor any street really, after a certain time of day.
In big cities, women are prey. But not only women, and not only in big cities.
Little country roads aren't safe either.
Obviously, at this rate you'd never leave your own home.
Not to mention that in your own home you can be a victim of domestic violence.
Even at home you have to be on your guard.

It happened a few years after her rape.

She'd taken the high-speed subway, ignoring all the precautionary rules. She'd stepped into the carriage without looking around.

She should have been careful, the corridors and platforms were deserted. She should have been careful, even though it was three in the afternoon, even though it was the middle of Paris, even though the sun was shining brightly.

She'd got on at Javel station.

She was reading.

What was she reading again? She can't remember. Everything that happened just before the event has been wiped from her memory. She knows she never finished that book. It stayed in the carriage.

She'd already been reading on the platform. She got in without looking up from the page. She sat on the first folddown seat by the doors.

The doors closed. The train set off. A few seconds later there was a noise and flash of movement. She felt something cold and sharp against the back of her neck, under her hair. She looked up and saw a human dick pulled out from lowered pants, erect in front of her at eye level. She heard a voice saying clearly: Suck me or I'll kill you.

She felt a shiver down her back, and a strange, sinister calm spread through her. To fend off the most immediate danger, she grasped the wrist of the hand holding the blade to immobilize it as best she could. Then she looked up and saw the face that this voice, this wrist, this blade, and this dick belonged to. She saw an open mouth and bulging eyes. She knew without a shadow of a doubt that he was high as a kite.

She thought: Here we go, it's happening to me. In theory at this point she should have seen her life flash before her eyes. Her grandfather, the house with the blue shutters she'd lived in as a child, Sainte-Euverte. But not at all. She imagined the future, her mother, the world without her. She saw the headlines in the next day's papers, imagined her face on the front page of *Libération* or *Le Monde*, which can't possibly be normal, which must be a unique pathology, which must have a name, an acute form of narcissism or furious megalomania or God knows what. Either way, it was seriously disproportionate because these things are everyday occurrences and the best there would have been in *Libération* or *Le Monde* was a small paragraph, in the society column on page 8. Perhaps half a page if after her death the man had been especially relentless. The higher the number of knife strokes, the more abuses he inflicted on her before finishing her off, the greater her chances of making the eight o'clock news. She just had time to see her image projected behind the presenter Patrick Poivre d'Arvor, a vast and rather flattering photo, when the man, who clearly had other things to get on with—even though this review of imaginary press and media coverage must have taken a maximum of an eighth of a second—showed signs of impatience. He made a slight movement of his wrist so that she felt the point of the blade against her skin, and he said the same thing again louder, as if he genuinely thought she hadn't heard properly the first time: Suck me or I'll kill you.

She held the wrist more tightly, trying to move it away from her neck a bit, looked back down at the dick, and tried to reason, as she'd read somewhere it was advisable to do in these situations, even though it seemed strange entering into conversation like this with an erect penis. But that didn't last long because the man immediately drove the knife blade in a little, proving to her that this was urgent and that neither he nor his dick was in any mood for discussion. This time she felt her skin giving way over a fraction of an inch, the blood beading on her neck.

She closed her eyes.

The problem of course was not fellatio per se. Fellatio per se was something Juliette practiced willingly, although preferably with people she knew and for whom, if possible, she even felt a degree of attraction. As it happened, there was nothing appealing about the erect dick before her. What's more, it was giving off a strong stench of urine, which really bothered her because she'd unfortunately inherited from her grandmother a very acute sense of smell, which, as everyone knows, is cause for far more inconvenience than pleasure.

But that wasn't the worst of it.

The worst of it was this scene was taking place in the late 1980s, and any sexual promiscuity with a junkie—or a presumed one—carried a certain number of risks about which Juliette was very well informed.

The subway train was making a terrible racket, it must have been running parallel to the Seine, it was hurtling along, in a few minutes they'd draw into Champ-de-Mars-Tour-Eiffel station.

She urgently needed to make up her mind. Juliette had to answer the Shakespearean question that confronts every human being at some point in his or her life, which was confronting her anyway in that high-speed subway train, on that summer afternoon, in all its brutal simplicity.

*To be, or not to be.*

*To live, or to die.*

*To suck, or not to suck.*

Actually let's stay downstairs, sweetheart, said Juliette.
Okay, Mommy, Emma replied meekly.

A few stations farther on, three men piled into the carriage just before the doors closed and climbed up the stairs to the upper level. There were cries, the sounds of a scuffle. Juliette held her daughter tight. No one downstairs moved, all the passengers seemed to have turned to stone. It went on for several minutes. Then at the next station the men came down and fled along the platform, followed by the other passenger, whose face was streaming with blood. Only then did someone set off the alarm.

The train stood still for a long time. Men in uniform arrived and busied themselves on the platform. Juliette couldn't make out whether or not the aggressors had been caught.

He got sliced, someone said.

All that to steal his cell, sighed a woman sitting beside her.

What happened, Mommy? Emma asked.

She tried to explain the situation, without lying, but without terrifying her either. You're not in any danger, I'm here to protect you, baby.

And as she said these words, she was bitterly aware of how ridiculous they were, how hopelessly powerless she was to protect anyone. So she buried her face in her daughter's hair and squeezed her close.

They'd only just arrived home when the phone rang. Your son wanted to say good night to you, said Olivier. Still shaken, Juliette tried to describe the episode on the train but soon gave up. He was hardly listening.

I'm going to put Johann to bed now. But call back later, please, I'd like us to talk.

At around ten o'clock, when Emma was finally asleep, Juliette called Aubigny. The phone rang for a long time before Olivier eventually picked up. He was out of breath. I was in the garden, he said.

They exchanged a few niceties, but Olivier wasn't very talkative.

Did you want to tell me something?

Nothing in particular, he replied.

How are you feeling? She persisted.

I don't really know, he said evasively. I need time. And you? She hesitated.

I don't feel like making big pronouncements, she said, but you've broken something, I think.

*She'd ended up on the platform, alive.*

She'd planned her strategy well. She'd given him a hand job as best she could, trying to make sure his pleasure culminated precisely as the train drew into Musée-d'Orsay station.

As the carriage stopped, right when the pneumatic door closure system gave the characteristic *tshhh* that means it's unlocking, the man was gasping, on the brink of ejaculation. She'd shoved him with all her might, pushing the knife away from her at the same time. He'd lost his balance and fallen to the floor. She'd launched herself at the door, lifted the handle, and landed on the platform just as the *ding* sound announced the doors were about to close.

The doors had closed, the train had left, the man hadn't moved.

She'd looked at her hand, which was shaking slightly, and hadn't seen a single drop of sperm.

She'd gone into a drugstore and bought a bottle of disinfectant and completely emptied it over her hands.

She didn't press charges that time either.

She'd only glimpsed her attacker's face, anyway. She wouldn't have been able to make an identikit picture, well, maybe of his dick, but that wouldn't have been enough, that would surely have been tricky, as far as the inquiry was concerned.

# 8

Juliette is walking along the street. It's the day after Olivier left for Aubigny, so it's Monday now. It's time to go back to work. Unlike Olivier, she has no vacation time to use up. She took all her days together during the school holidays, as had been agreed with her company. The alarm this morning woke her from an exhausting, twisted dream: She was at a holiday club in Tunisia or somewhere like that, she wanted to go back to swim in the warm sea but wasn't allowed to, she was being forced to stand among strangers in scorching sunlight to play a game whose rules she didn't know. She found it hard to get out of bed, feeling shattered with a thick head and stiff limbs as if she'd had a night of heavy drinking. Probably the Bromazepam, she's gotten out of the habit of taking medication to help her sleep. She dropped Emma at school and then headed unenthusiastically toward the subway to go to work.

She came out at Villiers station and is now walking along the street, elegant in jeans and a tailored jacket with her bag slung across one shoulder. Men watch her, and for once, she notices. When Juliette walks along a street, men usually look at her, and she just looks at her feet. People often comment on this. Her feet or something else: the sky, a shopwindow, someone begging, or a child playing. So used to sensing the attention of men that she doesn't even realize it's happening. But this morning is different, there's the unfamiliar blast of air on the back of her neck, making her shiver a little, she should have worn a scarf, but no, that would have been ridiculous in this weather—they're saying it's going to be over eighty degrees—it's just that she has short hair now and it's still early in the morning. It's more to do with the fact that there's a new fragility in her, like a crack in porcelain, and it's making her seek out eye contact with strangers today when she normally scrupulously avoids it—mustn't behave like a tease, mustn't encourage advances. She wants to catch their eye so she can cling to that attention and read in it the fact that she's still beautiful, still young and desirable, despite being tired, despite being betrayed.

She goes into the converted eighteenth-century mansion block that houses Galatea Networks' offices, waves to the receptionist, and pours herself a coffee in the bar area of the cafeteria. In the pretty tree-lined courtyard through the bay windows, coworkers are sitting at a teak table, having an animated conversation. The decor is refined, luxurious without being ostentatious, something you'd associate more with a fashion empire or a publishing house than a company that specializes in new technology. But the founder and CEO of Galatea Networks, one Denis Madinier, is a brilliant and eccentric fiftysomething, an aesthete with a soft spot for medieval architecture and baroque art. With his newly acquired fortune he's apparently bought himself a Cathar château and is having it renovated stone by stone. A few years earlier he'd kept a similarly close eye on the conversion of the mansion where he'd chosen to set up his young company when it started to grow. The staircase rising up from Galatea's entrance hall is monumental, with a magnificent banister in sculpted raw oak. Juliette lets her hand trail up it every morning on her way to her office on the second floor. She never takes the elevators.

When people ask Juliette what she does in life, she says she's a "technical project manager," which doesn't mean anything to anyone. If they probe further, she adds that she works in tandem with a "commercial project manager" who's also her immediate boss, although he's younger and less qualified than she is. This is partly due to the fact that she's "technical," therefore not so well remunerated as if she were "commercial." (At this point the person she's talking to is usually completely baffled. Exactly what is the mysterious economic equation by which the person who sells an ultra-sophisticated computer system is worth more in a company's view than the one who managed to design and perfect the system in the first place? It defies the most elementary logic but appears to be a generally accepted fact, and anyway, that's just the way it is.) This difference in salary of course also derives from the fact that Juliette is a woman, and her two periods of maternity leave, not to mention the four-day week she secured after Emma was born, have not helped her professional progress, to say the very least.

Besides, Juliette shares her office with other "technical project directors"; she works in an open plan space. Which is significant in what happens next.

Recently the atmosphere at Galatea Networks has been electric. Rumors of a hostile buy-out from a competitor have put everyone on edge. Some suspect that now that his company is quoted on the Alternative Investment Market and he's hit the jackpot, Madinier has no more pressing business than to sell the enterprise off to the highest bidder and put his feet up in his thirteenth-century château. That must be what her coworkers are talking about in the courtyard. These rumors are in fact very well founded; the future will be proof of that. But for now Juliette couldn't give a damn. She stays there, standing alone at the bar. Then, once she's finished her coffee, she goes up to her office to get her files together before slipping down to the basement for the coordination meeting that takes place every Monday morning.

There's still no one in the meeting room besides the general manager, Chatel, and the commercial project manager, Pissignac. They're standing, coffees in hand and deep in conversation, only half aware of Juliette, whom they greet with an absentminded nod. Neither of them seems to notice she's had her hair cut. This doesn't surprise her. Management takes sexual harassment very seriously. None of the directors would risk complimenting a coworker on her new hairstyle. Feeling strangely invisible, Juliette sits down and takes out her files just as Chatel casts a knowing eye over Pissignac's new suit; it was made to measure by the tailor he recommended to him. Pissignac effects a cool, detached attitude and, not wanting to be outdone, goes into ecstasies about his general manager's shoes; Chatel promptly promises to give him his shoemaker's address. Juliette nibbles her pencil. She's waiting patiently for her bosses to stop chatting about fripperies so the meeting can finally start.

It's not until the end of the morning that Olivier calls her. A quick word to ask whether she'd be kind enough to call back because he's gobbled up (his words) all his phone credit. Obviously she finds this strange. Because Olivier usually complains when he opens their cell phone bills and is always trying to convince her to switch to a cheaper contract. Seeing we never use up all our minutes anyway, he says.

It looks as if this month is the exception that proves the rule.

So she calls him back and says: Hey, you seem to be making a lot of calls for once.

On the other end she hears the same little laugh he's given a few times in the last few days, the one she doesn't quite know how to interpret.

For once, yes. That little laugh, which may just be embarrassment but which does actually sound like a flattered little laugh, satisfied even. Can Olivier really be feeling satisfied deep down for the pain he's inflicting on her? The word that comes to mind is "smug." That's it, a smug little laugh. She must remember to tell him this laugh doesn't suit him at all, in fact it literally makes her want to throw up. But now's not the time. She'll have to tell him one day, when things have calmed down.

He's getting ready to take Johann to play on the beach. He doesn't mention "the other woman." Juliette still doesn't know anything about this other woman. She still doesn't want to know anything. More than once over the course of the long weekend Olivier attempted a few confidences, but she immediately made him stop. I don't want to know, she'd said. I couldn't give a shit about her life, I don't even want to know her name. She's putting all her energy into not thinking about them, not imagining anything, and the incredible thing is she's almost managing it. For three days she's managed to ward off the image of Olivier sleeping with another woman; she's driven it out of her mental field of vision with all her strength. She feels that if she allows it to take shape in her mind, the mental picture will then follow her everywhere forever, like an image of mutilated bodies that you just can't forget, like that beggar she once saw in Lisbon: He appeared from nowhere, brandishing his stumps before her eyes; she hadn't had time to look away, and those stumps come back to her with no warning, they wake her with a start in the night. She knows this will be the same, the image of another woman's body intertwined with her husband's is a hideous vision that would loom between them every time Olivier put his hand on her. If he still puts his hand on her, that is, if they stay together for years to come. I so wish this had never happened, she thinks for the hundredth time. I so wish I could erase it.

They've hung up. As the hours go by, while Juliette stays glued to her computer screen, drafting a reply to an invitation to tender that she's been working on for several weeks, the vague feeling of disgust provoked by Olivier's laugh morphs into a far more familiar fear. Olivier is alone with their son, that's for sure. But the very thought that he might be spending hours on the phone with this woman causes her absurdly, unbearably intense suffering.

It occurs to her for the first time that she might be the one with a problem. Why doesn't she just chuck him out? This inability to accept loss, the idea of being unloved.

Although she always resisted psychoanalysis—she was too rational for it, too impatient, and also associated it too strongly with her mother—though she did have to spend some time with therapists after her rape. One of them once asked her to speak out loud to the five-year-old girl somewhere deep inside her who had been abandoned by her father. Feeling ridiculous, she'd gone ahead and after only two words had started sobbing. Weirdly, it did her good at the time. She's tempted to try it again, slightly curious to see where that younger Juliette has got to now, because it's been a while since she's sent any news. But she soon gives up. It's not a good idea at work. Particularly when your office is open plan.

Changing tactics, she searches through her e-mails for the one she received recently from a long-lost boyfriend who tracked her down on the Internet, and while she's at it, she calls him. This is fantastic, he says. They agree to have lunch together soon, although she stays as vague as she can about dates. Franck asks her a bit about her life, then sums up: So, you've settled down? She laughs feebly and asks: What exactly do you mean by that? —Well, you meant so much to me... —Adventure, freedom, she cuts in derisively to smother the sadness and regret washing over her. —Um, yes, but, you know, we're getting older...No, it's fine. Just have to watch our weight. —That's not a problem for me, she says. He laughs. —You're lucky. I'm on a diet.

Later she walks out of the office, and at the end of the corridor, near the restrooms, she leaves a message for Olivier. There can't be any signal where he is, they must be down by the sea. I just wanted to tell you I'm not feeling great. I said earlier I was fine, but I'm not. I'm not fine at all. I'm having anxiety attacks, I feel like I'm going to pass out.

After hanging up, she wonders exactly what she said, what her voice sounded like. She's tempted to replay her message. There's nothing to stop her from calling Olivier's number again and listening to the messages, he always uses the same pass code, and she can't imagine he's taken the precaution of changing it. She toys with this possibility a moment, then rejects it, rejects the thought of hearing an unfamiliar woman's voice saying things she doesn't even want to think about. She thinks of those Eastern figurines with their hands over their eyes and blocking their ears. See no evil, hear no evil. If only she didn't have to know the evil. She hadn't asked any questions, after all. She doesn't believe the truth is always a virtue.

As she comes out of a meeting that afternoon, she finds a text.

"What I want is for us to carry on together. If that's still possible."

She can't help noticing he's found the most economical way of saying it, now that his credit's used up. Olivier's never been a man for grand declarations. He's the type who thinks acts are enough. And Juliette now realizes she has nothing to show for this love, for these ten years of life together. Two children, an apartment, but not the tiniest little letter, the tiniest scribbled note to prove they love each other, anything to tell her when it was they stopped loving each other.

The public transport system is completely paralyzed by strikes at the moment, so she decides to walk home. In spite of everything, Olivier's message has gone some way to dispelling her fears. She feels less jumpy. When she's walked for an hour, the vibrations of her cell tell her she's been left a voice mail from the house in Aubigny. She keeps on walking, not wanting to shatter her precarious sense of calm prematurely.

Just before she's home, still in the lobby of the building, she listens to the message. Olivier wanted to know whether Johann likes omelets. She looks at the time, no point calling back about that, they're bound to have eaten already. As she goes up in the elevator, she wonders whether his text said: "All I want is to carry on" or just "What I want is to carry on." Out on the landing she checks. He said, "What I want." So that doesn't preclude him wanting other things.

Carrying on seeing this girl, for example. She exchanges a few words with the nanny, kisses her daughter, and rushes to the shower. She's dripping with sweat.

Emma, who still sucks her thumb, comes to look at her naked.

How can you tell when you have milk in your boobs? she asks.

You can't really tell, she replies. It's just when you're nursing, your breasts get bigger, and sometimes a little bit of milk comes out.

I'd really like to have milk in my boobies, Emma says. But what I'd *really* like is to have hot chocolate. I'd like to have a whole bunch of things, apple juice, chewing gum, McDonald's. That would be cool.

Very cool, sweetheart, Juliette agrees. Very useful.


# 9


About her rape, the real one, there wasn't much to say. It had been a nonviolent rape, which is the ultimate kind of rape, the kind that drives you really nuts, because you didn't fight, you didn't struggle, you were a passive victim, as they say, it sounds so easy, doesn't it? So she'd been not only raped but passive, two harmless words but two complete mindfucks; it took her a while to realize this, even longer to get over it. It was the early eighties, and no one even talked about passive victims, and from a distance, from close up even, from the man's point of view, a passive victim looks very much like a consenting woman, as long as you're not really looking, as long as you don't pay attention, especially when, like her, she sleeps around a bit without making the boys beg, when she considers herself liberated, as she did at the time. She'd been twentysomething, but she was far from a virgin; she could hardly blame the guy, she had only herself to blame, meaning she hadn't fought or struggled, she'd been paralyzed with fear.

Basically it was the kind of rape that makes the guy think it was exactly what she wanted, little bitch; she'd often pictured him going home as if nothing had happened, kissing his wife, he was a nice, regular guy, the marketing type with a beautiful car, most likely a company car, what does it matter? In fact she believed it too, that nothing had happened, she'd done everything she could to believe this, and she'd succeeded, almost, give or take a small detail, really very small, like a few years of lost youth, a career stopped in its tracks, a sudden all-embracing inability to project herself into the future. While her contemporaries who'd graduated at the same time as she had swept up all the best jobs in international consultancy firms or went off to study at MIT, she'd put all her energy into carving a gaping hole in her résumé, living off menial work, spending hours under her comforter, drinking tea and eating tranquilizers; this little excuse for a life had gone on for a good three or four years, with the predictable consequence that she would one day end up as an obscure project manager reporting to a Pissignac, but that was the least of her concerns. She no longer saw anyone, had decided to read Proust, Balzac, and Zola and all of Russian literature from Gogol to

Gorky, she didn't know what she was looking for or what she was running away from, she was just trying to survive, the therapists put it all down to her mother, her depression, the whole thing, and she agreed, or the fact her father abandoned her, yes, that was also a possibility—and what about the tranquilizers in all this? To be fair, she wasn't sure she'd ever really told her therapists about the rape, couldn't be sure she hadn't thought it was completely insignificant, she was in total denial, no, it's true, at that point it's not about resilience anymore, it's denial, plain and simple, unless it's just stupidity, plain and simple stupidity, either way that's what happened, it was her own personal victory, she thought, that in the middle of the total disaster that her life had suddenly become, she denied the, let's face it, obvious cause-and-effect connection. It was her way of resisting her very private downfall to convince herself that the rape had nothing to do with it, was unconnected, just a passing incident, in fact in the early days she talked about it openly, with a sort of lightness that amazed people—my goodness, the naivety—she talked about it occasionally, not making a song and dance, she even made goddamn jokes about it, what was she thinking? She thought that in this day and age and in her country it was no longer a dishonor to have been raped; this wasn't Berlin in 1945, when girls who'd been passed around fifteen Soviet soldiers then found their fathers handing them ropes to hang themselves with, this wasn't Iran or Libya, and if there was one thing she knew for sure, it was that her own personal honor and pride lay elsewhere. But she soon realized how wrong she was because it may well not be a dishonor, but most people seem to have very fixed ideas about how a girl who's been raped should behave, about how she should talk about it, and the way Juliette talked about it meant that a lot of people had unpleasant doubts as to how true her story was. So she'd stopped the talking, but gradually, insidiously, something of those doubts had insinuated itself into her and festered into guilt. Afterward, every time she read a newspaper report or the firsthand account of a rape victim who'd fought back and got away, a living model, so to speak, or even statements from the family of a girl who'd fought and been killed for it, another model, perhaps even more so, just a dead model, every time she read things like this that talked about purity and courage, she felt judged; she couldn't do anything about it, she felt an anger bubbling up inside her, a rage, she didn't know who it was directed at, at the man? No, strangely, she no longer thought about him at all. At those victims? No, of course not, nor their families either. At herself then, it must be, because she hadn't fought or struggled, and at all the preachy people who think, to themselves but who still manage to insinuate clearly, that if you don't defend yourself at least a little bit, then you must have been consenting. What would it have been like if she'd really told the truth, if she hadn't invented the knife?

It had come to her in the very early days, just like that, to protect her from other people's judgment, on a reflex, when she talked about it, she said the guy who'd picked her up in his car had threatened her with a knife, instinctively predicting that most people would be incapable of under-standing that even without a knife the fear had been the same, the fear had been overwhelming, paralyzing. What exactly would you do, alone with a guy stronger than you in the middle of nowhere, by the side of a deserted road, and anyway, what did she actually know about it, maybe this guy did have one, a knife, after all, hidden in his glove compartment; all he needed was the opportunity provided by a little modicum of resistance, and he would get it out. That's what her friend Jean-Christophe, the only person to whom she'd admitted her lie, had told her, and even if she didn't really believe in it, in the marketing-guy-who-has-a-flick-knife-in-the-glove-compartment-of-his-company-car, it had done her good hearing it. It did her good hearing that in spite of everything, yes, she *was* a victim, that for once what had happened to her wasn't entirely her fault, her fault, her fault her fault her fault.

Finally, and luckily, five years after her rape there was the high-speed subway thing.

It had done her so much good, ridiculously much, a real head case, a real knife, a proper, unambiguous attack with no shadow of a doubt, in the middle of Paris in the middle of the day, and not the tiniest chink for her guilt to worm its way in and take up residence; it retrospectively justified all her lies.

Thanks to her attacker on the high-speed subway, she'd started getting better.

Not very long after that, she'd met Olivier.

She now realizes it was only after this that she'd felt her life had begun, with marriage or perhaps motherhood, it's hard to say and even harder to swallow, diametrically opposed to her feminist convictions, but there it was, every little girl's sad, sad brand of insanity, it was only then that she'd stopped waiting, stopped constantly projecting herself into a possible future or not projecting herself at all, started living in the present that was her life. Olivier was the love she'd been waiting for, and it was a miracle how well they got along, she never stopped marveling at it, except for this thing he had with words, so unlike her, this problem he had with saying things and perhaps even more with hearing them, but she didn't think it was serious, thought it would sort itself out with time, it hadn't sorted itself out. On the contrary.

# 10

So, did you call your lawyer? Olivier asked lightly when he called her later that evening.

She didn't think that was funny.

Did you get my text? he asked.

Yes.

But we need to talk about us, because we can't go on like before. I've told her I don't want to see her anymore, and I want to rebuild things with you. Now we need to talk about you and me.

Let's do it then, she said, totally trusting.

The torrent of criticism that then descended on her left her speechless. Without even drawing breath, Olivier launched into a long monologue in which he randomly accused her of never wanting to make love with him anymore, of always criticizing and belittling him, pointing out, by the by, as he often did, that there was no point in her claiming this wasn't true because he was sure he was right. She tried several times unsuccessfully to convince him that accusations like these weren't, in her opinion, the best preamble to a constructive discussion. He just carried on, saying that on top of everything else, she couldn't deny she had sexual problems.

She tried in vain to parry his blows but failed to interrupt him. He eventually stopped, concluding that he wanted to continue living with her but "on certain conditions," and she was suddenly gripped by an overriding anger, a huge, uncontrollable anger.

On certain conditions. He wasn't asking her forgiveness, it didn't even occur to him to say he was sorry.

Would it fucking kill you to tell me you love me? she thought. And with the safety zone she usually forced herself to maintain between her thoughts and their vocalization now dangerously reduced by the state of rage she was in, there was a sort of multivehicle pileup in her brain.

Would it fucking kill you to tell me you love me? she heard herself screaming.

Then she hung up and, huddled on the couch, started crying.

Luckily he called back right away, and she gradually calmed down. By mutual consent they decided to put off the rest of this conversation until later, and once they'd hung up properly, wishing each other good night this time, bearing in mind that Olivier would be home the following morning, Juliette started thinking. From Olivier's endless catalog of grievances she'd retained two things: (a) he felt he was constantly being criticized, (b) you can't deny you have sexual problems.

To the first point, there was a lot to say, but you'd have to go right back to the beginning of their relationship, the fact that she'd never been able to say anything to him without his interpreting it as a criticism, never been able to express the least disagreement without his feeling it was a personal attack, without provoking hostile reactions, his I-don't-understand-why-you-say-that-when-I-know-perfectly-well-that-deep-down-you-agree-with-mes, his you-can't-feel-like-that-it's-just-not-possibles, and even his full-on I-don't-believe-yous. You'd have to trawl back through everything, which meant that beyond their first two years of marriage, which were idyllic, she'd felt she had no other way of settling their differences than to hold her tongue, to say amen to everything, to keep their relationship alive all on her own until, two years ago now, she'd had enough; she rebelled and thought of leaving him, and—true—at that point she'd stopped being very nice, for example when she said she wasn't sure she wanted to grow old with him, but first of all this was the truth, then the complicated bit was working out how it had come to that.

To the second point, she wondered what he was talking about. Sexual problems, yes, she'd had a few—after her rape, it would have been extraordinary if she hadn't—but nothing very serious, were they even actually problems? Let's say she'd started having fantasies, violent fantasies, that frightened her a bit. She'd mentioned this to Olivier shortly after they met, not making too much of it, in passing, for fear of shocking him, as a strange but probably inevitable reaction to the attacks she'd experienced, and that had faded with time. He hadn't asked any questions, and the subject had never come up between them again. Was that what he was referring to? Because on every other score she thought her sexuality was pretty normal and reasonably fulfilled, she had an orgasm every time they made love or nearly, no particular hang-ups, few taboos. No, she definitely couldn't see what he meant by her "sexual problems."

Eventually she remembered something it had taken her ten years to acknowledge: Words didn't have the same meaning for him as for her. It was one of the main difficulties they had, a stumbling block, worse than a stumbling block, a real obstacle course, with ditches of misunderstanding and walls of incomprehension. Juliette found it exhausting, it drove her crazy.

Perhaps he was talking about desire.

If in Olivier's terms "having sexual problems" meant "not wanting him so much," then he wasn't wrong.

In the last few months she'd refused his overtures several times. If Olivier had asked her why, she could have supplied a whole raft of excellent reasons, the most obvious being that she was completely exhausted in the evenings, and that since Emma had stopped having an afternoon nap, those special times at the weekend when most of their sexual activity had been concentrated had fallen away. If she had dug deeper, she could have found more, like the fact that she'd always been the one to take the initiative with lovemaking and in the end she'd gotten fed up. If he wanted her, he only had to ask, do something to awaken her desire, instead of turning sharply toward the wall with a bloody-minded sigh when she pretended to ignore his advances, as had happened several times recently. But as usual, Olivier preferred to retreat into silence.

As she thought this over, Juliette gradually regained her confidence. The fact that only moments ago Olivier had finally, and for the first time, verbalized his frustration was actually a good sign. Not the verbalization of desire she'd always hoped for, but still a good sign.

If that was the root of the problem, if it was only about sex, it wasn't very serious. Her physical compatibility with Olivier had been immediate, from the moment they met. And now, having licked and inhaled every inch of Olivier's body, it had become more familiar to her than her own. Rightly or wrongly, Juliette felt that once the potentially strong but inevitably very fleeting allure of novelty was over, no other woman could give him more pleasure than she could—or as much, even.

It was just that she needed to act quickly. A lack of desire wasn't insurmountable, but since Olivier had told her he was being unfaithful, Juliette had noticed with terror that something not unlike disgust was building inside her. Soon, she could tell, making love with her husband again would fill her with the same revulsion as putting on a pair of panties already worn by a stranger. She could see that this comparison suggested an ugly possessiveness and a possible loathing toward her own sex, but she preferred not to dwell on this. Now wasn't the time.

When Olivier came home from Aubigny the next day, she said, I've decided we're only going to say nice things to each other for ten days, okay?

He went out to buy flowers. He put the children to bed, then she led him off to their bedroom to make love. We mustn't wait, she said, otherwise I'm worried I won't be able to touch you anymore, it's like falling off a horse, you have to get straight back in the saddle.

They gave each other quick little kisses, he smelled good, she trailed her lips over his body, saying: I'm sorry if I haven't loved you enough lately.

He lay back passively, saying: I don't know, I hadn't thought of it like that.

You do realize this isn't how this is supposed to happen? she said, smiling. You do realize theoretically I shouldn't be the one saying sorry?

He was far away.

After making love, they fell asleep immediately, tired.

The following morning she went off to work, and Olivier stayed at home, doing little chores and looking after the children.

When she arrived home late in the evening, he proudly showed her the telephones he'd set up in her absence. On top of the bases and cordless phones they already had by the front door and in their bedroom, he'd added two more handsets, passed on to him by a coworker, one in the living room and one in the kitchen. She wondered how much point there was having four phones charging in an 810-square-foot apartment, given he was always saying they had too many machines plugged in and spent his time putting the TV and other appliances on standby to save electricity.

He instantly hit the roof. Always criticizing. He did think he deserved a bit of gratitude for the day he'd spent doing it.

Gratitude, thought Juliette. You had to pinch yourself to believe it.

Their conversation very quickly grew heated. She didn't understand what he was going through. He slumped down on the couch with tears in his eyes. If you think this is easy for me. This is about love, you know, he said.

She felt as if he'd slapped her, she turned and pummeled his chest. Really, it's about love. No, you hadn't told me that.

Then, very abruptly, their anger subsided. Let's go to bed, he said.

A noise in the corridor silenced them. Emma was curled up on an armchair in the hall, listening to them.

Juliette took her to bed with her and asked her exactly what she'd heard. You were talking about a hurty place, a hurty thing Daddy did to you. Juliette tried to explain that sometimes people who love each other could hurt each other without meaning to, like Emma did with her brother, nothing serious, nothing to worry about at all.

The following day, having run out of vacation time, Olivier went back to work at the newspaper.

Sitting in front of the TV that evening, he cried again. Juliette watched him, a dead weight of fear in the pit of her stomach.

I warn you, I'm going to tell Florence everything. I need to talk about this to someone.

If you like, whatever, he said.

# 11

It was eleven in the evening, and the party was in full swing. The whole local gang was there, plus a few friends of friends, the manager of the bistro across the street, and a teacher from the children's school. Squished onto a tiny balcony, Pierre, Stéphane, and Paul were talking to Olivier while inside, twenty or so people divided into little clusters were eating amid happy, noisy chatter, some sitting at a round table, others on the couch with their plates on their knees and their glasses at their feet. A few guests were also sitting on the floor, and some had opted to stay standing, using the marble mantelpiece to park their plates.

This is delicious, what we're eating here, what is it?

And so she was like, That's really not the school cooperative's job, you know!

Guess what, I've won a trip to the Seychelles…way outstripped my targets for the first trimester…best sales figures in Europe…

It's beef maté, an African dish with peanut sauce. Amidou gave me the recipe, you know, Babacar's mom.

And where have you got to with moving your premises?

Two hours, every morning. And swimming three times a week.

According to the mayor, they're going to be rehoused in hotels, but I don't trust him; he keeps smoking us out, plus all the hotels in the neighborhood are full.

Peanut butter.

Sure, we're not guaranteed there won't be some new social program, anyway; speaking objectively, there are far too many of us.

How many subscriptions do you need before you can open?

I made some once with bananas, that was good too.

Juliette had arrived a good hour before everyone else and had helped Florence in the kitchen. In the hallway she'd bumped into an odd character but had made the decision not to pay any attention. You often came across odd characters in this building. Paul was a psychiatrist and saw patients at home. His professional ethics were exemplary, and he scrupulously respected patient confidentiality, except with his wife, who, for her part, didn't feel beholden to anything, and so she thrilled everyone in the neighborhood with stories about crazy people. Florence had been an archivist for a daily paper, but since it had gone into bankruptcy, she spent her days at home and had become quite an authority on the many and varied neuroses afflicting our modern society at the dawn of the twenty-first century. Juliette asked her where she'd got to in her search for work. Florence shrugged. The newspaper industry was dying, and Florence wasn't optimistic about her chances of finding a job anytime soon.

Luckily more and more people were depressed, which balanced out their household finances, and Paul worked very late into the evening every day.

She then asked Juliette how she was doing, and Juliette told her the whole story while Florence peeled onions, these two factors combining so perfectly that it wasn't long before they both were in tears.

Paul, who'd just finished his consultations, had appeared with a beaming smile before gauging the situation at a glance and disappearing without a sound.

I hope you're not expecting me to give you advice, Florence said, sniffing. Last time I gave advice in a situation like this it was a disaster.

I'll just mind my own business, she added pointedly as she went back to chopping onions while Juliette peered at her questioningly with watery eyes.

When Florence's friend Isabelle had fallen in love the year before, Florence had encouraged her to discuss it with her husband, who'd promptly thrown her out. Her *grand amour* with Nathan had lasted only six months. Isabelle now lived alone with her cat; her children no longer spoke to her, she worked forty-eight hours a day and was well on her way to becoming an alcoholic.

So I just keep my mouth shut now.

Juliette shrugged.

I'm not expecting advice.
You should talk to Paul, Florence suggested. He saw you crying, anyway; he'll ask me what's going on, and I don't want to lie to him.

You can tell him the truth, it doesn't bother me.

No, I'd rather you did it. He really likes Olivier, he might understand better than I do, and he could talk to him.

She went to find Paul and stood him in front of Juliette (Juliette has something to tell you), then went off to deal with the children.

I'm surprised at this coming from Olivier, said Paul. I wouldn't have thought he was so …shallow.
What can we do? he added.

Nothing. I just need to be able to talk about it, that's all.

Now they all were eating their maté, which was slightly overdone, and Juliette was watching Olivier laughing with Paul and Stéphane.

Hard to believe that he was crying just a few hours ago and that he's going through this great thwarted love affair, don't you think? she whispered to Florence.

Béatrice sat down near them, plate in hand.
Who are you talking about? she asked.
You don't know him, Flo replied. A friend's just found out her guy's having an affair.
Béatrice had recently separated from her daughter's father, who had cheated on her continuously throughout the few years they lived together.
It's the time of year, Béatrice said lightly with a shrug. Every time Philippe had a new relationship it started in springtime. Tell your friend not to worry too much, they calm down in the fall.

Apart from Béatrice and Nourredine, the bistro manager whose wife had stayed at home, all the other guests had come in couples. Most of them had been married about ten years, like Juliette and Florence. Which made sense because they'd gotten to know each other through their children. They all seemed to get along well with their partners, they even still seemed to be in love with each other, but that, Juliette thought, was what you saw from the outside, you couldn't know what was really going on between them. The previous year, when Laura and Thierry, and then Béatrice and Philippe had announced they were separating, they'd all been dumbfounded, as if a building they walked past every day had suddenly collapsed before their eyes. Marriages are like that, edifices that seem to be built to last for centuries and then sometimes crumble in an instant, eaten away by some invisible dry rot.

Serge, who'd just arrived from the theater, joined Paul and Stéphane on the balcony and gave each of them a kiss on the cheek before giving Olivier's cheek a pinch.

Still got skin like a baby and the body of a young man, haven't you?

Olivier gave a modest half-smile.

They segued into one of their favorite topics: exercise, weight loss, and cycling. Stéphane was dieting, and Pierre was training for a marathon.

As for Serge, his status as a sometime actor left him with a lot of free time to spend at the gym, lifting weights and working on his body. He displayed his abs before his male friends' admiring and envious eyes while their wives looked on wearily, absorbed by their own conversations about work and politics.

Look at them. You'd think we were at the Turkish baths. Florence giggled.

They'd do better to pay their wives a few compliments, Béatrice added. Look at you two, not an inch of flabby stomach, but you were the ones who carried their babies.

Juliette nodded thoughtfully. How long was it since Olivier had told her she was beautiful? If she commented on this, he would shrug and say:

You know perfectly well you're beautiful. Everyone tells you so.

You're right, she grumbled sarcastically. Too much positive reinforcement from other people. It's good to be knocked down a peg by your partner.

And anyway, she added, if you'd ever set a foot at Galatea, you'd know that's not the case.

At Galatea Networks banter and gallantries were seen as serious professional errors. Having chosen a scientific career, Juliette had long since grown used to moving in a male world, but her current coworkers' sanitized chilliness meant she missed her days back at engineering school, where she'd acted with impunity on all fronts, reaping the benefits of her intelligence without sacrificing any of the advantages of being a woman. She was one of the few girls in her program, and probably the prettiest; her fellow students and even her lecturers fell over themselves telling her that. And yet no one would have dared question her competence or contemplated setting limits on her freedom. This was most likely why she'd soon stopped hanging out with "women's groups." She felt the battle was won, sexual equality achieved, there was no need to fight anymore. She wondered, very briefly, whether she was still a feminist. Surrounded as she was by men who really were feminists, as much as or even more so than she was, starting with her husband, she could no longer really be sure.

She caught Florence's eye, and Florence, who over the years had developed the ability to read Juliette's thoughts, smiled at her. Both of their husbands came pretty close to the masculine ideal they'd dreamed up some twenty years earlier. Like the other men in their tight-knit group, they were actually almost perfect specimens of the new father species. They changed diapers, made up bottles, and met each other along the banks of the river on Sundays, carrying their babies on their backs or in pouches or comparing the suspension of their brand-new strollers. (When Johann was born, Olivier had invested in an all-terrain King Roller Cruiser, but Paul's Maclaren High Trek Duo, complete with shock absorbers and disk brakes, wasn't bad either.)

All the same, painful though it was for Juliette to admit, it was when Emma was born that all the problems between Olivier and her had begun.

She'd almost immediately had a horrible feeling of abandonment. Olivier was besotted with his daughter, and Juliette not only felt she no longer existed in his eyes but constantly had to fight back the feeling that he was robbing her of her role as a mother. In the early weeks she still had a secret weapon: She was breast-feeding. Olivier brought Emma to her in their bed and stayed beside her while their daughter suckled, gazing at them both with a tenderness that was a pleasure to behold. But Juliette was prepared to swear she'd seen a glint of envy in his eyes several times. Luckily for him, it hadn't lasted long. By force of circumstances Juliette had had to wean Emma and go back to work at the end of her maternity leave, when the baby was less than three months old. And then Olivier had been free to unleash his paternal fervor. He'd developed a phobia for sudden infant death syndrome and would wake Juliette ten times a night, oblivious of her exhaustion, leaping out of bed to check that the baby was still breathing. Then he started perfecting original techniques for preparing her bottles and changing her diapers, techniques whose only merit, as far as Juliette could see, was to double the amount of time devoted to these tasks and were only a damned nuisance with no counterbalancing upside, but Olivier wouldn't hear it, and to avoid arguments, she'd given in to his demands. He'd suddenly become a baby expert, he spent his life on the Internet comparing experiences with other parents. Juliette had been lucky enough not to suffer the baby blues and had thought that this birth would bring her some sort of fulfillment, but she couldn't look at her daughter in her husband's arms without feeling terribly jealous—jealous of who? Of him? Of her? Probably both. She was torn between anger at being dispossessed and a feeling of abandonment, without allowing any of this to show, of course. What exactly could she complain about? She too had most likely made mistakes. In their defense, neither she nor Olivier knew what a father was meant to be: Juliette had seen hers only two or three times in her entire childhood, and like her, Olivier had spent many years in boarding school. Even if they both had been closer to their fathers, the previous generation's example wouldn't have been of any use to them. They were decoding a new way of life, and everything had to be invented.

Juliette would never have admitted it to anyone (forgive me, Johann, I love you), but her decision to have another child very quickly after Emma was born was not so much out of a true longing for one as dictated by a fierce urge to be done with this infernal triangle where she was constantly getting between Olivier and her baby, partly out of nostalgia for their life as a couple, but also for fear that Emma's intensely close bond with her father could end up turning the child into a psychopath.

The stereo was playing Noir Désir's song "Le Vent Nous Portera."

Does anyone understand the words to this song? Pierre asked. I'm not kidding. Who gets it? "I'm not afraid of the road / Gotta see how it goes, dip in your toes / Meandering around the small of your back ..."

Forget about it, someone answered. It's poetry.

Around midnight couples started leaving. The baby-sitter meters were whirring. Juliette, Sylvia, and Béatrice went over to the group formed by Paul, Serge, Olivier, and Stéphane to suggest it was time to go home. Stéphane had launched into a long saga about an affair going on at work.

Marchand's convinced he's the kid's father. So I asked, How can you be sure? She is a bit weird, this Marion.

Can you recap for us? asked Juliette. We missed the beginning.

My boss had a thing with a chick in the department.

That's not a good start, someone commented.

Stéphane threw his head back and laughed out loud. Oh, you said it. Especially because they're both married.

So what happened?

So she got pregnant, and now she's come to my boss, Marchand, threatening to tell his wife everything.

And what about her husband?

Well, her husband thinks the child's his, obviously. But this Marion couldn't give a damn. She tells Marchand she's getting a divorce anyway and he's the love of her life. She calls his house in the middle of the night, she insists he give her the same gifts as his wife, or she'll spill the beans. He's starting to get freaked out.

He's right there, said Paul. But how come he told you all this stuff? He's your boss, right?

Yes. I don't know. I think he's kind of flattered, actually.

Flattered by what?

Stéphane's fascinated by this story, Sylvia interjects. Marchand's using it as an opportunity to show off in front of him.

Wait up, though, this *is* a pretty unusual case, Stéphane said defensively. This Marion is gorgeous. You can't help thinking that if a girl like her gets into a state like that, then the guy must have something special.

Oh wow, I must be dreaming, said Sylvia. It's pathetic.


When they were back at the apartment, Juliette, who'd had far too much to drink, decided to make love to Olivier, as she had every evening since he came home. The moment they were in bed she pressed herself up against him and started kissing him, but for the first time he pushed her away. Stop it.

Surprised, she drew away from him to look him squarely in the eye, then dropped her head on the pillow without breaking the eye contact.

No point staring at me like that, said Olivier. Anyway, I totally know you don't really want to.

This was what he did when he didn't want something: He blamed it on her.

You're wrong, she said. But she didn't push it any further, turned toward the wall, took far too many Bromazepams, and crashed.

The following Monday, the Monday after Pentecost, she found it impossible to get up. Olivier took the children down to the square. When she finally emerged, she went to do the shopping, then headed to Buttes-Chaumont with the children to find Florence, as they'd agreed the day before. At lunchtime she tried to have another conversation with Olivier.

You're always very eloquent, he said, when it comes to demonstrating how useless I am.

The following night she woke in tears at two in the morning and shook Olivier in bed: Promise me you will leave me my children. Please.

He woke with a start, horrified.

It's never been about that.

I don't want joint custody. I don't want to see my children every other week.

Stop it. I swear it's not going to happen. Anyway, joint custody is a dumbass idea.

He put his arm around her and added, I don't want you to be hurt.

# 12

The question is: Exactly what do *you* want? asked Jean-Christophe, holding his cigarette at arm's length, his elbow resting on the back of the banquette, while with his other hand he wafted away the smoke that was obstinately drifting toward Juliette. In the brasserie's large mirror positioned just behind him, she could see his reflection in three-quarter shot from behind, and he looked like a great two-headed octopus waving its tentacles.

Juliette thought before giving an honest answer.

Right now I want to hurt Olivier, I want him to suffer, she replied.

Jean-Christophe sighed, being careful to exhale toward the ceiling, which made him look peculiarly exasperated.

Yes but, well, that's not going to get you anywhere, no, don't let yourself get sucked into that, he protested. Not revenge, I mean, you're above all that, seriously.

No, he went on, watching the scrolls of smoke vanishing overhead, as if he were talking not to her opposite him but to a higher power in whose view Juliette's little ups and downs could only possibly appear laughable. No, the question is: Do you want to carry on living with him, or do you want the two of you to separate? In the second instance, the steps to take are simple. But watch out, there's a very heavy price to pay, and you mustn't underestimate it. Ending up on your own with two children, especially when they're as young as yours are, and in Paris as well, it's not very easy.

And if I want to continue living with him?

Jean-Christophe lowered his eyes to look at her, nodding sympathetically but delighted that Juliette had chosen to submit the thornier option to his wisdom. He granted himself a long period of silent reflection, still staring at her through half-closed eyes, before slowly starting to speak again.

Well, it's one of two things: Either he's in love, you insist he leave her, but would you then be able to forgive him and would he too be able to forgive you for stopping him from going through with this? Mind you—I'm thinking out loud here—if he's really in love, if she's really the love of his life, he'll leave anyway, so you can also decide to let things run their course...

He paused for a moment.

Or...Juliette continued inside her head because, enslaved by her Cartesian logic, she was still waiting for the second alternative.

But nothing came. By all appearances, Jean-Christophe had finished. He'd stopped talking and was darting inquisitive, probing looks at Juliette. She hesitated for a moment, then shook her head.

I'm too frightened, she replied. If I wait for things to run their course, if I don't fight, he'll do whatever she wants. He's like that, he'll go with whoever wants him more.

She's remembering when she met him, and the Maria episode, thought Jean-Christophe. At the time he'd been surprised to see just how devastated Juliette had been by the breakup with Olivier, when she'd known him only a few weeks. He was even more astonished three years later, after Juliette and Olivier had gotten back together, by the speed with which she convinced herself he was the love of her life and had dived headlong into marriage. There was no denying it: Juliette had wanted Olivier much more than the other way around. He'd just settled for being loved, with his usual nonchalance.

Okay, so if it's weakness you're worried about, then you have to be hard, Jean-Christophe said emphatically, bringing his fist down firmly on the table to punctuate his words. There are some very scary women, you know that, who'll stop at nothing to get what they want. *She* has nothing to lose. If that's what's going on and you want to keep him, then you have to take no prisoners. He mustn't see her or talk to her anymore.

Juliette wondered how Jean-Christophe had come by this expertise in matters of the heart, this oraclelike wisdom when, as a homosexual, he'd never—at least officially—maintained a single lasting relationship. Probably from reading, because he was impressively well read and, as everyone knows, literature is crammed with situations like this. It was also bound to be from various people's personal accounts, gleaned over the years: He showed such sincere interest in people that everyone confided in him, and this must eventually have constituted a significant body of experience from which he could easily deduce a few general rules.

She thanked him for his advice and left feeling relaxed. The subway was still on strike, so she kept thinking things over as she walked from Opéra to her office. Her lunch with Jean-Christophe had done her good. The business about a price to pay made everything clearer: No, she didn't want to pay the price of separating from Olivier. She shuddered at the thought of years spent battling over choices relating to the children, battling without any love, with no attempt to understand each other.

She decided she wanted to keep him, and she was going to fight.

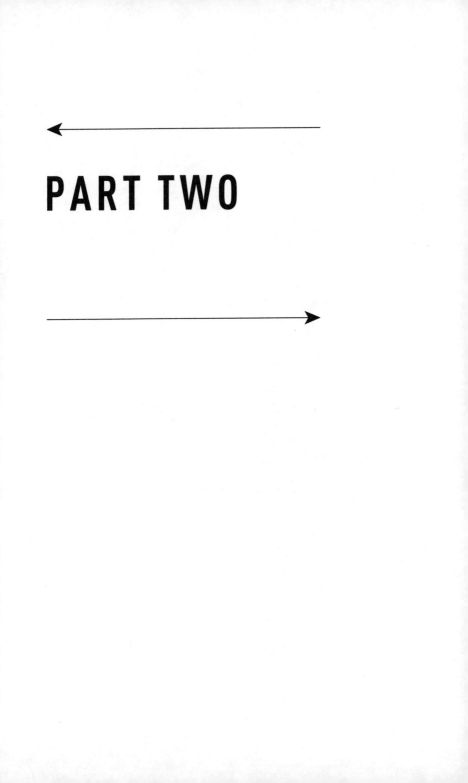

# PART TWO

PART TWO

# 13

Juliette's plan of action had been hastily established: to make love to Olivier every day and to stop this girl from poisoning their life. The first part of the plan was easier to put into action. After putting the children to bed in the evening, she went to bed herself, freshly showered, and was quietly surprised to notice how much she wanted him. When, after an hour's wait, he came to bed at ten o'clock, she was half asleep and her desire considerably blunted, but she galvanized herself and made love to him as best she could, with a skill that she hoped reflected her experience but didn't exclude a dash of inventiveness. Olivier proved docile and cooperative, as usual. Her enjoyment was slightly dulled by cramps in her feet; since the warm weather had set in, she'd been wearing sandals she wasn't used to. But it was very pleasing all the same, and she was rewarded for her efforts when, as she lay next to him afterward, she heard Olivier sigh: My, but it's good making love to you.

Since her husband had come home from Aubigny, Juliette was still refusing to talk about the "other woman"; she still didn't want to know her name or how old she was—nothing. But with the odd question here and sentence there, she was starting to know far more about her than she would have wished.

Her name, which started with a *V*, but which Juliette refused to say aloud.

(V for Victoire, just like V for Victory.

Yes, her name meant Victory.

Even if she'd been called Agatha or Josephine, Juliette would have struggled to speak her name.

But Victoire was just too much…)

How he'd ended up at her apartment one day for a reportage he was doing on the thorny issue of the Islamic veil, which was dividing the left wing. Should the wearing of Islamic veils be forbidden in schools? In the name of her feminist convictions, Victoire had defended every Muslim girl's right to pursue a secular education without having to deny her religion. In the name of her feminist convictions, she could have defended the exact opposite stance, as many of her fellow feminists did, denouncing the veil as an intolerable symbol of the patriarchal oppression of which these schoolgirls were victims. But the stance V adopted had the huge advantage of appearing bold, breaking ranks with the majority view in the Socialist Party, and therefore inevitably creating a buzz about her. Which had certainly succeeded, and the newspaper's editorial team had decided to run a portrait of her. This was to coincide with International Women's Day on March 8.

I thought it had been going on for three weeks, Juliette said, amazed.

Yes, I only met her then. After that there was a lot of e-mailing.

Along with her mandate on the city council, V was chairwoman of a feminist organization She & He are Equal, which Juliette had vaguely heard of; she'd noticed its self-consciously clever and auto-referential acronym SHE!, which was always followed by that shrieking exclamation mark.

SHE! belonged to the neofeminist movement known as differentialism and was largely inspired by a radical American model that denounced the Simone de Beauvoir–style aspiration toward a neutral universality in order to promote a specifically feminine identity endowed with many fine qualities and in every way superior to its male counterpart, virility. In France, parity in politics had been legally instituted in June 2000, just in time to favor V's election to the city council in 2002, which was fortuitous. It was also supported by a woman philosopher very much in the public eye, a woman who in private was Prime Minister Jospin's wife, and this was even more fortuitous for V because it usefully reconciled her feminist convictions with her political ambitions: The former left-wing leader had officially withdrawn from public life but still had some influence over his comrades, and thanks to him, V had managed to establish favorable connections with several key Socialist Party figures.

Of course Olivier hadn't told Juliette all this in those terms, stating only that V was close to the philosopher. But thanks to her impressive powers of deduction, and by putting together the facts, the dates, what she knew about politics, and the few elements of V's character known to her, Juliette had managed to come up with a few plausible hypotheses, and it was unlikely to be long before they were confirmed. Her instincts—her superior woman's instincts—had done the rest.

Olivier had also told her that after he'd interviewed V, the newspaper had invited her to take part in a roundtable about secularity, in Bordeaux in June. A roundtable that Olivier, as co-organizer of this series of debates, had to attend.

Lastly, he'd told her that V was divorced and had a six-year-old son.

Juliette would go on to notice with interest how Olivier, who was so scrupulous and exacting about details where his journalistic work was concerned, proved vague on the subject of V, because she'd actually never been married and her little boy, Tom, was only three.

But, she thought, this vagueness wasn't very significant.

In fact it didn't mean anything at all.

So it would have been ridiculous to take him to task on it.

And what did she do with her little boy when you were at her apartment?
I never saw him. Her mother looks after him, I think.
Oh, said Juliette.

Since Olivier had mentioned them, Juliette had been obsessed with the thought of those debates in Bordeaux when he would inevitably see V again. She made the most of this moment of intimacy to suggest going to Bordeaux with him. The idea made him smile. He made a joke of it, and she felt hurt.

Don't take this too lightly, she said. It's not a game.
He immediately became serious, almost gloomy.
No, he said, staring at the ceiling. It's not a game. She sometimes scares me.

Scares you? Juliette turned to look at him, surprised. What are you scared of?
I don't know, he replied. That she'll show up here maybe. But don't worry, she doesn't have our address.

Juliette didn't understand.
What would she come here for?
To ask you to let me go. To tell you I don't love you.

Juliette lay there in silence for a moment.
If that's what you've told her.

He didn't answer. Of course that's what he'd told her. She didn't push it any further.

Over the next few days, life seemed to go back to normal. Except that when Juliette called Olivier one evening to ask what time he would be home and he didn't answer either at the paper or on his cell, a nasty suspicion reared its head. She sighed as she realized this was now her fate, and would be for some time to come. How long did it take before you trusted someone again? She left a message for Olivier, asking him to call her back, and five minutes later the phone rang when she was taking a shower. He'd been in the paper's archives department; he was on his way. The little pang of pain eased.

"She sometimes scares me." Juliette was intrigued by these words of Olivier's. Could you be in love with someone and be scared of them? Perhaps naively, she had trouble imagining it. Wasn't love synonymous with abandon and trust? She decided to consult the expert on the subject and sent Jean-Christophe an e-mail from the office. She didn't have to wait long for a reply:

From: JC
To: Juliette
Sent: Thursday June 12 2003 15:10

Of course it's possible. Some women are a bit extreme and they use all sorts of strategies to achieve their ends. Some are genuinely dangerous: threatening to commit suicide or upset third parties or cause professional ruin...
I would find it unacceptable for you to suffer this sort of blackmail because you're less aggressive. The best solution would probably be for you to scare Olivier even more than the other woman does, but could you do that? Either way, you've confirmed my conviction that he mustn't see her anymore,

because otherwise he'll be more and more scared and could
end up giving in to her in spite of himself.
Lots of love
Jean-Christophe

Juliette read the e-mail several times. Scare Olivier? She
felt as if there was a whole section of man-woman relationships she hadn't known existed till now. She'd prefer not to
take any risks, and to stick to her initial plan. Every evening,
in their bed, sometimes even when they were still on the
couch in the living room, she pressed herself up to him and
started stroking him. Since the party at Florence's house, he
hadn't rejected her again. He lay back and let her get on
with it, amused, flattered, turned on, or all three at once, in
any case consenting. After they'd made love, he lay on his
back with half-closed eyes and sighed contentedly; then he
pulled her close and kissed her affectionately.

Bolstered by these encouraging signs, she again brought
up the subject of going to Bordeaux with him.

He gave a noncommittal wave. There's plenty of time, he
said, maybe I could go there and back on the Saturday, miss
the Sunday events, not spend the night there.
Things can happen in the daytime too.
He shrugged.
If there's one occasion where nothing could happen, it's
these debates. It's one conference after another, everyone
knows everyone…
Oh, she said, you never know, the lunch break, a patch of
cool grass.

Come on, he said.

They were evading the issue. What she wanted him to do was say he was determined to break up with the woman. He couldn't not know that.

One evening he came home late; it was a deadline day. Juliette felt exhausted. She had settled the children and gone to bed herself. He got in at around ten o'clock and slipped silently into their bedroom.

You okay? I'm feeling beaten down, she said. Why? he asked. She smiled gently. I don't know. I've had some issues recently.

She was woken in the night by a burning sensation between her legs, and it grew only worse over the course of the following morning. Unable to bear it any longer, she called the doctors that afternoon and was given an appointment in half an hour.

This time she wasn't alone in the waiting room. When she walked into that big, stuffy lounge, there was already a man waiting. He was simply dressed and looked North African. The Haddou-Duval clinic's clientele clearly wasn't as well-heeled as its address might suggest. The cost of a consultation was actually very reasonable. So there are some normal people who live in this neighborhood, Juliette thought. Unless, like her, they just worked in one of the many offices housed in the buildings on the rue de Miromesnil and the rue La Boétie and were using a break to find a bit of relief from their psychosomatic aches and pains, spawned by stress and their work conditions. Juliette was always amazed when, at the end of her appointment, the doctor spontaneously offered to prescribe her several days off work for just a sore throat. Of course she refused; that wasn't her style.

When it was her turn, Dr. Duval (or Haddou) shook her hand and, exactly as she had a few days earlier, asked: What can I do for you?

Juliette hesitated for a moment.

I have this painful burning sensation, it may just be a yeast infection, but like I said the other day, my husband's having an affair. He says he used a condom, but well, I'd rather check we haven't caught something.

The doctor hadn't contradicted her, so it must be the same one as last time. She prescribed a full course of tests for Juliette, for yeast infection and all STIs.

Go right away, she told her. And avoid having intercourse until you have the results.

She saw the consternation in her patient's eyes.

That's not very easy right now.

The doctor nodded. Of course, she understood. No, Juliette definitely shouldn't stop making love with her husband, particularly in this situation.

It would just be better if you used a condom for a few days.

Juliette wondered whether all the cheated-on women in the Eighth Arrondissement used her strategy of making love to their husbands every night.

Before she put the prescription in her bag, she glanced at the letterhead. Dr. Haddou. Wrong again.

That evening their neighborhood was having a street party. Trestle tables had been set up on the pedestrian road outside the Cité Lepage nursery school. It had been nonstop since the beginning of June. What with end-of-year shows, the school party, and various birthdays, their group of friends had met up with their kids pretty much every evening. They'd had a succession of picnics at Buttes-Chaumont, and Juliette mostly went along on her own with Johann and Emma, while Olivier had to stay late at work—or somewhere else. She tried not to think too much about his schedule, clinging to the fragile assurance he'd given her that he was determined to end his affair. But as the days wore on, as she felt increasingly keenly that she was on first-name terms with every blade of grass in the park's lawns, she started loathing the place.

As she walked toward Cité Lepage, Juliette glanced over at a narrow passageway flanked by dark, ramshackle, abandoned buildings. A few months earlier the local authorities had decided to knock these blocks down and evacuate the families, most of them immigrants, who were occupying them illegally. Backed by the nursery school teachers, the whole neighborhood had mobilized itself to ensure these families were suitably rehoused and their children could finish the school year in acceptable circumstances. The passageway looked deserted, but there was still washing hanging out to dry on a first-floor balcony. If you leaned out one window and stretched your arm, you could touch the building opposite and, by contorting your head, could glimpse a slice of blue sky. Bags of garbage had been left outside a door; it was a hot evening. It could easily have been Naples.

Flo was waiting for her outside the school with Hector and Jeanne. The moment they saw their friends, Johann and Emma let go of their mother's hand and ran over to them squealing. Juliette kissed Florence and, exhausted, dropped down onto the steps, taking it upon herself to give a welcoming smile to people arriving, their arms laden with drinks and junk food. Flo sat beside her and eyed her kindly.

Is Olivier not coming?

He's still at the paper, Juliette replied with a shrug. Or somewhere else. He has a lot of meetings and discussions at the moment.

Flo tried to reassure her. After the disaster on April 21, the Socialist Party was trying to rise from its ashes. You would expect the opposition to cash in on the growing protest movement by launching offensives and debates left, right, and center in anticipation of future elections.

Are you worried he's with her, is that it?

Juliette hesitated.

No, she said eventually. He said he wanted to end it. I believe him.

Moments later Olivier arrived at last. Pierre and Serge, each with a plastic cup of red wine in hand, greeted him with loud exclamations.

So, how are the fluffy Socialists doing? asked Pierre, who was pretty far left himself. Say, you're working crazy hours right now!

Olivier was smiling, apparently relaxed.

Anyway, it seems to suit you. You're looking fantastic. Is that a new shirt? asked Serge.

Still sitting on the steps, Juliette watched Olivier from a distance and wondered whether he'd noticed she was there. Deep down, she thought, he thinks this whole thing is fun. He's happy, kind of proud.

When she stood up to take Emma to the restrooms in a nearby café, she heard Olivier call out to her, and she turned around. He was running over to her, looking worried.

Where are you going?

With a tilt of her chin she pointed to their daughter.

Emma needs to go pee.

Oh, Olivier sighed. I thought you were leaving without saying anything.

She shrugged.

Of course not.

Back home, once the kids were in bed, she told him about the burning that had been torturing her since the day before.

It kind of sabotages my plan to make love to you every day, she said. And I can't help thinking this is all I need, you bringing some nasty infection home to me.

Staring him directly in the eye, she added: Did you really wear a condom?

He held her gaze, insisted that he had.

It's probably nothing then, she said. A chance thing. A weird coincidence.

Questions were going around and around inside her head.

What is her job exactly? Is that a real job, being on the Pantin council? Being chairwoman of SHE!? No, that's not a job.

Theoretically, she's a teacher.

Oh yes, she went to the École Normale Supérieure. You told me that. She's not just anybody. She went to the École Normale Supérieure. If you only knew how little that impresses me.

I can't have said that. Not like that. It sounds like my father.

You said: She's not just anybody. She went to the École Normale Supérieure.

If that's true, if I did say that like that, that's really pitiful.

When you came home late in the evening, were you with her?

It might have happened once.

And how many times did you make love?

He gave a little laugh: It's easy to count it up, you've done it yourself. There was the first time, the last time, and three weeks in between.

(That first evening she'd said: How can she ask you to leave us, you've seen her what? Six times, ten times...)

How many?

Well, I don't know.

You just said it was easy to count up.

If I were like you, I'd already have counted it up, but I can't do it. You do it. Ten times?

Ten times in fifteen working days, that's almost every day.

Well, no then, less. Then it's not ten times.

The mental pictures she'd at first refused to countenance (don't tell me anything, I don't want to know) were becoming increasingly unavoidable, obsessive.

# 14

The gynecologist she finally decided to consult—she was so over the twins—gave her a kindly look. He'd called the lab for the first results of her tests. There was a dubious bacterium, they were doing a culture.

So, Juliette asks, can it only be caught through sexual contact? Are you sure?

Absolutely, yes. If it's confirmed, you'll have to inform your partners, they'll need to be treated too.

Her partners. She quashed a sarcastic comment.

When Olivier came home that evening, she was in front of the TV, watching a report about the war in Iraq. He sat down beside her and, not even looking at the screen, put an arm tenderly around her shoulders.

Is it good, what you're watching?

She put it on mute, and without turning toward him, her eyes pinned on some tanks advancing through the ruined suburbs of Baghdad, she replied, I saw my gynecologist, he called the lab. There's a dubious-looking bug, it could be an STI. Well, it may be nothing, they need to do a culture, we'll know on Friday.

Olivier sat in silence for a moment.

I just can't believe it, he said.

If that's what it is, it's something you can only get from sexual contact. I told him that you'd had an affair but that you'd told me you'd used protection. He said maybe not enough. Basically, if you didn't use a condom for everything, absolutely everything, oral sex, I don't need to draw a picture, enough already.

He didn't reply. She sighed.

So, it's possible.

Yes, he muttered, what you said, yes.

There was an explosion on the TV screen. Women and children running, trying to take shelter. She felt a sort of bubble of emptiness in the pit of her stomach.

He laughed briefly. I don't know, it's just so unlikely, the probability that I would cheat on you multiplied by the probability that I catch something...

He's playing with statistics, she thought. She felt she was gradually slipping out of her depth and he was playing with statistics.

She asked him, again, something along the lines of: But how could you do this to me, how could you not protect me? She said: I'm impressed by your capacity not to feel responsible. It's just like when you left the car unlocked overnight in the street and the radio was stolen. You always have a good excuse. It's never your fault.

His face changed abruptly. His smile vanished, his face hardened, she was almost startled. He turned to her, his expression suddenly resolutely hostile.

Oh really, it's just like that. You think I didn't feel responsible for the thing with the car radio. Well yes, I do, believe it or not, I do feel responsible. And besides, there were genuine reasons why I'd forgotten the car was out that night, but let's not go there. Do you have more examples like that, of times when I didn't feel responsible?

She tried to reply, he cut her off.

You just keep thinking about that goddamned thing I said, it's going around inside your head on a loop: It happened to me. But that was just something I said. Do you want the truth? I'm totally responsible for what happened to me with her, extremely responsible, even, if you really want to know. And if there's something else going around on a loop in your head: You gave in to the first temptation, you never had any urge to cheat on me for ten years, and at the first opportunity—bang! Well, that's not true either. Of course I've been tempted.

She reeled slightly under this avalanche of words. He was saying the opposite of everything he'd said up till now; she didn't know what to think anymore, she didn't understand anything anymore. But what she really wanted, most of all, was to stop this onslaught of violence. She begged. Olivier dropped his voice.

Anyway, we need to wait till Friday, he said. It could be nothing at all.

Juliette got through the next day at Galatea Networks as if in a fog. Olivier called her in the morning about God knows what practical subject, the car, a tax bill; she replied in monosyllables. Are you okay? he asked. Not great, she said.

She used her lunch hour to research STIs on the Internet, tried without success to get hold of Jean-Christophe. He was at a seminar in Venice.

That evening she was in such bad shape that Yolande offered to put the children to bed. She accepted with relief and went to kiss her kids good night. Are you sick, Mommy? She hugged her little boy tight. You don't have a diaper tonight. You won't wet the bed, will you? You're a big boy now. No, he said, and I won't come into your bed.

She gulped down half a Bromazepam and before going under listened to Yolande reading the children a story. She didn't hear the door snap shut, but soon afterward Olivier came into the bedroom and sat beside her on the bed. She pretended to be asleep; the tranquilizer was having its effect, she was relaxed, unwilling to lurch back into crisis. She just wanted to rest, sink into sleep. He started crying beside her, noisily, with the clear intention of waking her. She kept her eyes shut. So he said, I love you, cried a little louder, touched her leg. She couldn't pretend now. She took his arm. Why are you crying? I love you, he said again, I don't want you to be unhappy. I haven't thought about anything else all day. She didn't say anything, just listened. She felt good all of a sudden, she pressed herself up against him, and they stayed there in each other's arms for a moment. Then he kissed her gently on the eyes. I'll leave you to sleep. Sorry I woke you. You can wake me whenever you want to tell me you love me, she replied. A moment later she sank into a deep sleep.

She woke the following morning feeling rested, having had an excellent night. For the first time in a long while no child had come and snuggled against her in the night, and even Olivier hadn't woken her when he came to bed. Which was lucky because they were planning to go to the theater that evening. As they did every September, they'd taken out a subscription to the Comédie-Française. The last show of the season was Jean Racine's *Esther*.

On her lunch break she decided to stop by the lab. As she walked along the sidewalk, she remembered very clearly how she'd felt in the same circumstances twenty years earlier, going to pick up the results of the tests she'd taken as a precaution after being raped—why couldn't she stop thinking about this whole rape thing right now? Luckily, on that occasion the results had been negative, but AIDS had come on the scene shortly afterward: AIDS, which you could say had put sex back in its rightful place, a question of life and death, and anyone who'd forgotten that, who, like her, had treated sex lightly would be punished. The terror had dogged her for months. It was a long time before she'd found the courage to have that test, fearing some form of immanent justice, not so much because of the rape as because she'd had many lovers, convinced deep down—thanks for this, Sainte-Euverte—that divine retribution would strike her down for being so easy, a girl of such loose morals.

Walking the last few yards to the medical analysis center, she was amazed by how different it felt this time. This time if she was ill, it wouldn't be her fault—*her fault her fault her fault*—and her anxiety was considerably less intense as a result. When she finally had the test results in her hand, her eyes widened in disbelief. The results were positive, if you could call it that. Juliette hadn't caught just one piece of shit but three: yeast, a urinary tract infection, and mycoplasma. Slightly dazed, she called her gynecologist, who confirmed what she'd just read and told her to come to his office as soon as possible to pick up a prescription for two different antibiotics. Juliette promised to come by later in the day.

In the first instance she felt perversely satisfied by this tangible, clinical manifestation of the wrong that had been done to her. This couldn't just be brushed aside anymore: She was now objectively and indisputably a victim in the whole business; Olivier would have to admit that. Then it suddenly occurred to her that if, despite his insistence, despite his claims, Olivier hadn't used condoms, then V could also be pregnant by him. And the thought chilled her to the core.

When she returned to the office and sat down at her computer, she found an e-mail from Olivier:

From: Olivier B
To: Juliette
Sent: Thursday June 19 2003 12:14

Want to ask your forgiveness
And ask you to trust me,
Because we haven't lost each other, because we still have a
ton of things to share, because there still are and there still
will be so many ways to prove we love each other.
Olivier

Soon afterward he called her on her landline.

I've been trying to get a hold of you for ages, he said. Well?

I just got back, she replied. I went to the lab. It's positive. So you'll have to be tested, and she'll need treatment too.

There was a moment's silence on the other end of the line.

Okay, so we need antibiotics, that's all, right?

Just then Pierre-Yves, one of the computer analysts who was working on the Magellan project with Juliette, came over to her desk and hovered there, hanging back slightly, waiting for her to finish her conversation. She cut it short and hung up quickly.

Five minutes later, when she'd answered Pierre-Yves's questions, she called Olivier back.

I wanted to say, there's no point rushing to tell your little playmate about this; wait till I tell you what the thingy's called.

Too late. I already called her.

She had that empty feeling in her stomach again.

What exactly did you tell her? You don't even know what it is.

I told her you had an STI and I'd let her know by text what it's called. I had to tell her because she's seeing her gynecologist this evening.

And then he promptly changed the subject.

Are we still going to the theater tonight?

Yes, she sighed, of course.

From: Juliette
To: Olivier B
Sent: Thursday June 19 2003 15:08

Subject: Thingy
The thingy's called UREAPLASMA UREALYTICUM and it's a
mycoplasm.


From: Juliette
To: Olivier B
Sent: Thursday June 19 2003 15:21
What I'd really like is for you to tell her what the thingy's
called so she can get treatment, and for you to ask her to get
out of your life—and mine, while she's at it.


From: Olivier B
To: Juliette
Sent: Thursday June 19 2003 15:28
I've sent the thingy's name.
And I've told her, again, that you and I are having a hard
time, and I want to end all contact with her, even by phone, to
rebuild things with you.


From: Juliette
To: Olivier B
Sent: Thursday 19 June 2003 14:47
Thank you
J xx


At four o'clock Juliette went into a meeting on the
Magellan project. The work wasn't shaping up as well as
they'd thought it would. Apparently they had some serious competition on this one, and the clients hadn't waited
to hear Galatea Networks' bid, on which Juliette had
been working for several weeks, and had made substantial

alterations to the project. Whole swaths of functionality had been cut, including—significantly—the one for which she felt confident she'd found the most apt solutions. On the other hand, other key functionalities had been added, meaning more than half the work needed to be redone from scratch. The commercial project leader, Juliette's alter ego on the job, had assured the client this wasn't a problem, and a new bid would be compiled very quickly. Juliette laid into him, and the meeting went on longer than anticipated. She emerged completely strung out. She needed to race to the theater and wouldn't have time to stop at the gynecologist's to pick up her prescription.

She made such an effort to rush that she arrived on the place Colette with an hour to spare. She took a seat at the Café des Colonnes, ordered two whiskeys in quick succession, and smoked several cigarettes. However this all ended, there was now a clear risk she'd come out of it an alcoholic druggie for the rest of her days. She'd count herself lucky if she managed to avoid lung cancer. Weirdly though, the waiter who took her order didn't seem to notice he was dealing with a wreck. In fact he couldn't do enough for her, called her mademoiselle and bantered with her. It did her good. She glanced at her reflection in the mirrored wall and was somewhat reassured by what she saw. Not bad. She wasn't in top form of course, but given the circumstances, it could have been worse.

The show started at eight-thirty. At eight o'clock she stood, paid for her drinks, and walked across the square.

Olivier was waiting for her with the tickets in the theater lobby. They went into the Richelieu auditorium and took their seats in the orchestra. Olivier steered her, holding her arm, and this gave her a peculiar buzz. Recently any physical contact with him seemed to be invested with new significance. Or a significance that had been missing for a long time.

I don't know anything about this play. I haven't even had time to read the reviews. How about you?

I don't know it either. I know the story's from the Bible.

We should have bought a program, Olivier fretted. We're not going to understand a thing.

This irritated Juliette.

Come on, we should be able to manage. I know *we* didn't go to the École Normale Supérieure, but we're not exactly dummies.

Olivier shot her a sideways look, wriggled deeper into his seat, and didn't unclench his jaw for the whole performance. They left the theater some distance apart, like strangers.

A little later, when they were home in the kitchen and had calmed down, they started talking about the shitty STI—those were Juliette's words.

Now, of course, she told Olivier, your girlfriend's going to say she doesn't have anything.

She already has, he replied. She told me it was impossible, she hasn't slept with anyone for years.

Oh really. If that's true, I'd better get in touch with the Vatican. I'll be the first woman to have caught an STI by immaculate conception.

It was strange, Olivier didn't seem to give V's declarations any credence, but he didn't seem to hold it against her either. He reported what she said as he would have done the words of a child, with a sort of affectionate indulgence.

Confronted with this inconsistency, Juliette dared ask the question that had been plaguing her all afternoon: How did you know she was seeing her gynecologist this evening?

I'd already told her there was the possibility of an STI.

When, though? I thought you'd asked her to stop calling you.

Yes.

And she called you?

Yes.

And you spoke to her?

Yes.

When was this?

I don't remember, two or three days ago.

What did you say to each other?

Stuff about work, and she was having a housewarming party, she's just moved to a new apartment. She wanted to tell me what she'd done to the place, how she'd decorated it, that sort of thing, you see what I mean.

She saw very well. I can't do this anymore. I'm quietly falling apart in front of your eyes, and you're still chatting away with her. Why didn't you tell me?

It didn't mean a thing.

The following night Juliette had a dream featuring a punctured, sagging globe whose continents were no longer in the right places. She was probably in Greenland, but Greenland was no longer in the Arctic and was all the wrong shape.

In the morning she returned to her desk and started at square one again on the Magellan project.

At about eleven o'clock the telephone on her desk rang, and a woman's voice asked to speak to her.

That's me, she said.

The person on the other end introduced herself as if Juliette ought to know who she was, but none of it meant anything to her. Juliette thought it must be someone from the client company handling the Magellan project, a woman she'd met once but whose name she'd forgotten.

I'm not sure how to introduce myself, the voice went on, it's a little awkward, I'm Olivier's girlfriend.

Oh, said Juliette. Right. Give me your number, I'll call you back from my cell. I can't talk here in the office, it's open plan.

She instantly loathed the voice. More than the voice, the tone of it. Too polite, falsely humble, rather plaintive. But in under a minute she was standing in the courtyard dialing the number she'd written down on a Post-it. She didn't wait to hear what the other woman wanted to say to her. Instead she started talking herself, gazing at her surroundings as if seeing them for the first time. The tables made of teak and steel, and their matching chairs. The glass roof overhead, designed by a famous architect.

I don't know exactly what Olivier's told you about our relationship, she said, or what conclusions you've drawn from that, but he and I still love each other. And we still make love to each other, you know. Otherwise I wouldn't have caught that thingamajig.

I know, the other woman replied. He hasn't contradicted that.


The paving stones, the door standing open to the cafeteria, and people from the marketing department coming into the courtyard.


I don't know how old you are, Juliette said. How old are you, actually?

Thirty-three.


Juliette was amazed. Olivier had said V was much younger than he was; he talked about her as if she were practically still a student. She'd deduced that V must be twenty-five, twenty-eight at the most. But in the world of politics the notion of youth was skewed. She felt a twinge of envy as she remembered she'd already felt old at thirty. That was right before she'd met Olivier, she was only just emerging from the black hole she'd descended into after her rape, and she felt her life was over, before it had even started.


She kept going.

Thirty-three, okay, you're not eighteen, you're not a little girl, you should have some idea, then, of the risk you're taking embarking on an affair with a married man.

You're wrong there, the other woman said. This isn't at all like me.

Juliette sighed.

I didn't necessarily mean personal experience. More a sort of grasp of life. Even without going through it yourself, you just have to have read a book or two. Which I think you have.

I'm happy to play the role of the wicked seductress if that's what you want, V replied without picking up on the jab, but that's not how it happened. He's the one who came looking for me, if you must know.

Her tone of voice was firm, the voice of someone who was in control of herself and who wasn't going to be walked all over. In a minute she's going to say she has witnesses, thought Juliette. She had a sudden mental picture of an accident, of a jointly agreed statement for the insurance companies, of two women drivers squaring up to each other next to a damaged car. Except this was about a couple, it was about her marriage, a couple reduced to little pieces of badly crumpled metal.

I don't doubt he did, she said to cut short this line of argument. There was no doubting Olivier had behaved badly in all this, but she felt that the question of blame, so crucial in a road accident, was utterly secondary here. I don't doubt he did, it takes two to have a relationship. But why won't you leave him alone *now*? Has he asked you to stop calling him or not?

He asked me not to call him today. He didn't say in general.

Juliette said nothing for a moment, while she absorbed this. Either she'd misunderstood or Olivier hadn't made himself very clear.

So why did you call him again earlier, why are you still sending him texts?
He never asked me not to send him texts.

The conversation was going nowhere. Not knowing what to say next, Juliette decided to ask why V had called.
Olivier's unhappy, she said. I love him enough to accept that he stay with you.
That's very generous of you, said Juliette.
But let him keep seeing me.
He hasn't asked that of me. And you're not really giving us that option, I don't think. You have a nervous breakdown if we go to the cinema together.
There was no connection, she said, I was ill that day.

Pissignac came into the courtyard, talking animatedly with a coworker. Juliette took refuge in the hall.

Galatea Networks' monumental staircase.
That recess in the corridor behind the restrooms.

I don't want my relationship with Olivier to end, said V.
Neither do I, I don't want *my* relationship with Olivier to end, Juliette replied.

How long had this conversation been going on?

She was now sitting on the stairs.

But he's not tied to my apron strings, you know, said Juliette. He's a free man. I don't watch him like a hawk.

The large contemporary painting hanging in the hall, the doors open to the cafeteria. Every year the CEO of Galatea Networks, the great Madinier, commissioned an abstract work of art and hung it in pride of place in the hall. He must have gotten some sort of tax benefit from doing this. Juliette had never looked at it properly but gazing at it now, she thought she could clearly make out a face in the bottom right-hand corner of the canvas. She stared at it, her eyes bulging.

Listen, you're in love, you've known Olivier a month, let's be reasonable about this, for you he's just an option, you'll fall in love with someone else in six months' time. For him and for me, it's our life, ten years, two kids. Leave us in peace, like he's asked you to. You could have thousands of different relationships.

V's plaintive little voice hardened.

And marriages, then. Shitty marriages like yours. There are thousands of them too.

There was a long pause. The face in the canvas dissolved again; all Juliette could see now were crude, increasingly indistinct blobs of color, a droplet splashed on her hand.

Right. I'm going to stop there, I think. I'm going to hang up, I have work to do.

Fifteen minutes later, or an hour, or two, V called back, this time on Juliette's cell phone—Juliette hadn't thought to hide her number. In the meantime Juliette had had that horrible feeling of only now hitting on what she should have said, and she'd thought through everything she'd failed to say.

She cut V off straightaway.

Listen, what I suggest is you stop calling him. And if your relationship is that important to him, that vital, exceptional, irresistible, he'll end up getting back in touch with you, he's bound to. But let him think and make the decision for himself.

The other woman interrupted. Her voice had changed since the previous call. It was shriller, more rushed, almost a hiss.

There are things you may not know, she said, and you need to know them. Did Olivier tell you he came to my apartment three days ago and we made love and he told me he loved me?

No, said Juliette, he didn't tell me that.

Well, perhaps you should know that. I can understand you're hurt, but.

Of course I'm hurt, said Juliette, but what exactly are you looking for?

She was walking in circles on the porch. Her hands were shaking.

You want me to be disgusted by him so I throw him away and you can pick up the pieces, is that it?

Not at all, said V. It's just—

Maybe we should stop right there then, Juliette interjected. I'm going to call Olivier and let him explain, that's a bit more dignified.

The staff of Galatea Networks was starting to come out in small groups to have lunch. Juliette hung up, walked out into the street, and called Olivier. She was on the verge of a nervous breakdown, almost running, as she tried to find a quieter place, and shouting into the phone to be heard over the racket of cars. Olivier was shouting on the other end too.

It's not true, he bellowed. I swear it's not true, she's talking garbage.

I swear to you, Juliette, Olivier shouted, I don't know why she called you to tell you that, she's flipping out. It's kind of a good thing, it means she wants it to end too, I can't see any other explanation. Trust me, it'll soon be over, I swear.

Juliette walked on until she came to a square near the Saint-Augustin Church. The streets of Paris were so noisy. The din around her was deafening, but it was nothing compared with the chaos inside her head.

She sat on a bench and decided to call Florence.

One of us three is crazy, she said. Her or him or me. Or maybe two of the three, that's possible.

Come right over, said Flo, drop everything and come to my apartment. I'll wait for you here.

I'll stop by the gynecologist to pick up my prescription for the antibiotics and I'll be there.

Olivier called her back soon after that: He was worried, he couldn't get hold of her at the office, he wanted to know where she was. She eventually told him, and moments later he was there. They sat down together on the terrace of a café. She listened to him, her expression unreadable.

It's true, he said, I went to bed with her on Tuesday, she spent the whole day begging me to go see her new apartment, when she calls I can't hang up on her, I can't be cruel. I thought it didn't matter, that you'd never know. But I didn't say I loved her. I have said it to her, before, but not in the last few days. I told her that if I said I loved her, it would mean I was going to leave my wife, and that's not going to happen.

Tuesday. The day she went to the gynecologist. While she was being told she'd caught this crap and the gynecologist was talking about her "partners," he was sleeping with her. And it was when he came back from V's apartment that evening that he'd thrown all that aggression in her face.

I don't understand why she's doing this, he said. The next step would be for her to send you the letter I wrote her in Aubigny.

What had he put in that letter to make him so afraid? She can send it, I won't read it, said Juliette.

She was outside the theater yesterday evening, Olivier went on. She was waiting as we came out to take a look at you. I'd spent three hours on the phone with her in the afternoon, she had the same tantrum as the day we went to the movies.

Juliette sat in silence for a long time before making up her mind to comment.

She sure has a problem with movies and theaters. She doesn't mind us making love, but she clearly can't deal with us going to a show together.

He laughed, reassured to see Juliette more or less back to her normal self.

So anyway, she went on, what was the verdict? We weren't exactly at our best when we came out of the theater.

Olivier was still smiling, amused.

No, she said we didn't suit each other at all. And she wasn't at all impressed by how beautiful you are.

Juliette nodded.

And what did you reply to that?

He shrugged. Nothing, obviously. I just saw it as the words of a jealous woman.

He admitted to Juliette that when he was leaving V's apartment to come home one evening, she'd sent him a text: "I wish she were dead."

He hadn't replied then either.

# 15

The next day, Saturday, the much-discussed debates were happening in Bordeaux. Olivier had asked a colleague to stand in for him on the Sunday and decided to make a round-trip on the Saturday. When V heard the news, she called him several times, leaving dozens of messages, but he didn't call back. Instead he just sent a text telling her she shouldn't worry, he'd be there on the Saturday afternoon as scheduled to chair the roundtable in which she was participating.

He and Juliette didn't sleep much that night. Despite several attempts, Juliette hadn't succeeded in persuading Olivier to say he was sick and to cancel his trip outright. In the morning, though, he did take the precaution of changing his departure time and not catching the 9:09 train, as planned. Victoire knew he had a reserved seat with other journalists, and she was bound to be waiting for him on the station platform.

Olivier checked the times for the next train on the Internet, then they made themselves a coffee and waited, their eyes pinned on the kitchen clock. At 9:12 Olivier's cell phone rang. He picked up. V had just walked the entire length of the train and realized he wasn't on it. She was beside herself.

Olivier hadn't put on the speakerphone, but she must have been shrieking because more than three feet away Juliette could hear a distorted voice, although she couldn't make out the words. Olivier talked to her calmly, kindly. It was the first time Juliette had heard him speak to her. It felt strange, and extremely unpleasant.

I changed my ticket, I'm still at home…Yes, of course I'll be there, don't worry…I'm with Juliette, we're just having a coffee…No, she's not coming with me.

Then there was a silence.

Juliette tilted her head questioningly at Olivier. Explanations were being requested from the other end of the line. Olivier stammered, clearly uncomfortable.

Listen, what happened yesterday was, well, pretty violent...

She watched him tying himself in knots, not saying the words that she, Juliette, wanted to hear. Things like: It's over, I don't want to see you anymore, stop calling me. She could prompt him with dozens of lines like that if he was short of inspiration, simple little lines that would make everything clear. Why were they so difficult to say?

In the end he hung up, then got up to go to the train station. She caught hold of his arm. Call me while you're there. He held her gently to him. Don't worry, nothing can happen, there'll be four hundred people in the room.

When Juliette called him sometime later, he was on the train. Something had just occurred to her.

She doesn't know you're catching the train back this evening, does she? She thinks you're spending the night there.

No, she does know, of course she does.

When and how had he told her? A mystery. But Juliette was getting used to not asking too many questions and sticking to the ones that really mattered.

I know she's going to try to get you to miss your train. I know she will, she'll do anything to keep you in Bordeaux for the night, so please don't get trapped.

Don't worry, there's no danger of that. Anyway, I already have a voice mail full of abuse on my cell.

What's she saying?

Oh…you make me puke, the pair of you, that kind of stuff.

There was a music festival on that evening. Juliette went out with the children to meet Florence and Paul at a café. They were joined a little later by Stéphane and Sylvia. Juliette had had no news of Olivier since the morning. She called him at around eight o'clock to let him know where she was. By then he should have been on the train. But his cell phone was still off. She could feel the panic rising.

This isn't right, she muttered to Florence. If he'd caught the train, he'd have sent me a text by now.

Nearby a band was making a terrible cacophony playing Rolling Stones covers. Johann was hanging on to her leg, sniveling, and Emma was exhausted too. Juliette decided to go home. She'd only just shut the door when Olivier called her. He was trying to find them, her and the children. He seemed relieved to catch her at home, and moments later the two of them were sitting comfortably in the living room. His train had just been a bit late, he said.

He described the day, the succession of roundtables. V had sat near him and said she was sorry.

Sorry about what?

About the voice mail she'd left that morning, I guess.

He played it for her. It went something along the lines of:

I wish you good luck with your nice little wifey, she's got you back under lock and key, at least I've helped bring you closer. I hope for your sake that in five years or maybe ten you'll find a love like the love I was offering you, full of freedom and trust.

Yeah, right, thought Juliette.

He'd replied, of course, to say he forgave her, that that wasn't the issue.

Then, as predicted, V had tried everything to stop him from going home to Paris.

It was a nightmare, said Olivier. She followed me to the station, she was crying, she bought a ticket from a machine and got onto the train with me. I spent the whole journey with her in my arms, it was the only way to stop her screaming. When we reached Paris, I literally had to run away, then I stopped and waited for her. When she caught up with me, she clung to me, so I started running again. It was a nightmare. But what could I do? he asked. I really can't attack her physically.

Just then his phone started ringing. He put his head in his hands.

She won't stop, he said. I can't take it anymore.

The ringing went on, tirelessly, stopped for a moment as the call was switched to voice mail, then started again. Olivier put his cell on silent. But sitting there on the table, it shuddered and bucked like an animal caught in a trap, refusing to be reduced to silence. It kept on giving out muffled rumblings that sounded angry and threatening. In the end Olivier turned it off completely. Juliette's immediately took over.

It's her, said Olivier. Don't pick up, please.

Juliette had a mounting feeling of suffocation. V had obviously put her number in her phone's address book after their conversation. Olivier was watching her anxiously.

Juliette, I swear to you I thought about you for that whole journey, I was holding her in my arms thinking I could tell you the truth. I had to calm her down, I couldn't do anything else.

I guess.

He took a deep breath.

There's something else you need to know, then it'll be over, then that's it. She came to Aubigny.

The evening I got there she called me, she said she was on the freeway. I shouted no, told her I was putting Johann to bed. He asked me, Why are you shouting, Daddy? It was horrible. She arrived later, you called me back like I asked you to, it was awful, do you remember, I was out of breath, it took me five minutes to catch my breath, she was in the garden, I didn't want her to interrupt our conversation, I was worried she'd come into the house any minute, and you'd know she was there.

Juliette remembered, yes. She was still in shock about what had happened on the train, but yes, she'd called to say good night to Johann, he'd asked her to call back later, he'd taken a really long time to answer the call, he was out of breath.

What could I do, he said. I wrapped her in a blanket and carried her to the top bedroom, we made love, she wanted

to sleep with me in our room, I said there was no way, that
Johann would come into the bed, and I didn't want him to
find her with me. She said it didn't matter, children understand everything. She wants to spend a night with me, it's an
obsession. In the morning I left early, before she woke, to go
to the beach. I put Johann in the car and left like a thief, then
I called her and insisted she leave before I got back.

What else could I really do, he said.

Juliette's whole body tenses, and her skin prickles at
the thought of her little boy finding another woman in his
father's bed. She can picture Johann still half asleep, slipping
silently into the bedroom, tottering on his little legs, oh her
little bunny rabbit, lifting the sheet on autopilot, as he's done
a thousand times, and then his horrified eyes widening as he
sees a stranger's body, a body that isn't his mother's, naked
obviously, and why not her pussy while we're at it, assum-
ing she sleeps on her side, her pussy on a level with his eyes,
when she, Juliette, has always made a point of wearing panties in bed since having kids. Or worse, it's too dark for him
to realize something's weird, or he's kept his eyes closed, he
clambers into bed without a thought in his head, her little
boy's so good at climbing, he heaves himself up, and there
we are, he lies down next to her, against her breasts, and
suddenly he doesn't recognize his mommy's shape or her
smell, he can't work out where he is, or who he is, his world
turns upside down, and this other woman starts laughing,
she thinks it's funny, the expression on his face, she even says
it doesn't matter, kids understand everything. Juliette could
commit murder.

If that had happened, she says, it would have been the end of you and me.

I know, Olivier replies. And she probably knows that too. That's why she wanted it so badly.

So what did you do?

I stayed upstairs with her, not for very long. I got up very early, the minute she was asleep, like I said, I ran away, I took Johann and ran.

She plays it through in her mind. Johann alone on the second floor, in his little bedroom, in the silent countryside, getting up in the night and finding his father's bed empty, not even rumpled, all the lights are off, he's all alone in this empty house, his father's left without him, abandoned him, she knows only too well what it can do to you suddenly not having a father, feeling totally alone, abandoned, he cries out in terror, and it wouldn't take much for her to start screaming too, she's struggling to hold back the tears.

Olivier holds her close, covers her in kisses, reassuring her as if she were the child all of a sudden, in a way he's never done before. Their love's in bad shape, but they still have this, the powerful love they share for Johann and for Emma, a love they share, the child of their own love for each other, and something the other woman can never, never take from her.

It didn't happen, Juliette. Johann didn't wake up. I went down to check on him several times, I left all the doors open deliberately. If he'd cried, I'd have heard him.

She calms down in his arms. They're lying on their bed, locked in each other's limbs, both flinching every time a door opens or closes. She doesn't have our address, does she, you're sure? No, he says. I'm sure she doesn't.

There's still music playing outside.

Do you think she followed you?

I'm sure she did, he says. She's out there somewhere looking for us, she knows I live near the place Stalingrad. She must be looking around all the café terraces for us.

Both their cell phones are switched off. They should sleep. They sleep.

Sometime later Juliette wakes in a panic, she strokes Olivier to wake him, he instantly has an erection. What's the matter, honey, why aren't you sleeping? Still half asleep, they make love; it burns her terribly, but it also feels so sweet, sweet as a dream. Eventually they climax together, softly, in silence, and this goes some way to soothing them.

We've never made love like that, says Olivier.

Juliette looks at him, surprised.

In the early days, surely, wouldn't you say?

Not even then. You've just made love to me like you would to a lover. And there's something I want to tell you, because you may be wondering: I never think about her when we're—Never.

She believes him, obviously. All the more readily because the thought hasn't occurred to her until now.

Then they try to get back to sleep, their bodies molded together in their favorite position, both lying on their sides with her pressed up against his back, with one arm around him. She can tell that through the thick curtains it's almost dawn. But Olivier isn't breathing the way he normally does when he's asleep. Maybe he too is lying there motionless, listening to his own heart beating, eyes wide open in the gradually dispersing darkness.

# 16

Of course Juliette knew Olivier was lying to her. She wasn't stupid. She'd gotten a sense of this watching him operate with their friends at Buttes-Chaumont the day he canceled his trip to Rome. And it was confirmed for her later, when V called her at work, and then again when Olivier told her about the night at Aubigny. She knew Olivier wasn't being as open as he was trying to appear, that his determination to break up with V wasn't as wholehearted as he was telling his wife it was. She knew men like him found it difficult to take drastic action; they liked keeping their options open, having fallback positions and escape routes, and they rarely embarked on affairs of the heart without keeping several possible exits wide open. Just in case. So as not to be left looking like a dick. One evening Olivier had said: I'm frightened. Frightened I'll end up losing both of you. Juliette hadn't reassured him. It really was a possibility.

She knew he was still lying to her, but she didn't know just how much. She felt she was standing on the banks of a frozen lake, studying its surface. Apparently frozen, but just how deep was the ice, hard to tell. There's no way of knowing whether it's a treacherously thin film or an ice field as solid as terra firma, whether you can trust it, putting one foot forward, then the other, without the ice giving way, stepping out without any fear of sinking straight to the bottom, instantly frozen, swallowed in those hypocritical waters. Still doubtful, Juliette edged along, clinging to overhanging branches on the bank, the intangible, dependable details that proved Olivier wasn't completely taking her for a ride. The fact that he'd changed his departure time to Bordeaux. The fact that he hadn't picked up V's ten thousand phone calls that evening of the music festival. Ever since she'd seen his cell phone spinning on the kitchen table, twitching and bucking, giving off muffled cries as it lay dying, she'd had a good feeling about it. She now saw it as an ally.

The day after the music festival, Olivier got Juliette to listen to the dozen or so messages V had left on his voice mail that evening. Played one after the other, interrupted by beeps and the synthesized voice giving the time of the call, they gave an acute sense of an unfolding drama; they were a striking illustration of the ravages that passionate love can effect on a particular, fragile sort of imagination. The recording would have made a good one-act radio play about twenty minutes long, in the same vein as Cocteau's *The Human Voice*. It could have been called *Chronicle of a Breakdown Foretold*. It was fairly restrained at the start with a "Call me please," then it crescendoed with a few "I beg of you" 's, some "You can't do this to me" 's, screams, groans, a beep, then silence. The last call came at six in the morning.

Olivier wanted to see her reaction. He didn't seem to realize how painful it was for Juliette to be thrust into the intimacies of her husband's relationship with V. She was suffocating, suddenly battling the feeling she'd been shoehorned into their embraces, sandwiched between them, fighting to break away from their intertwined arms. But maybe it really was already over between them, in which case Olivier was actually pushing her into the middle of the battlefield, into the no-man's-land between what were now enemy lines. This thought was something of a relief: Olivier's apparent indifference, the very fact he was making her listen to these messages seemed to confirm that he'd chosen his camp and decided firmly and definitively to break it off.

What are you going to do? she asked.

Nothing, Olivier said. I don't intend to call her, if that's what you're asking.

Just then, as if in response to this announcement, he received a text on his cell phone: "I beg you. There's nothing worse for me than your silence." This accentuated the agonizing impression that V was in the room with them, hiding in a corner, behind the door, under the table, waiting to pounce.

Olivier thought, then started typing on his phone. Juliette got up to make another coffee. When she sat back down, Olivier showed her the text he'd just sent:

"You need to stop torturing yourself."

You didn't say you need to stop, she said.

He didn't respond to this. She didn't say anything for a while, sitting drinking her coffee in silence.

Have you actually told her you love me? she asked.

Yes.

How did you tell her?

He hesitated.

I told her I couldn't love two women at once.

Juliette nodded.

So you didn't tell her you loved me.

Olivier sighed. Juliette felt very clearly that right now he wasn't sure he loved either of them, and he would have given anything not to be having this conversation but to be in a café with the guys or out fishing with the kids.

Juliette took Johann and Emma to the swimming pool, and Olivier went to the office to help the Web team upload the videos of the previous day's debates. When he came home, he was ashen. He tried to pretend everything was fine and he hadn't heard from V, well, just an e-mail. But everything about him belied this claim, and it wasn't long before he snapped under Juliette's probing eyes. As he could have predicted, V had come to the office.

I bumped into her right away, she was waiting for me on the sidewalk outside. She was drugged up to the eyeballs, it was scary. This isn't about love anymore, d'you see that? We've moved on. She really is a wreck. We talked a bit, for a few minutes, if that, and she broke down again, like that evening when I called you, about the movies, an epileptic fit, that's what she told me, either way it was quite a sight. She asked me to use her cell to call a friend of hers, some guy called Tristan, who I met at her apartment the first evening. He came immediately. He glowered at me like he really hated me and said he'd already had to scoop her up on the place Stalingrad last night, she'd passed out, he took her back to her place by taxi, he had to come back this morning to pick up his motorbike, which he'd left outside the subway station.

A pause.

According to him, these aren't actually epileptic fits, just really violent anxiety attacks, there's nothing anyone can do, they're not really dangerous, you just have to wait for it to pass. She's on medication, she's been on sick leave for two years, she hadn't told me that, of course.

That's the icing on the cake, said Juliette.
So what's this Tristan like?
Okay, said Olivier. Not exactly friendly, but sensible. I told him I'd like to talk to him. We agreed to meet in a café tomorrow morning, then he took her home.

Juliette nods. Another long pause. Olivier bites his lips, snaps the joints in his fingers, on edge.

You should have seen the way he looked at me. Like I was a torturer, a Nazi. Am I really that tough on her? I feel like the worst asshole of all time.

Of course not, says Juliette.

He peers sideways at her, apparently not convinced.

I'm not sure I can trust you on that one. Maybe Tristan can help me get things straight.

Let's hope so, says Juliette, whose knuckles are completely white from balling her fists; she's having to suppress the urge to scream, and deep down she's thinking, Yeah and what the hell is this condition she has, what exactly is this condition?

No, really, I'm interested, I'm even very interested. What's this condition that makes everyone feel sorry for you, you're forgiven everything, everyone's hopelessly indulgent toward you, you don't care who you step on, but you can have a nervous breakdown in the street, sit on the local government and hound people on the phone, have a political career at the expense of national education, sick leave, my ass, and everyone thinks it's fantastic, everyone's taken in, and you're a role model for all women, a left-wing icon, a figurehead for new feminism. Well, if that's how it works, I'm sick too, I'm sick with the pain of it, but nobody gives a shit about that, I need to calm down, come on, breathe, there's a good girl, there you are, now breathe again, breathe in and breathe out, that's it, you hang in there, good girl, calm down, you're going crazy.

# 17

V's friend arrived a few minutes late, with his motorbike helmet under one arm, and stopped in the doorway to the café to scan the room before going over to Olivier with a surly expression. He was no giant but had an impressive build, and while he took off his biker jacket with its armored inserts and hung it on his chair, he radiated such hostility that Olivier couldn't help feeling slightly apprehensive as he pictured a physical confrontation between them should the conversation take a bad turn.

To his relief, Tristan actually proved understanding. He showed no surprise as he listened to Olivier's account of how V had followed him all the way to Normandy and also onto the train bringing him home from Bordeaux, how she'd waited outside his office block and called him the whole time despite his pleas to stop, refusing to accept his decision to break it off.

Is that really what you want? Tristan asked. To break it off?

He was staring at Olivier with piercing, intensely dark eyes. Olivier hardly hesitated at all.

Yes, he said.

Tristan didn't respond for a moment, then nodded with something that Olivier interpreted as incredulity but it could also have been pity, or dismay.

Did you make that clear to her? Tristan asked.

I think so.

Tristan then asked Olivier to tell him the exact words he'd used, he was very persistent. Was he sure of his decision, it was absolutely crucial he didn't leave room for any ambiguity in what he told V, he mustn't show any hesitation, if not, she wouldn't waste a moment jumping into the breach and going back on the offensive. Meanwhile Olivier tried to explain how helpless he felt in the face of V's fragile state of mind, the tenderness he felt for her, and how difficult it therefore was for him to use words that were bound to sound brutal, particularly now he'd seen the hysterical reactions produced by his more or less timid efforts so far. But Tristan swept these objections aside with a flick of his hand. Olivier was fascinated by his self-assurance, which implied in-depth experience of situations like this with V. After a few minutes he couldn't help asking him whether this was the case. Tristan didn't answer. Instead he pointed to where he'd left his cell phone on the table. It had just received a text from V: "He must love me. I need him to."

At this point in Olivier's description of the conversation for Juliette that same evening, she stiffened visibly. "Need." She loathed that word. Need had nothing to do with love. The very idea of appeasing a physical need, when it came to sex, disgusted her. In her own personal experience she would only admit to feelings of desire, which could sometimes be violent, but desire made no demands, and when desire was fulfilled, it produced only a sense of wonder and gratitude; unlike need, which was demanding and ill tempered and went hand in hand with a sense of entitlement, of rights that one person believes they have over someone else, as if love could ever be anything other than a gift, a miracle between two people.

What are you thinking? Olivier asked.

Nothing, said Juliette. How did it end?

I've pretty much told you everything. I was surprised she'd sent him that text, I didn't know she knew we were meeting.

Do you think he was there on assignment?

Perhaps. Anyway, right at the end he told me he wouldn't have a moment's hesitation if he were me. He's married too, he has three kids, but he's been in love with V for years, he'd dump everything in a flash if only she wanted him.

It was so huge Juliette couldn't help laughing.

Sounds like you've found the perfect person to talk to.

Olivier didn't smile.

One thing's for sure, he said. This morning I realized she's not going to work this out for herself. I need to do it for her, and I just can't, it would be like throwing her off a cliff.

Having exhausted other options, Juliette had looked for a family therapy center and persuaded Olivier to go to a meeting there with her. They arrived together at lunchtime the following day.

The therapist was a youngish, kind-looking woman who showed them into a bare, impeccably clean room, furnished in a soothing Zen-inspired style. She sat down with them in white armchairs around a small, round glass table on which there was an orchid in a single-stem vase, and she asked them to explain, one after the other, why they had decided to come.

Olivier spoke first and, in answer to the psychologist's first question to him, he reiterated that he didn't want to leave Juliette. He also said:

I felt I had a right to have this relationship.

A right? the therapist echoed, raising her eyebrows. "Right" is a very strong word. Who gave you that right?

He hesitated. I don't know. I felt I had the right, everyone was doing it.

Why did you talk to your wife about it?

A pause.

It was a relief, I think.

Wasn't it a way of asking her to protect you from this relationship?

He hesitated again, said, Perhaps, yes.

When it was Juliette's turn to speak, she described V's phone call and froze when she heard the therapist's response:

I feel a lot of compassion for this young woman.

Did she hear that right? The shrink was full of compassion for the Other Woman. Clearly none for her, though. As usual, Juliette had no right to any compassion. But no. She'd misunderstood. The therapist repeated what she'd said: I feel you have a lot of compassion for this young woman.

Olivier was amazed, he seemed to find this comment bizarre.

You know what? That's true, Juliette acknowledged after a moment's silence. I understand her, I think. I can see aspects of myself in her, myself ten years ago. She's not completely alien to me.

A while later she added: I'm really struck by how little Olivier's done to protect me in all this. How little he's ever done to protect me.

You're the one protecting him, the therapist said, nodding. You're protecting him, you're protecting your children, and you're protecting this young woman. What about you, who's protecting you?

No one, said Juliette. I think that's why I came up with those infamous words "I'm not sure I want to grow old with you." At thirty I really wasn't that bothered about it. But as you get older, your needs change. Maybe one day I'll want someone to take care of me.

After the session they both felt slightly calmer, and they said good-bye on the sidewalk before heading back to work. Olivier held her to him and gave her a long, lover's kiss.

I'm going to call her, he said. I think that session helped me see more clearly what I have to say to her.

Have you heard from her since this morning? Juliette asked.

I've felt my phone vibrating in my pocket all morning. I must have eighteen messages.

When Juliette reached Galatea the following morning, still on the sidewalk outside the main entrance, she called him.

I wanted to tell you something very important: If ever, in a week, or six months, you have to sleep with her again, if ever that happens, please, please don't give her the choice of getting pregnant. A woman like her would do anything to hold on to a man. I know you won't think it's possible, but I know she's prepared to do anything.

I don't have any intention of sleeping with her again, he said. But I understand.

Later in the day Juliette tried to get hold of Olivier again, without success. His phone was permanently engaged. When she finally managed to speak to him, she asked whether he'd heard from V, and all he managed was a restrained "I had an e-mail, everything's fine."

At eight o'clock that evening he still hadn't called, as he usually did, to say what time he'd be home. She was suddenly overwhelmed by anxiety, distraught that he still couldn't see he must never leave her with no news like this.

She called Flo in tears.

When he finally came home, he looked surprised.

I didn't think you'd be in such a state. I actually thought I was home early.

This is pure hell, she said.

He sighed.

It's moving on, I promise.

He came over to take her in his arms, but she pushed him away and went out to find a handkerchief; he wandered off, hurt. She immediately regretted her rejection and looked around for him. He'd slumped into an armchair in the living room.

I know it's pure hell, he said. I know. Afterward we have this whole question of taking care of you…but what I'm doing right now, trying to stop this, telling her it's over, that's taking care of you too. It really is.

She blew her nose and came to sit next to him, head held low.

How could you do this to us? she said. Then, crestfallen, she added, Was it really that exceptional, with her?

He shrugged, tired.

I don't know what to say. We've had exceptional times too, you and me.

We have, she said. When the children were born, for a start.

Yes. Our marriage too.

She looked at him in astonishment. She'd never imagined that being married had meant so much to him.

Yes, our marriage.

After a pause she continued: We are moving on, but we've fallen so deep into a hole, there's such a long way to climb back up before there's the same trust.

She hesitated before asking him whether he'd heard from V today, hesitated a moment longer, and then eventually murmured slowly and quietly:

We've come this far, tell me the truth. If you really want to look after me, I want to know what's going on with her, the facts but also what you tell her, because right now what you say means as much as what you do. It's not going to be fun for me, believe me. Believe me, I'd rather not have to hear this, but I'm asking it of you. Otherwise your lies will end up driving me crazy.

He sat there in silence, gazing blankly ahead.

Then admitted unwillingly that V had sent him two e-mails. The first said: "Okay, I get it, it's over, but I must be allowed to talk to you on the phone." The second, a little later (or was it the other way around?) expressed her anger: "You got what you wanted. Now you can fix this pathetic little thing you have with your wife."

Every word seemed to take a toll on him, to torture him. Juliette looked at him, puzzled.

Anyway, Juliette said, we don't have the option of staying together while you carry on seeing her, even if we, you and I, could manage it. Given her reactions, it just wouldn't be possible, you do agree, right? He agreed, but still looked devastated. Juliette took his hand. She could never have guessed that at the very moment she was begging him to tell her the truth, Olivier was still lying to her. Feeling increasingly uncomfortable, he was aware of his wife studying him. He'd had lunch with Victoire, and before they'd parted a few hours earlier, she'd given him a copy of Simone de Beauvoir's *The Woman Destroyed*. He'd leafed through it, read a few pages. The story of a married man who has an affair and ends up leaving his wife, you see, some men do, you see, it *is* possible, V had said. He put his hands over his eyes so he no longer had to look at the distress in Juliette's expression.

# 18

Juliette was counting the days until the summer vacation. After several rainy summers in Normandy, she desperately needed some sunshine. She'd applied for her holiday time from Galatea back in February; it was always a real headache organizing the project directors' schedules because the company didn't shut down for August. In the end she'd agreed to take her time off in two blocks, and they'd arranged to go away to Italy for a fortnight right at the beginning of July. She'd rented a house by the sea, in the coastal part of Tuscany that was more affordable than Chianti's luxurious villas with pools, especially in the first two weeks of July; besides, with children as young as Johann and Emma, private pools were a nightmare, whether or not they were fenced. No way did she want to be jumping up from her deck chair with her heart beating like a drum as she scanned the area to see if one or other of them was still there or checking fifteen times a day that she or Olivier really had shut the gate to the pool. She'd chosen the house on the Internet, an old stone building with rudimentary comforts, but it seemed to ooze charm, nestled in olive groves. She loved olive groves, and Olivier sometimes joked about it, saying she might not even have noticed him if he hadn't had a name that reminded her of olives. She would smile, careful not to contradict him.

It was June 24. In just over a week, Juliette thought, they'd be miles from Paris and miles from V, and the vise that had tightened around her heart would let up a little, even though she knew their problems would still be far from over. Only the day before she'd had the lucidity to tell Florence: He'll never choose, I know he won't, he'll wait till one of us—her or me—gives up the fight. When Florence looked skeptical, she went on emphatically: Olivier's like that, he always has been. He waits to be chosen. He stays with whoever hangs on hardest. She'd given a little tilt of her chin, as if to say you'll see, and hadn't said another word, her face unreadable.

Olivier wasn't working that day. It was the first day of the summer sales, and he was planning to buy himself some shirts. He never really went shopping, once a year at the most, and apart from the presents she occasionally gave him (usually sweaters, soft and very comfortable ones she'd love snuggling up to), Juliette didn't get involved with his wardrobe. He didn't have anything left to wear. Then he'd go visit his brother, who'd been admitted to the Yvelines private clinic a few days earlier following a motorbike accident. He called Juliette at work at the end of the morning to tell her his plans and mentioned in passing that for several hours now V had been trying nonstop to get hold of him. Tired of resisting, he'd eventually replied and had lied to get rid of her, saying he was out of Paris for the day.

When Juliette took Olivier's call, she was in the cafeteria with Joséphine, a coworker from HR to whom she'd just told the whole story. It was weird, not at all in Juliette's nature, this sudden need to talk, to confide in someone she liked well enough but who wasn't one of her close friends. Joséphine did actually seem surprised, and Juliette noticed this, but she couldn't help herself, it was like an overflow system, there was no containing it, the words flowed of their own accord, with no hint of anger, calmly, and always with a touch of irony. If anyone asked, How are you? She'd reply, Not so great, my husband's cheating on me, her voice even as she waited for the other person to wince, which they unfailingly did. Of course there was an element of provocation in this, like with the doctor the other day. Her choice of words was party to that. They weren't her words; that was immediately obvious. She could have said: Things aren't great with my man, or even, I have relationship issues. That would have been more in character than this phrase that sounded like the advice column in a cheap magazine. But maybe she was reassured by the amazement she could see in people's eyes, maybe it reinforced the feeling she had that this wasn't really happening to her, that this sort of French farce belonged to another time and place, and she was being made to act it out against her will. It wasn't in her repertoire at all, hardly surprising she was pissed about the role, she was totally miscast, someone would eventually realize. When her phone rang, she broke off halfway through a sentence to take the call, listened, and then, after a moment's stunned silence, hung up.

That was him, she said. Passion, my ass.

Joséphine looked at her inquiringly but didn't dare ask her question. She didn't need to anyway; Juliette was already going ahead.

This other woman won't stop calling him, she desperately wants him to go see her and he says he won't go, he's in the Galeries Lafayette and the sales are on and he's had enough of this, he just wants to buy himself some clothes.

Joséphine's eyes widened.

I thought he was in love with her.

Juliette turned the palm of her left hand toward the ceiling to mean "go figure."

Me too. But hey, he really *does* need some shirts.

She felt the comedy of her words rising up through her irresistibly, and soon she could no longer contain a burst of nervous laughter. She quickly put her cup down on the bar to avoid spilling it, laughing so hard she was crying. She eventually quieted down and wiped her eyes. Joséphine was staring at her, speechless.

Damn, you're strong, she said. I admire you.

Juliette accepted the compliment graciously. Her ego wasn't exactly having a party right now, it was always good to hear compliments. Joséphine's admiration turned her lunch break into a precious moment of glory that she then spent in a beauty salon having her toenails painted in preparation for their vacation. Then she went back to work slightly more relaxed. Olivier called her that afternoon as he was getting on the train to go see his brother, then again three hours later to tell her he was in Versailles, waiting for the next train back into Paris Saint-Lazare, and he didn't have much battery left. His voice was different this time, almost flat, and Juliette, who'd recently developed an extraordinarily sensitive ear for the tiniest variations in the tone and modulations of her husband's voice, was immediately anxious.

Is something wrong? Is it your brother?

No, it's nothing to do with him. It's her. I'm frightened. It might be better if I did go see her, after all.

Juliette's heart instantly started hammering in her chest. She didn't say anything, waiting to hear more.

That asshole Tristan called me. He says I can't do this to her, I can't treat her like this. And if anything happens to her, he'll hold me responsible.

He sounded frantic, was almost shouting. She could hear the bustle of the railroad station in the background, contrasting with the studious atmosphere in Galatea's offices.

Juliette glanced around. Her immediate neighbor was typing busily, his eyes trained on his computer screen and headphones over his ears. A couple of yards farther on, two of her coworkers were leaning over a document, talking quietly. She swiveled her chair slightly away from them, pressed the phone to her lips, put her left hand over her mouth to screen it as best she could, and spoke as softly as possible, but still loudly enough for Olivier to hear, concentrating all the persuasiveness she could muster into her voice.

Don't go, she said, and she was irritated by a feeling that, because of all these constraints, her voice sounded false, not genuine, she recognized the voice she used when she read the children stories in the evening, when she was being the snake or the mermaid or the witch disguised as a fairy. She panicked to think she wouldn't be able to convince Olivier, pictured him in all that pandemonium of trains, lost, buffeted between V's wails, Tristan's outbursts, and his wife's artificially sweet voice, but she went on all the same, with all the energy of despair.

Don't go, I beg of you. It won't solve anything, in fact it'll make things worse. Come here when you get off the train. Or I'll come wait for you at the station if you want.

He interrupted her.

I have no more battery, I have to go.

She kept the phone to her ear for a moment, listening to the busy tone. Had he just hung up on her or had his cell phone cut out suddenly? Sadly, she was inclined to think it was the former. She looked at her watch. Quarter of seven. She didn't hesitate for more than a second. She stood up, grabbed her purse, and left the office, leaving her computer on and papers all over the place. She fled without explaining anything to anyone.

She pelted down the stairs.

Out on the street she ran. She ran as if her life depended on it; she ran to the nearest subway station. From Villiers, it was a direct line to Saint-Lazare train station.

She had a meeting with Pissignac scheduled for seven, and he waited more than twenty minutes for her. He asked her coworkers where she'd gone. As no one had any idea, he ranted and, in front of witnesses, descended into openly misogynistic comments before stalking off in a rage. At about nine o'clock the only project director still there took off his earphones and switched off his work station. On his way out he hovered in the doorway and looked back into the now deserted open plan office. He went over to Juliette's desk and, tactfully avoiding looking at the contents of her e-mail inbox, which she'd left open, he saved any active files and turned off her computer.

Juliette waited in vain for Olivier at Saint-Lazare. It was ridiculous and she knew it, it was pitiful even, at the age of forty, after ten years of marriage, racing around the subway and then the station, finding the right platform and then waiting, in tears, the succession of trains, a hundred figures glimpsed, the accelerating heart rate, the beginnings of a step forward, then dropping back. Taking her cell out a hundred times, trying to contact him yet again, getting his voice mail, hanging up before the end of the first word. She's running up and down, talking out loud, sobbing. People cast an embarrassed eye over her as they pass by, the more sympathetic among them ask her: Is everything okay, miss? Can I help you? She shakes her head, notices in passing people still call her *miss*, that's a good sign, says: Thank you, I'm fine. It's absurd, but the good news, the thing that saves her from total misery, is that no one takes her for a forty-year-old, and it's actually true, right now inside her head she feels twenty or fifteen or even five, inside her head right now she's a young fiancée, a little girl. People don't make enough of this, but the age someone is now doesn't obliterate the other ages they've been, all the ages a person has been coexist inside them, piling up, and then one particular age takes precedence depending on the circumstances. At the end of the day the whole question of age relates only very vaguely to how long it's been since you were born; well, that's what she feels anyway.

Either way Olivier doesn't show up. Waiting here on the platform for him doesn't make much sense. After quite a while this becomes obvious—even to Juliette, even in the terrible state she's in. She just can't understand how she missed him, but that's what happened. The rush hour is over, train arrivals are growing fewer and farther between, the crowd in the concourse is dispersing, it's evening already. Olivier is with V by now, or on the way to her place; she can roll around on the floor, screaming like a hysteric, it won't change a thing. She can see that's what passersby think of her, Oh my lord, they're thinking, another hysterical woman. Right, so V doesn't have the monopoly on that, Juliette now realizes. She might even be able to fight her on this front, if she wanted to. Nothing could be easier, after all. You just have to stop thinking about anything, empty your head completely, and surrender to the fear eating at your stomach. You just have to forget you have two young children waiting for you at home, relying on you, who see you as the center of the universe. Only here's the thing: Juliette wouldn't be able to do that for long, to forget about her kids, and anyway, she's pretty much had enough of the pitying way people are looking at her. So she decides to calm down, pack away her hysteria, lean against a pillar, and light a cigarette.

She doesn't think about anything as she smokes, her head weighed down by so much crying, her muscles aching like after a heavy night's drinking. She sobers up slowly, comes back down to her life.

She's now completely calm. She feels the way you do when everything's over. She knows she's lost.

She dials her home number to talk to the children's nanny.

# 19

As soon as Juliette called him, Jean-Christophe jumped on his scooter and rushed to Saint-Lazare. She'd fallen into his arms, explained the situation, and begged him to take her somewhere for supper. On the phone the nanny had eventually agreed to watch the children till midnight, but no later. Juliette could tell from her tight-lipped voice that it didn't suit her at all. But for once Juliette had had no scruples about abusing her kindness and forcing her hand. However strong her love for her children, she currently felt quite incapable of going home to read them stories about Prince Charmings while Olivier was making out with V.

As she might have expected, Jean-Christophe had chosen the coolest and probably the most expensive restaurant in the neighborhood. He was finishing placing their order and was selecting the wine when Juliette's cell phone rang. Olivier had just arrived home and was surprised not to find her there. She felt a flash of intense relief as she asked him how on earth she'd missed him. He explained tartly that he'd gotten the wrong train and had caught one that went to Montparnasse station. His voice still sounded strained. He'd only stopped by the house to recharge his phone. He wanted to know whether she'd be back soon so he could let Yolande, who was visibly sulking, go home.

Juliette hesitated.

Of course, she said. Tell her she can go now you're there.

He sighed, exasperated.

Don't pretend you don't understand, he said. I can't stay.

I don't see why not, Juliette replied.

I have to go see V. I'm worried she'll do something stupid.

Since admitting to his affair, Olivier had respected the code set by Juliette without a murmur, never letting himself pronounce V's name in front of her, and when he needed to mention Victoire, he settled for referring to her by her initial, as Juliette did. More often than not he didn't even have to; a simple "she" was enough. Juliette was privately amazed that even in this crisis situation, when she felt he was about to explode, he still respected this tacit agreement.

Don't go, she said, staring at Jean-Christophe, who was looking past her impassively, apparently absorbed in perusing the photos hanging on the wall facing him.

A moment later she jumped up and instinctively pulled the phone away from her ear. On the other end Olivier had started screaming.

Tell me what I should do, then, just tell me, if you're so sure of yourself. You know if she offs herself, it'll be over between you and me too.

Juliette felt that even though her phone wasn't on speaker, Olivier's cries must be audible as far away as the next table. As for Jean-Christophe, he hadn't missed a word. He'd stopped pretending he wasn't listening, and with his chin resting on his hands, he was watching Juliette attentively, inscrutable.

Juliette closed her eyes.

I want this hell to stop, she enunciated clearly.

Olivier said nothing for a moment, then replied more calmly, I told you I would need some time.

Don't go, Juliette said again.

Olivier's reply felt like a slap, a threat.

Okay, he said with a hard edge in his voice.

Then he hung up.

Juliette put her phone down on the table. She felt terrible. She raised her eyebrows to secure Jean-Christophe's approval.

Right?

Jean-Christophe shrugged.

Yes. I guess.

Is that it? I guess?

You could also let him go. From what I know of this girl, if he leaves you for her, he's likely to be kicking himself very soon and to come groveling at your feet.

Juliette shook her head, not convinced. Still, she hesitated. She herself had made a kind of phony suicide attempt in early adulthood, when she'd seen her then boyfriend kissing one of her best friends. She'd retaliated by taking every pill she could lay her hands on until he gave up trying to stop her, called an ambulance, and started swallowing pills himself. Between them they'd emptied the entire contents of the medicine cabinet, contraceptive pills included, before the emergency services arrived. It all ended with a double stomach pump, and the following day they'd made love in the confines of a single bed in the hospital before being thrown out by a horrified nurse. Quite a good memory really, looking back.

But well, she was twenty at the time.

What if she really kills herself?

Jean-Christophe smiled, softened by such naivety.

She won't kill herself. If there's one thing I know for sure, it's that.

How do you know?

People who commit suicide don't talk about it all the time. They just do it one fine day.

He looked away. The smile had been wiped off his face, and Juliette suddenly remembered that his mother had taken her own life when he was a teenager, before she, Juliette, had met him. He'd found her hanging when he came home from school. Juliette was furious at herself for carelessly introducing such a sensitive subject and tried fruitlessly to think of something to say to make up for it. But Jean-Christophe was smiling again with hardly a hint of bitterness in his casual expression.

Juliette was still hesitating. She was strung out, fiddling with her phone.

What's to say she won't do something dumb just to scare him? If I stop Olivier from going to see her and she swallows a bottle of pills on the strength of that, he's going to hate me.

That's for sure, Jean-Christophe agreed.

Juliette thought it over a little longer, then picked up her phone again and dialed the home number. Olivier picked up right away, after hardly half a ring, which gave Juliette the unpleasant impression he was expecting her call.

Yes? he said in an amiable voice, at odds with the previous phone call. He was clearly confident he'd won this hand, and it infuriated Juliette.

So, what are you doing? she asked coldly.

I don't know, he said. Why are you calling?

He's got her cornered.

Juliette sits in silence for a moment, lost. Olivier waits patiently on the other end. She starts talking again slowly. The words are stuck somewhere between her brain and her mouth; they're having trouble getting out.

You know if you go see her, every second you spend with her will be hell on earth for me?

Olivier becomes even more gentle. He can tell she's about to relax her grip, and he's suddenly not her enemy; he's back to being her partner, her lover, the person who shares her problems.

I do, he says tenderly, putting an arm around Juliette's shoulder's with the sheer magic of his voice. Of course I know that.

She makes herself continue.

And what are you going to do when you get there? Will you make love to her?

He hesitates.

No, he says. She'll want to, no doubt about it, she'll do everything to make it happen, but no. And she's got the STD anyway. No. I'll just try to calm her down.

This conversation is surreal. Juliette is staring at the table-cloth, her cell phone pressed to her ear, rubbing her forehead with her free hand. Her hands are shaking. She's picturing what the next few hours will be like if she gives in, and all at once it comes to her: He's asking my permission to go see this girl, and here I am giving it to him.

In a flash, she sees the sequence of events. She sees the consequences of what she's about to say perfectly clearly, many miles and many years from now. It's weird suddenly being clairvoyant, she just found out she's a medium, she has visions, illuminations.

A disheveled, tearful V clinging to Olivier like a ship-wreck survivor clutching a piece of wood, throwing her-self at him, kissing him, unbuttoning his shirt. He resists and resists, and of course gives in eventually. Because he's only a man after all, and it's a recognized fact that men can't resist, it's in their nature to take a female who offers herself, that's just the way it is, they can't fight it. And all the drama of tears too. So they make love. Without a rubber, given the state they're in. A rubber would tarnish the image of doomed lov-ers, of all-consuming passion. In a month V's pregnant. A child of Olivier's and V's in their lives forever, in Johann's and Emma's lives.

Whatever else happens, whatever decisions they may make. The irreparable.

No, she says.

Silence on the other end.

She takes a deep breath, looks up at Jean-Christophe, and repeats firmly:

No. Listen to me. I'm going to have dinner with Jean-Christophe, and you're going to stay home with the kids.

Fine, Olivier says, his voice soft and almost toneless, a frightening voice. So I'll tell Yolande she can go home, I'll call V and tell her you're not coming home and I can't leave the kids on their own. Mind you, it gives me a brilliant excuse not to go see her.

Exactly. Perfect.

But she's likely to show up here, I warn you.

Juliette takes it upon herself to ignore the threat, pretends not to notice anything strange about the way he said this. She just promises to be home before midnight and hangs up.

*Alea jacta est.*

The die is cast.

All's fair in love and war.

Right from the start, right from Olivier's first mention of this on the phone—I'm seeing a girl, I told her I was going to the movies with you, and she started screaming—Juliette was obscurely aware of a fight looming behind all this, a fight that V was waging against her. She feels as if this other woman wants to impose a character on her, a character that has nothing to do with who Juliette really is, the uptight little bourgeois, the wifey who only makes love in the missionary position, the mathlete who inevitably knows nothing about passion; but Juliette refuses to be a pushover, it's a question of pride, everyone puts pride in what they choose, and if Juliette's pride lies in having had thirty lovers, in having been raped, abandoned, aborted, and not wanting anyone's compassion, well, that's her incontrovertible right, and no one can stop her. And the more this goes on, the clearer the idea becomes in her mind; it's even starting to make her really angry, the way V's so sure she's superior, superior with her fancy school, superior with her career, her love, her suffering, even her rape.

She's thinking all's fair in love and war, but those are just words, and this is not a war, there's nothing humane about this battle, it's a fight between two females, a scramble, carnage; she can tell V wants to pull her apart, tear her to pieces—I wish she were dead—and she's got it just as bad herself, the intrinsically peaceful nature of women, give me a break, women are females, full stop, and females, when they have young, are worse; in fact, when they have young, that's when they become dangerous, that's when they're unstoppable, that's when they can kill.

Juliette smiles at Jean-Christophe. Now that the decision's been made, it's like having a weight off her shoulders. The waiter brings their meal. She digs into hers hungrily.

She does call back a little later, though (yes, she does trust him completely as a father, but) just to check that:
a. Olivier didn't somehow manage to persuade Yolande to stay
b. or even sneak out once the kids were asleep.

Recently she hasn't been so confident about how well she knows him.

He picks up. Yolande has gone home.

Perfect, says Juliette. Then she adds: I just wanted to check there was someone with the kids.

He doesn't respond to the provocation.

I've just called V's house, he says. There's no reply. She must have gone to bed.

Juliette hangs up without saying anything else. The rest of the evening with Jean-Christophe is almost jolly. They chat, linger at their table. Jean-Christophe is on his scooter, so he doesn't drink much, meaning she downs almost the whole bottle herself. At the end of the meal she's laughing out loud and smiling at him gratefully: He knows her so well but never judges her and has never hurt her. In times like this friendship seems to have much better qualities than love, particularly passionate love; it makes you really start to wonder why people go to such lengths to live as couples.

When they leave the restaurant, Juliette still really doesn't feel like going home, so Jean-Christophe gives her a ride around Paris on his scooter, driving it quickly and skillfully, with bursts of acceleration; she has her arms around him and is pressed hard up against his back. She can feel his muscles and his bones, the warmth and heartbeat of an adult body next to hers, but with no sexual subtext, incredible how soothing it is. She watches the streets filing past, feels the draft on her bare legs. She feels good, better than she has for several weeks.

When she puts her key into the door to the apartment, it's one minute to midnight.

The lights in the hallway are on, but she can't see Olivier. He must be in the living room, reading. She goes straight to the kitchen to take her antibiotics and fills a glass of water at the sink. When she turns around, Olivier is framed in the doorway. He's making the face actors make in films when in self-defense or accidentally the nice hero has committed a murder and staggers toward his wife, dazed, the blood-spattered knife still in his hand. He doesn't say anything. Neither does she. She doesn't want to ask any questions. So he goes and collapses into the armchair in the hallway and puts his head in his hands, then lifts his head back up and looks her in the eye. She's followed him as far as the kitchen doorway and waits there, taking little sips of her glass of water. She studies her husband objectively, with a critical eye, and deems his performance a little too theatrical. She's no longer frightened of whatever he has to tell her. She even has a rather delicious feeling of not giving a damn, not minding what he says.

She came here, he says.

Juliette doesn't waver. Stares at him.

She started knocking at the door, I was putting the children to bed. I looked at her through the peephole, she was out on the landing. I called Tristan, and he was waiting outside in a car, he said there was nothing he could do to stop her. I wanted her to stop knocking, so I opened the door, just a tiny bit, I asked her to wait there until Johann and Emma were asleep, she dropped down onto the doormat. Later she came in, I sat her in this chair—he indicates the chair he's on, the one in natural-colored linen, Juliette's favorite, her birthday present, she'd asked for it because that had been the only way to get Olivier to buy it, he'd thought it too expensive. She didn't get further than the hallway, I swear to you.

He's looking at her beseechingly, his eyes loaded with reproach. She still doesn't say anything, and her silence doesn't tell him anything he wants to know. He's getting angry now.

What else could I do, tell me that! Her psychiatrist called her on her cell while she was here, he gave her a hard time, but she was in no state to listen to him, she threw her cell on the floor. In the end Tristan came up, he said, That's enough now. I went down with them to help get her in the car. I left the kids alone, less than five minutes. As soon as we were in the street, we let go of her, and she tried to throw herself under a car right in front of us.

Juliette listens.
You let her in here when the kids were asleep, she says evenly.

He looks exasperated.

What could I do, Juliette? Did you hear what I said? She threw herself in front of a car *right in front of me.*

Right in front of you, of course. She sighs, suddenly exhausted, but very calm. Next time she comes here, I warn you, I'm calling the cops.

He looks at her as if she's just said something obscene. What the hell, did you hear that, did you hear what you just said?

I mean it. It's each for himself now, each of us has to save our own skin. I'm going to bed, I have my annual meeting with Chatel tomorrow.

She heads for the bedroom, and he follows her.

She makes her point clear without raising her voice: Olivier, I really want to sleep.

He looks at her with his hunted-animal eyes. I don't understand how you can treat me like this. What have I done to you?

She snorts feebly.

What you've done to me.

# 20

Juliette called Florence the following afternoon. She'd managed to do some damage control in her meeting with her general manager, but now felt exhausted. As usual, she told Florence, Chatel had left the door to his office wide open throughout their meeting, giving her the exasperating impression he was afraid of her, as if she were a panther about to eat the lion tamer, whereas with Pissignac he would shut himself in there for hours on end to talk about God knows what.

Florence laughed. Juliette asked whether Paul would be kind enough to give her a refill prescription for Bromazepam and also whether she could come over to their apartment to get some rest at the end of the day when she'd finished work. Florence said of course she could, she must come over whenever she liked.

The previous night, after their conversation, Olivier had walked out of their bedroom, slamming the door. He'd slept fully clothed on the couch in the living room. In the morning she'd said:

I've thought about this. As far as I'm concerned, this whole business is over. I don't want to hear any more about it. So I'd like you to take some things, get out of the house, and only come back when it's completely finished. When I can be sure that woman won't show up at my apartment the minute my back is turned.

His face was expressionless as he replied:

I really don't understand why you're reacting like this. Why now, I mean. What I did yesterday was just a continuation of what I've been doing for days and days to get this to stop. We didn't exactly have a picnic, you know.

Maybe not, she said. But it doesn't make any difference to me. I've always said I had limits, and I didn't even know myself what they were. Well, here we are, we're there. Now I'm saying stop. Each for herself. I'm protecting my children, and I'm also going to protect myself from now on, seeing no one's doing it for me.

Fine, he replied icily, if that's what you want. Can I at least give the kids their breakfast or do I have to leave right away?

When she came out of Galatea that day and headed over to Florence's apartment, Juliette didn't have the heart to trudge down into the subway. She took a taxi. She'd lost twelve pounds in three weeks, her cheeks were hollow, and her eyes had dark rings under them. Paul came to say hello between two consultations and was taken aback when he saw her. When she asked if he'd give her a new prescription for tranquilizers, he hesitated and sat down across from her, preoccupied.

How do things stand with Olivier? he asked.

I can see it all more clearly now, I think, she said. This isn't about jealousy anymore. I'm convinced this girl is crazy and destructive. I want her out of my life. And him too, if she's still a part of his life. I feel relieved now that I've made the decision.

It's true. You look like you're feeling better, Florence agreed.

Paul looked at his wife as if she'd lost her mind, but she held his gaze.

I promise you, she insisted, she's looking better.

He decided not to contradict her, settling for an imperceptible shake of his head. Juliette, on the other hand, gratified Florence with a real smile, the first since she'd arrived. Her face instantly softened and came alive, which reinforced Florence's theory about the performative power of words, a theory to which Paul, who'd been an analyst for twelve years, did not subscribe.

He was immediately on the counterattack.

Now you need to get hold of yourself physically. You're a pretty scary sight.

Juliette's smile vanished. Tears welled up in her eyes. Florence shot a fierce look at Paul, and he stopped what he was saying, sheepishly acknowledging defeat.

Have you heard from Olivier since this morning?

Juliette gave a disenchanted shrug.

I had a text just as I got to work: "Trust me. I'll call you this afternoon. You are my life." And he's been trying to call constantly this afternoon. I just switched my phone off.

Do you want to go lie down for a while? Florence suggested.

I'd love to, Juliette replied, getting to her feet meekly. I feel like I haven't slept for weeks, I'm dead on my feet.

She fell asleep almost before her head touched the pillow. She was woken by the landline ringing and tried in vain to get back to sleep, then resigned herself to getting up and joined Florence and Paul in the living room.

That was Olivier, Paul told her. He wanted to know if maybe you were here. I told him you were resting.

Juliette sighed. At that exact moment the doorbell rang.

I'll go, said Paul.

It was Olivier again, in flesh and blood this time. He smiled at Paul with the half-embarrassed, half-proud expression that, since his affair began, he'd been wearing in front of people who knew about it. Paul did not return his smile, settling for a handshake, then he stepped aside to let him in. Florence came over to them and kissed Olivier on the cheek before conveniently remembering something that urgently needed her attention in the kitchen. As for Paul, he'd already vanished.

For a moment Olivier stood in silence in front of Juliette, who was sitting on the couch and hadn't moved an inch. With a resigned shrug, she gestured to the space next to her.

Sit yourself down.

He did as he was told, maintaining his silence, which Juliette quickly deemed ridiculous, so she forced herself to break it.

So, where are you at?
You want me to tell you about it?
Well, you're here.

He told her. He'd seen V that morning, having arranged to meet her in a square. It was on his way there, he thought it worthwhile pointing out, that he'd sent the text to Juliette—"Trust me, you are my life"—before switching off his cell phone for a few hours, for fear she might try to get hold of him.

At this point in his account, Juliette gave a small sigh, which Olivier didn't seem to notice. Or if he did notice it, he didn't understand what it meant.

He and V had talked at length, calmly. It was really good, he said, even though it started very badly.

Why did it start badly? asked Juliette.

Just before we met, I called Tristan to ask whether he had her psychiatrist's number. The asshole couldn't think of anything better to do than call V and tell her I was trying to have her institutionalized.

Not a bad idea, said Juliette.

Olivier ignored the interruption. During their conversation, he told Juliette, he'd made things much clearer to V than he ever had before, reiterating the fact that whatever V insisted on believing herself, it had also been really special when he and Juliette met ten years earlier.

Juliette cut in again. As usual she was weighing his every word, even though she knew perfectly well how exasperating he found it.

Whatever V insists on believing? What do you mean? What does she think?

I have no idea. But I guess she thinks you and I have a marriage of convenience.

Great, said Juliette. Keep going.

I told her, again, that my life was with you, we've built something together, and I don't want to lose that. We talked through the times when I fooled around, when I was irresponsible, like planning that trip to Rome, and saying things or letting her say things that might have led her to believe that even though I'd always said I wasn't leaving my wife, it was still a possible outcome.

Such as? Juliette asked, thinking about one of the things V had said—I wish she were dead—that Olivier had not picked up on.

Like when she said: I've never been so happy.

And did you reply: Neither have I?

No, I didn't tell her that. No, I don't think I ever told her that. But it's true that in the first flush of love, I must have told her I was experiencing feelings I hadn't had for a long time. Yes, that's true.

Filled with an infinite sadness, she nods in silence.

And also the fact that I spoke to you so soon, she told me that made her feel I wasn't the kind of guy who'd have a mistress for years but never leave his wife.

He pauses briefly before going on.

I also told her there were some things I might have said to her that I wouldn't ever say again, particularly about sex.

Oh, said Juliette.

You and I have both noticed the last few times we've made love that it's never been so good between us.

No, not both of us, Juliette thinks. I never said that. But she's used to him thinking he knows what she's feeling better than she does herself.

Even in the early days? she asks again.

No, never, Olivier replies. I told her that…[another pause, he's floundering]…I told her that with you recently it had also been…[inaudible]…that you could also…[inaudible]. Basically, I told her that she could easily meet someone next week and have something just as special.

Juliette doesn't understand a word, but she knows it's important; she tries in vain to get him to say it again. She's well aware of the superhuman effort Olivier has to make to talk about this. He looks overwhelmed.

Yes, well, anyone can find it, I mean.

She gives up trying.

So?

So we managed to agree we have to let some time pass. She deleted my number from her cell phone right in front of me. (Another sentence comes back to Juliette like an echo: She threw herself under a car *right in front of me*! How theatrical, Flo said later — and it's true, V must have at minimum 379 entries of Olivier's number in her texts and her call history.)

How much time? Juliette asked. Forever?

No, said Olivier, we didn't say forever. It seemed obvious we meant we had to let the summer go by, but we didn't actually arrange to meet in September. The question now is: I don't know whether I should change my number.

Juliette gave a chuckle of surprise.

That's a bit radical, isn't it? she said.

Olivier clicked the joints in his fingers nervously.

Yes, but well, it sends a clear signal. Oh, I don't really know. We'll see.

A pause.

Otherwise she showed me her test results. So she does have the thingy, you know, that thing, like you ...

I'd have been surprised if she didn't, said Juliette.

...and she's HIV negative.

Some good news at last.

Olivier looks at her with a perplexed expression, not knowing what to think of her attitude. She smiles at him and, encouraged, he keeps going.

What are you planning to do now? Are you going home?

Of course. I need to see my little bunny rabbits.

Okay, well, I'll go over and take some things, then I'll look for a hotel. It's going to dig a bigger hole in the overdraft, but the way things are ...

Go to a friend.

I don't have any friends, he says.

Stéphane.

Olivier shakes his head.

I really don't feel like talking to him about it.

Okay, a hotel then, she says, although she's lost track of exactly what the point of this is.

Still, it's a relief to think he won't be there when she gets home.

After he left, she and Florence went out for a drink on the sidewalk terrace of a bar.

He doesn't get it, said Flo. He's not going to get it. And he doesn't have it in him to say "I don't get it." Paul and I have listened to you every day, what you're saying is clear, it's very clear. When Paul talked to him, he tried to make some points to him, Olivier said yes, but by the end he was saying the exact opposite, and Paul says he understands what you mean when you say Olivier doesn't listen to you, he doesn't hear what you're saying.

Juliette nodded glumly.

When did you say his mother died? Flo asked.
The year before we were married.
Aha, she said. And you became a mother too, that changes things a lot for men.

# 21

Olivier hadn't left.

When Juliette arrived home that evening, he seemed to have kept his promise. The drawers where he kept his socks and underwear were still slightly open, and his blue overnight bag had disappeared.

Juliette spent the evening alone with the children. Calm and properly available to them for the first time in weeks, she played Happy Families with an ecstatic Emma while Johann nestled against her, sucking his thumb, and fell asleep on her lap.

Then she went to bed and went out like a light. She woke with a start several times in the night, thinking she could hear noises in the apartment. She made herself stay where she was. The noises must be coming from the apartment above or below, the building was so noisy. She just wasn't used to sleeping alone anymore.

In the morning Olivier came into the bedroom in a bathrobe with a smile on his lips and a mug in his hand; he was bringing her morning coffee as if nothing had changed. She stared at him in astonishment. He stopped in his tracks.

Did you not get my message?

No.

I said I'd be here for when the kids have breakfast this morning. I waited till you were in bed before I came home, and I slept on the couch. I couldn't really see why I shouldn't be here. V gets it this time. There's no danger she'll go crazy again.

She made no comment and took her coffee with a thank-you, showing no objection. He could stay, it really didn't matter, she'd decided to spend the weekend in Brittany with a childhood friend. She'd just stop by the house after work to pick up the children on her way to the station.

Élisabeth's been asking me over for months, and you can't stand her. So now I never see her.

Olivier looked put out, but he didn't protest, sensing he had little hope of making her change her mind. Élisabeth genuinely was his least favorite of all Juliette's friends. He found her hard and pushy, and selfish, and the way she flaunted her homosexuality made him uncomfortable. Besides, Élisabeth certainly reciprocated the dislike he felt for her, and made little effort to hide it. He was worried about the influence their conversations might have on Juliette. But she just shrugged.

Don't worry, I'm not planning to talk to her about what's going on between us. I already know what she'll think, and I don't want to hear it.

The weekend she spent in her friend Élisabeth's little granite cottage felt somehow suspended, outside time, and she experienced it as a glimpse of what her life might be like if she and Olivier ended up separating. Élisabeth had no children. She taught French in a junior high in Morbihan and lived alone, surrounded by books and cats. She was very talkative, very clever, and very funny, wickedly funny. Lying on sun-loungers in her flower-filled garden, she and Juliette talked for hours across a range of subjects, although they all revolved around the same themes—Élisabeth's life, Élisabeth's lovers, Élisabeth's students and coworkers—punctuated by walks along the coast. Olivier's name didn't come up once, and as a result of this, Juliette felt carefree and cheerful in a way she hadn't for a long time. She laughed a lot. As for Emma and Johann, their weekend was absolutely unforgettable thanks to a new litter of kittens produced by Minette, one of the cats Élisabeth had adopted.

They arrived back in Paris very late on Sunday evening, after more than eight hours of traveling. There'd been a fire at Laval station, and all the trains had been rerouted to Nantes. When they finally alighted on the platform, the kids were so tired they could hardly stand. Juliette had the hardest time just dragging them to catch a taxi home. Olivier was waiting for them, very anxious. She'd texted him to warn him they'd be late. He'd left her several messages asking where they were and offering to come get them in the car, but she only picked them up once she reached Paris. When the taxi stopped outside their block, Olivier was out on the sidewalk. While Juliette paid the driver, he opened the door and scooped a sleeping Emma off the backseat. Then he grabbed the suitcase, and they went upstairs together, with Juliette carrying Johann.

When the children were finally in bed, Juliette dropped onto the couch in the living room, exhausted.

So what did you do this weekend?
Olivier still looked strung out. He gave an evasive wave of his hand.
Pretty much nothing.
Pretty much?
She called twice today. The second time was just after I heard the trains were rerouted. I didn't know where you and the kids were, I was waiting for you to call, I didn't want to stay on the line. She took it really badly, she thought I was just making stuff up.

Juliette sat in silence for a moment. Then she explained calmly how her feelings had changed since the previous Wednesday evening, given that he didn't appear to have a clear grasp of this.

You see, this isn't just about you and her anymore. I worked out that in the last week there hasn't been a single day when she hasn't insinuated herself into my life, into my privacy, she follows us to the theater, she calls me at work, she comes to our apartment, she went to Aubigny—

I know, he said. And you're right, it's not acceptable. And if she keeps it up, I'll tell her that. I really did get the fact that you asked me to leave. If that's what it takes, I'm prepared to go live somewhere else from tomorrow until we leave for Tuscany [he hesitated slightly]. Well, if we're still definitely going to Tuscany?

Juliette had thought about this over the weekend.

Yes, she replied, I think we definitely are. Unless something extraordinary, something I can't even imagine, happens between now and then.

This didn't seem to reassure Olivier. He was biting his nails.
Theoretically we only have another twenty-four hours.
Twenty-four hours?
She's going on vacation on Tuesday.
Mmm, Juliette managed. In theory. What did she want from you this evening?
For me to go see her at her apartment. Obviously.
Obviously.
Juliette felt a wave of panic washing over her.
She must be ovulating.
She wasn't joking. And she went on equally seriously: Olivier, if you see her before we go away, don't go to bed

with her. She wants to get pregnant, I'm sure she does. I know you don't think that's possible, but you don't know what some women are capable of. Trust my instinct. I know for sure.

I know, Olivier replied to her surprise. She wants my child. She's already said so several times.

Juliette hid her face in her hands. Please don't let it be too late, she thought.

Olivier put an arm around her shoulders and made her look at him.

Don't be scared, Juliette. I've done some thinking this weekend too. I'm very clear on some things: I don't want to see her again, for now. Much less sleep with her. But I also know I don't want to be—I can't be—brutal or violent with her. I think I know what to say to stop all this, but I can't bring myself to say it, even if it means it takes longer. She's fragile, I need to be gentle with her. I've had a few days of respite now—that's kind of insulting to her, saying it like that, but hey—and I know that's because I spoke to her on Thursday morning. I'm pretty confident, I think in a couple of months she'll feel differently, and I will too.

You think so?

I'm sure. It's not just disappointment in love for her, there's also the humiliation. She'll get over it.

Juliette nodded.

If you say so. Let's go to bed.

They stood up and started heading for the bedroom. She stopped him in the doorway.

Why don't you want to leave me? It would be so much easier.

He smiled, playfully.

You're right. Cowardice maybe?

Maybe, she replied seriously.

No, I don't think that's it. Because I love my life with you, because I think we still have stuff to do together.

He smiled again and added with a note of irony: Perhaps I love my wife after all. That's a possibility.

Neither of them had meant to, but driven by something that wasn't desire, something they couldn't have named, they started making love the moment they were in bed. Afterward she felt sad, she wanted to cry. Knowing she wouldn't get to sleep, she reached for her box of tranquilizers.

Olivier frowned.

So it was really worth making love, he said.

She didn't orgasm, she told him.

Why not?

I don't know, she lied. But it doesn't matter, it was good anyway, I'll have an orgasm next time.

Is that why you're sad? he asked.

No. I was sad before. I've been sad for a while.

Olivier was affectionate, as he always was after making love. Another of Juliette's grievances against him because in her eyes this tenderness bought with sex didn't hold much weight. She saw it as purely mechanical, an only slightly enhanced version of animal gratitude. And perhaps she was wrong there, just as Olivier was wrong to believe that loving words counted only if they were spontaneous.

It would be easier for me if I felt you loved me, she eventually admitted.

But, Juliette, I do love you.

I don't know. You never tell me you do.

I just did.

With any conviction, I mean.

Do you feel like I don't love you?

Yes, often. You give me quite a lot of proof of loving me, but at the same time I often get the feeling you don't love me.

He stared at the ceiling, thinking.

It's funny. She says the exact opposite. She never doubts for a minute that I love her. She just complains I don't ever give her any proof.

Juliette didn't answer. He turned to look at her and realized she'd fallen asleep.

# 22

The following evening, Monday, Olivier arrived home pale and exhausted. Things were beginning to take their toll on him physically too. V had harassed him on the phone all day, insisting they see each other, threatening to talk to his wife again. I've kept all your texts, she told him. You've made a commitment with things you've said and done. It would be too easy for you to pretend they never happened. Olivier had managed to calm her only by arranging to meet her the following day.

How interesting. She's *not* going on vacation, then? Juliette asked with affected detachment; it was a cheap shot, but she couldn't resist it.

She's delayed a bit. She's not going until Wednesday now.

Juliette shook her head. She'd been expecting this.
No point relying on that. She won't leave while you're in Paris.

Olivier put his head in his hands fretfully.
I'm scared, he said. I have a bad feeling about this. It's going to be hell until we go away.

Juliette thought for a moment.

Do you have any meetings at work this week? she asked.
He shook his head.
No, nothing.
Get out of here, she said. Leave with the kids tomorrow morning, I'll join you as soon as I can.
That's not stupid, he said after thinking it over briefly.

They spent the evening organizing the escape. The "exfiltration," they called it, to lighten the mood. Juliette was very calm, but he looked lost, relying heavily on her. Just after she'd made the suggestion, she went to the bathroom to wash her hands. He trailed after her and sat hunched on the side of the bath.

I don't know, he muttered.

Call the magazine, she said, knowing he was waiting for her to force his hand in some way. I think you should tell Thierry what's going on.

I don't know, he said again. Are you sure about this decision?

It was a strange question. She studied him for a moment before replying.

Decision? I don't get to make many of the decisions in all this. But I'm sure, yes. It's like defusing a bomb. There are risks attached, but it'll go off eventually anyway, and it would probably be worse. At least by doing this, you're protecting yourself from more blackmail.

He nodded and went off into the bedroom only to come back less than a minute later.

Was Thierry not there? she asked.

No, he was. I've done it.

Already? What did you tell him?

That I needed to get out of town, the shit's going to hit the fan. He doesn't know the whole story. He said of course, of course, listen, if you need to talk…I think he's pretty shaken up by this whole thing.

She sighed in relief, led him off into the bedroom.

Come and make love.

I don't know if I really want to, he objected.

That doesn't matter, she insisted, you don't need to do a thing. You can even think about her if you want, I don't care.

Once they were lying on their bed, she started stroking him tentatively, quite prepared to be rejected. But as usual, as ever, and it astonished her just as much every time, when she reached for his penis after running her hands over him a few times, he was hard. The antibiotics had worked well, and the burning sensation she'd had was now just a bad memory, and they made love as they never had before, at least for her, and she came, with him inside her, and couldn't remember when it last felt so powerful. Afterward she held him tightly to her, stroking his hair and smiling.

Let's sleep, she said. We'll get up early tomorrow to pack.

When she woke at around six, he was already up, filling a suitcase. She was worried he might have changed his mind overnight, but no, he seemed more determined than ever to get away. She helped him finish the packing energetically and efficiently, then woke the kids in a good mood. It had taken her less than five minutes yesterday evening to book a hotel room with three beds, in the Burgundy region, far enough from Paris to avoid any slipups.

At eight twenty-five she kissed the children in the car; by eight-thirty Olivier and the kids had left. Juliette went up to change and go to work. According to the plan they'd settled on, Olivier was to call V when he was already a long way from Paris and cancel the date he'd set with her the day before. After a lot of prevaricating, he'd taken his cell phone with him, and a phone card. The card was so he could contact V from a phone booth, telling her he deliberately hadn't taken his cell on vacation so he couldn't be contacted.

He was to claim Juliette was with him, and they'd all set off twenty-four hours early—nothing to make a song and dance about, Juliette had said. Olivier had nodded, nervous.

Juliette proved frighteningly efficient at work that day. She suggested she and her counterpart from the commercial side go to lunch together. Having anticipated a call from V to check the facts, the moment she arrived she'd spoken to the receptionist and everyone with workstations near hers in the open plan office, asking them to tell any strangers who called for her that she was on annual leave as of that morning. I'm being harassed, she told them grimly. No one dared ask for further explanation.

At around eleven, Olivier called from a phone booth. As planned, he'd switched off his cell. He'd just spoken to V, and it had gone well. She seemed to have been caught out and only made him promise to call back later. They were near Nemours.

I can't talk long, Olivier told Juliette, the kids are in the car in the sun. I already spent an hour on the phone earlier, they've had enough.

Juliette hung up, feeling momentarily relieved. Then she started thinking and became increasingly anxious. A whole hour on the phone, though. And worse than that, V had seemed reasonable. From Juliette's point of view, that was bad news. For a while now she'd had an obscure conviction that Olivier wouldn't extricate himself from this without a drama. If V was accepting their separation during this vacation, that meant it would all start again when everyone was home. Olivier's idea that the only way to end their affair gently was to keep on talking to her and seeing her would be reinforced. This would mean phone calls from Tuscany and endless discussions, complete hell for Juliette instead of the hoped-for break. And the ever-present fear that Olivier might capitulate again.

She set to work with dogged determination and told her coworkers that for family reasons, she'd be leaving on vacation that evening. She spent her lunch break working productively with dear Pissignac, bringing him up to date on current clients, very helpfully giving him all the technical information he might need to bluff his way through in her absence. Incredible how much she was getting done today, she thought. She was constantly frightened V would turn up at her office. For some reason known only to him, Olivier had admitted to V that he was alone with the children, and their mother wasn't joining them till the next day. Juliette had actually packed her bag that morning so she could cover their tracks by spending the night somewhere else, because she knew V had it in her to hang about outside their apartment to check if they really were away; but now that precaution was pointless.

Olivier called a second time at four o'clock, from a phone booth again. They were close to the hotel, and things were beginning to turn sour. He'd called V back as promised and was now gnawing his fingers in panic. She'd spiraled out of control, screaming things he couldn't even remember about Juliette. Don't pick up your phone in the next few minutes, he told her, I think she's going to call you. Juliette asked to have a quick chat with the children, but there was noise coming from outside, and they couldn't hear her very well. We'll call you later from the hotel, Emma told her.

All through the day clouds had been accumulating in the sky, and the heat had grown more and more oppressive. At about seven o'clock thunder started to rumble, and the storm broke. Having dealt with the last bits of unfinished business, Juliette left the Galatea building, slinking along the walls, hidden behind her umbrella. She was afraid to go home, eyeing every woman in the street, thinking she could see V in all of them. She loathed this feeling of being in a position of weakness. Not only did V know where she lived and worked, but she also knew her by sight, while Juliette herself, having never shown the slightest curiosity, had no idea what this woman she was forced to call her rival looked like. She's bound to be very pretty, she'd once said casually to Olivier, by the by. I don't know, he'd replied, I'm not sure she's really beautiful, let's say she makes an impression. Juliette looked around. A redhead. A scooter. She felt a bit safer once she was in the subway.

Twenty minutes later she stepped off the train and loitered for a while on the platform at Jaurès station, not daring to go up onto the street. Then she thought of calling Yolande because even though the children were away, she'd come over, as she did every evening, to tidy the apartment before their vacation. She asked Yolande to meet her at a café just outside the subway station. Then she braced herself, ran to the end of the platform, took the stairs four at a time, spilled out onto the street, and sped, head down, to a seat by the bar with her back to the window. A rather surprised Yolande soon joined her, and Juliette suggested they have a glass of wine together to celebrate the vacation. As she drank, she said everything and nothing, blurting out ambiguous musings, behaving as if her nanny had been in on her tormented conjugal circumstances for some time. Yolande listened sympathetically. I'm so sorry, she said several times. But you're right to fight. Women shouldn't put up with everything men throw at them. Juliette was lost in thought for a moment. Since this all started, how many people had told her she shouldn't put up with it? I could tell things weren't going well for you, Yolande was saying. I don't know whether you've noticed, but Emma's been different the last few days. No, said Juliette, I haven't noticed anything. Well, I have, Yolande reiterated. She's strained, on edge, she won't even say hello or good-bye to me now.

After a couple of glasses Yolande wanted to catch the subway home. Juliette held her back, begging her to escort her to the apartment before she left. Yolande obliged. They met no one on the way there, and in a flurry of apologies, Juliette finally let Yolande go. Once she'd closed the door and turned the key, Juliette sat at the kitchen table and called the hotel. Olivier had the strained voice she associated with difficult episodes. We're all in bed, he said. I want them to get to sleep, then I'll call you, but I won't talk for long.

Call as soon as you can, she said, I want to know what's going on, I'm worried.

Not long afterward her cell phone started ringing. Twice. Unknown caller. She didn't pick up. Instead she called Florence from the landline to catch her up on the latest events. But she was soon apologizing for having to hang up because her cell was ringing again. She let it shrill pointlessly on its own a good dozen times. This time a message was left. It was the famous Tristan, all polite and syrupy, apologizing for calling uninvited—I'm not sure how to introduce myself, it's rather awkward—no, that was what V had said when she'd called Juliette at Galatea, he said he was a friend of Victoire S—. This might seem like an unusual thing to do, but I wonder if you would be kind enough to call me back please, it's important, I'd be very grateful. Go fuck yourself, thought Juliette, slightly under the influence. Go fuck yourselves, the pair of you. How can this stupid creep, this moron, this asshole think for one minute that I have any intention of talking to him?

She ate the melon Yolande had prepared for her, poured herself some more wine—no, this wasn't alcoholism, it was just self-defense. On the phone to Flo she'd said rather incoherently and disjointedly, I'd do anything, you know, I'd even prostitute myself to stop that woman from having his baby, so Johann and Emma never have to spend a weekend with that madwoman. Her voice had been slurred, the link between her children and prostitution not very clear, but perhaps all those times she'd made love to Olivier without any real desire, doing it deliberately, willfully, using her knowledge of how to give him pleasure as a weapon in the war against V, all that had left its mark. As for Olivier and me, she'd said, we'll see, I don't even know if I still love him, I sometimes think I hate him.

Her cell phone and the handset of the landline, which lay side by side on the table, suddenly started ringing at the same time. Juliette sat there transfixed for a couple of seconds, staring at them, with her hand in the air, hovering over the two phones. She was sort of hypnotized. The cell phone display read: "unknown caller." The landline was an older model. It had no caller display. To pick up or not to pick up? And if yes, which one? It felt like a game, one of those enigmas Juliette used to like challenging her friends with at boarding school. She thought they were child's-play. All it took was a bit of logic. Most of her friends used to give up.

A man on death row is shut in a cell with two doors. One door leads to the scaffold; the other, to freedom. There's a guard by each door. One always lies, the other always tells the truth, but the prisoner doesn't know which is which. He's allowed to ask one guard one question before opening a door. What should he ask to save his life?

After thinking for a few seconds, Juliette made up her mind. Her hand came down firmly on the landline handset. Their number wasn't listed, and so far—by what sort of miracle?—V didn't appear to have succeeded in getting the number.

She could hear the fear in Olivier's voice.

Tell me when you're getting here tomorrow. Send me a text. I'm only switching my cell on for a few seconds at a time, I don't want her to know I'm using it. This is a disaster. I called her back again. It went really badly. Now Tristan's leaving me messages, he's picked her up in the street again. I'm terrified. I'm playing dead. I won't stay on the line.

Juliette thanked the heavens he was 250 miles from Paris and stuck with the children because he really couldn't abandon them there.

Have you had any messages, from her or him? he asked.

I haven't listened to them, she lied. There's a train to Mâcon at around ten, but I don't know if there are any seats left.

Dijon would work too, he said. Send me a text telling me when and where you're arriving, and I'll be there.

The note in his voice was scary. She wanted to tell him, as she had the day before, that it wasn't his fault; and to think that so far she'd been criticizing him for not feeling responsible. It's not your fault, my love, you can't be blamed for ending up with a madwoman, yes, they do exist, I know you've always been told the opposite, but that's because no one's allowed to say it, it's forbidden, totally forbidden, but it is the truth, not all women are necessarily kind, there are nasty women too, bad women, not the majority, of course, but they're still out there, tons of them, all over the place, and as for the crazy chicks, let's not go there, there are even more crazy ones, they're a dime a dozen, there are swarms of them, let me tell you about it, I was like that myself before I knew you, I was crazy sometimes.

Her cell phone rang again. It must be V this time. Why can't she just die, thought Juliette. And she was slightly horrified to realize she really felt that. A week ago—a week? It felt like months—Olivier had told her: If anything happens to her, it'll be over between you and me, and she'd been scared. Now she couldn't care less. Let her die. Let Olivier loathe her, Juliette, forever, let them divorce. Just don't ever let Emma and Johann spend a weekend with that woman.

It was late. She was tired and went to bed. She'd pack in the morning. She was dead drunk, anyway.

What was it V had said, again? Children can understand anything. Considering that, God alone knew what Emma might have heard the evening V came to the apartment. Children can understand everything. By what right did this woman think she could decide what her children could and should understand? She could feel the loathing rising inside her; she was discovering her inner she-wolf. Oh, so that's what it is, she thought before sinking into something as close to an alcoholic coma as it was to genuine sleep.

That's what it was.

The maternal instinct.

# PART THREE

PART THREE

# 23

Her express train arrived in Mâcon around midday. Juliette had tried to call Olivier as she was getting on the train, but his cell phone was still off; he was using it very sparingly and only to check messages. She had to wait quite a while in a deserted train station in the middle of nowhere before he finally arrived. The moment Johann and Emma saw their mother, they ran over to her, whooping loudly. She hugged them. Then they set about finding a restaurant for lunch and ended up in a pizzeria on the banks of the river Saône. As they drove, Olivier chose his words carefully in front of the children and said only that he'd had no messages from V or Tristan since nine-fifteen the night before. They didn't bring the subject up again until late afternoon.

They reached Annecy toward the end of the day and went for a walk on the shores of the lake, stopping and sitting on a café terrace for a drink. While the children played, Olivier finally told Juliette about the phone conversations he'd had with V the day before. During the first call he'd told V he'd left Paris, and she'd laughed. Did you come up with that idea after discussing things with your wife? she'd asked. He'd promised to call her back a bit later; that was a mistake, a real fuck-up, sighed Olivier, because it was then that he realized V believed they'd be seeing each other as soon as he was home from Tuscany. When he said they wouldn't be and that as far as he was concerned, they had to let at least the whole summer go by, Victoire had gone to pieces.

So it's over, is that it? she'd screamed.

I can't seem to say it, *you* say it, he'd replied.

Is that what you want, for me to say it, you're expecting me to say it's over?

That would be good, he'd enunciated with some diffi-culty. (He'd managed to convince himself that if he left the initiative for the breakup to V, at least the formality of it, then he'd be sparing her the humiliation and would there-fore be making it easier for her.)

The conversation had ended there. After that she'd left him messages: "Call me back, I beg you"; then Tristan did too. Next, Tristan had tried to get hold of Juliette; she checked the time of his call on her cell: nine-fifteen. And after that, nothing. Olivier looked terribly strained, but on the other hand, there would have been nothing to stop him from asking for news of V. So deep down, thought Juliette, he couldn't be all that worried. In fact a good proportion of the fears that had gripped Olivier overnight had dispersed during the course of the day.

I hope she's calmed down, he said. I hope she goes on her vacation tomorrow. She's meant to be going down south to work on her business school entrance exams with a student friend of hers. He's in love with her too, from what she was implying.

No kidding, said Juliette. Doesn't she have regular friends?

They sat in silence for a moment, looking at the polished, reflective surface of the lake. It was still early in the season; there was hardly anyone else along the shore.

In any event, said Olivier, now I do see the difference. Between saying: We have to stop this, it's impossible, which is what I said, and saying what I can't say: It's over, I can't do it.

Juliette wondered yet again why it was so hard, but she refrained from commenting in any way.

So?
So I'm planning to write her a letter for her to read when she gets home.
Saying?
I need to find the words, to explain basically why it's impossible but still do justice to our relationship.
Juliette wasn't sure she understood what he was saying.
To *your* relationship or *our* relationship?
Our relationship, yes, every time I try to explain things to her she says, So what we had meant nothing? I need to say, No, it didn't mean nothing.

Juliette didn't press the point. It was better to cling to the general principle that he still intended to break it off, and not dwell on painful details.

And what if she still calls you, in spite of the letter, what if she wants to see you?
I'll tell her it's impossible, I guess.

Impossible, again. Not "I don't want to." No. Circumstances beyond my control make our relationship impossible.

That evening, once they were alone in their room and the children were asleep, Olivier turned on his cell phone and checked his messages. Still nothing.

It's one of four things, said Juliette, who was also starting to find this sudden silence weird.

One of four things:
Either something happened to her yesterday evening, she's in the hospital in a coma or I don't know, but I don't believe it for a minute. Our friend Tristan wouldn't have denied himself the pleasure of letting you know.

Or you were very convincing, and they both think that not only did you leave your cell phone at home, but you're not even listening to your messages.

Or she thinks you're a bastard, she's dropped the whole thing, and we'll never hear from her again, but sadly, I'd be really surprised.

Or she's decided to freak you out in the hope you'll call her back.

Personally I'm leaning toward the fourth hypothesis.

I've been thinking over what you said earlier, Juliette went on, and I'm interested to know how you're going to make her see that it's impossible for you to be together. Because it would actually be pretty possible, if you look at things objectively. It would even be completely routine, marriages come to an end every day. Especially as your main concern is also being sure you do your relationship justice. Personally I don't think she's in any doubt about how exceptional, how remarkable your relationship is. On the other hand, if you want to make her understand, you might need to do justice to *our* relationship, yours and mine. What does she really think about that, in fact?

She probably thinks I won't leave you because I don't have the courage. Because of my Catholic upbringing too.

Juliette laughed.

Catholic, you? Did you tell her we weren't married in a church and our kids aren't even baptized?

Olivier shrugged.

Either way, the truth—and you know this perfectly well—is that your relationship isn't impossible at all. It would be better if you stopped telling her that. Otherwise it'll just start all over again when we get home.

You're right. It mustn't start again, Olivier said. I have to manage to tell her it's over. But I can't do it. I can't tell myself I'll never see her again. Because she's an important part of my life.

Hush, hush, oh, my pain. Juliette made a mental effort to lull the child she had once been in her arms and focused on her obsession once more.

Have you slept with her since the fateful day you visited her apartment?

No. But that's not a problem at the end of the day. It's almost meaningless.

It's anything but meaningless, that's how you make babies.

Olivier closed his eyes.

I know, Juliette.

The following day there was still no news of V. Juliette spent the day hoping for a kind gesture, a tender word. In their bedroom that evening, she wept softly as she waited for Olivier, who'd gone down to the car. What was the point in fighting? she thought. This frostiness, this lack of tenderness, it was such a far cry from the love she'd dreamed of. The husband makes the marriage; the wife makes the family. Where did she read that? This stupid maxim had kept popping up in her head over the last few days, tormenting her painfully. Once again, for the umpteenth time, she thought: Let him go, after all. But it was impossible to contemplate the Other Woman's triumph; more importantly it was impossible to contemplate her kissing Johann and Emma. The day before Olivier had laughed as he'd told her that, without even knowing them, V already really liked their children. Juliette's stomach had constricted.

She was still crying when Olivier came back. Just to pick at the scab and suffer some more, she came at it head-on and made him recap what was so "exceptional" about this relationship. So he told her again: It's true, I've never felt the way I feel now, at the age of forty-six, such abandon, the all-embracing tenderness, the eagerness to say I love you. Juliette cried out and started sobbing again. He sprang angrily to his feet, took a couple of strides toward the door, then came back.

I'm not talking to you anymore, he said. I won't talk to you anymore.

But we were in love too, ten years ago, weren't we? Is there no comparison? Was that nothing?

Of course it wasn't, he said, of course it was, maybe, it must have been, I don't remember it feeling the same, but it must be my terrible memory doing that.

Later, when he was a little calmer, he told her: But meeting you, you were the one. The one that started everything: marriage, the kids. I'm just saying that this meeting with her, meeting her, at the age of forty-six, in secret, when it's forbidden, I don't think I've ever experienced anything like it, that's all.

Abandon, he'd said. If he'd said it was violent, if he'd said it was a struggle, irresistible. All he'd said was abandon. He hadn't even put up a fight, hadn't thought for one moment about the pain he would cause her.

They go to bed, but Juliette can't sleep. She's obsessed with the thought that he can't remember being in love with her. And worse, with the feeling that the truth she's doggedly avoiding is right in front of her: He never loved her. That what she's always interpreted as difficulty expressing his feelings was just a genuine lack of love, that for him, the love he's feeling now may be the first.

She gets up to take another sleeping pill in the bathroom. What are you doing? he asks.

Taking a sleeping pill.

I thought you already took one.

I took a quarter of a Bromazepam, it's not enough. I'm taking something to really sleep.

He follows her and sits on the side of the tub, furious.

Then was this really worth the trouble? Why the hell am I doing this, why am I here, why am I doing this to her?

I was just thinking about what you said to me, she tells him, that you don't remember being in love with me. It hurts.

I never said that.

He sighs.

I've had enough.

Let's get some sleep, says Juliette.

The following day they didn't talk about anything.

It was safer.

As they headed for Italy in the car, they listened to talking-book CDs for the children. Thinking over it that evening, Juliette realized that through all those long hours of traveling, Johann had opened his mouth only three times.

The first to say: I like macaroni and cheese.

The second: When we get home to Paris, can we listen to *Winnie the Pooh*?

The third, Juliette had forgotten.

# 24

For a while now they'd been driving through a desolate landscape of industrial wasteland punctuated by hideous housing developments. Juliette snuck an anxious look at Olivier, who kept driving but turned to look at her with a sarcastic smile.

Are you sure about this house you've chosen?

She shuffled deeper into her seat and went back to staring at the road, chewing at her fingernails. As usual Olivier hadn't made any of the arrangements and had trusted her to choose a location. She was the one who wanted to get some sun, after all. When they finally found the house with the owner there expecting them, she could breathe again. The place was on its own at the end of a long dirt track. It was basic but clean, with a bigger garden than she'd imagined. From the second-floor windows they had views over the countryside, which stretched away below a village perched on a hillside. Before seeing them, they heard the bells worn by sheep roaming freely in a nearby pasture.

When the owner left, the sun was starting to go down. The children were hungry, and they decided to go eat in the village before unpacking. As they were leaving the house, Juliette's cell phone rang; it was a French number beginning 04, not one she recognized. She didn't pick up but went out into the garden, grim-faced.

Who was that? Olivier asked.

Your girlfriend, I should think, she replied tartly.

Olivier pulled a disbelieving face.

What makes you think that?

You said she was going somewhere near Nice to do this business school work, and I don't know many numbers beginning with zero four.

Why wouldn't she have used her cell? He objected before answering his own question: Oh, yes, so you wouldn't recognize the number.

After a silence he added, Did she leave a message?

Proof, if any were needed, that he was sure it was her.

No, said Juliette, V hadn't left a message. The evening was ruined all the same.

It's all going to start over when we get back to Paris, she told him. I'm sure it is.

I don't think so, he said. It's impossible.

The next few days all followed the same routine. In the daytime they played with the kids, went to the beach, or visited the area. Then in the evenings once the children were asleep, they sat under the arbor talking.

Under that arbor, Olivier was her prisoner.

Juliette exploited the situation quite willfully. She tortured him as she saw fit for entire evenings, bombarding him with questions that he previously wouldn't have tolerated for a minute before flying off the handle. He couldn't shirk them any longer and, deep down, had some sense of relief.

Under the arbor, Olivier was compliant.

The first evening, he told her: I was really convinced you didn't love me anymore. One time I even cried over this void that had grown between us.

I never stopped loving you, she replied, but I wasn't happy, I didn't know how to tell you. Because talking wasn't any use. I must have thought that only the fear of losing me would make you react. You see, it worked.

Not entirely the way I hoped it would, she added a moment later, but almost.

At times like this, Juliette finds herself thinking it's all for the best, even if the closing chapters of this story they're writing together are still unclear to her.
So she digs deeper.
She digs and digs, with words like little spades, little picks.

Don't you think, she asks, that there comes a time with love when it becomes unique because it's been chosen? Don't you think people decide to love, to keep on loving, or to stop loving? Wouldn't you say there's an element of will in love?

Yes, I agree with that, I think, he replies. Otherwise I wouldn't be here with you.

Later they would make love. It was no longer a strategy on Juliette's part. She'd referred to prostitution, but the truth was she'd rediscovered her appetite for the pleasure Olivier was so skilled at giving her. Of course she was always the one to initiate, to make those first tentative moves. But she was beginning to see that, as is often the case in a relationship, things she held against Olivier were the very things that had attracted her to him. And as it happened, his relative passivity meant she could give her own arousal time to develop, choosing her pace. Feeling him gradually stirring to her touch gave her a sense of power that culminated, without fail, in unusually intense pleasure. One night as she lay next to him, basking in the postcoital glow, she even joked about it.

Why's it never you who takes the initiative? It's always me who gets lumbered with that job.

He smiled playfully.

It was still good, though, it was worth the effort.

It was great, she replied.

So that's something to be said for it.

It was something to be said for it.

The days were less of a success. Olivier was always borderline irritable, with her and with the children, who—and this was probably no coincidence—proved a handful and uncharacteristically restless. One day they had a fight, and Emma bit Johann, who retaliated by throwing a stone at her head. Olivier was seething with anger; Juliette, appalled. I've had it with you! he yelled at the children. It was something he said increasingly often, and Juliette couldn't be absolutely sure whether or not she was included in that "you," but she wasn't under many illusions. Every time his temper boiled over like this, he and Juliette avoided eye contact, aware they were both thinking the same thing. The specter of separation was looming between them, and they were both terrified of it.

Then things calmed down.

To limit the risk of explosions, Juliette was mostly excessively conciliatory with Olivier, attentive to the point of servility. The house in Tuscany matched her expectations, and even Olivier agreed that it was a beautiful part of the world. Juliette wondered how she'd managed to let herself be trapped like this. How had she ended up doing cartwheels for this amicable but distant male who obligingly made love to her and occasionally put a hand on her shoulder but never felt the need to hold her in his arms or whisper fevered words in her ear? Trapped into being careful not to irritate him, not to contradict him, reduced to a submissive female role when she sometimes felt like screaming that he was a bastard, that he'd betrayed her trust, that he'd reduced them to a tawdry mediocrity she didn't want and didn't deserve, that she couldn't stand him. Would he one day acknowledge the wrongs he'd done her here? She was struck once again with the thought that she was letting her one chance slip through her fingers, her chance to get out of this marriage with Olivier as the bad guy, to reclaim her freedom with a clear conscience so she could tell the children later that she had done what she could. But then she immediately thought of V tucking Johann and Emma into bed and reading them a story before saying good night to them, and the image sent a jolt of pain through her, strengthening her resolve to win this fight and confirming her painful conviction that she had no choice.

One night she heard Olivier get up, then come back to bed next to her. The children weren't sleeping well; it was hot. Are you asleep, she asked quietly.

No, he replied, you neither?

No.

What's going on?

I was wondering why one time, not that long ago, you woke me in the night to tell me you loved me and why you haven't felt the need to do it again since.

I don't know, he said. That night I was suddenly acutely aware of what I stood to lose.

And you're not now?

I can't explain, he said. I see you, I look at you, I recognize the woman I chose, I think you're beautiful. But getting from there to feeling a need to say "I love you..."

They went to visit the Leaning Tower of Pisa. All through the day she was aware of her ignorance in art and architecture; she could read the reproach in Olivier's eyes because she didn't know what to say when she was looking at a statue. Or she was imagining this. As he often did, he walked quickly, not waiting for her, several yards ahead of her because she was keeping to Johann's speed. And he was the one who talked about togetherness, complicity. Most couples walk hand in hand or at least side by side, whether or not they have children. Juliette felt like an Arab wife, ten paces behind her husband. Later in the day she went into a post office to mail some postcards, and he stayed outside on a bench. It felt like she had to wait forever to be served. Bring on the day they invent stamp vending machines in Italy! she said when she finally came back out to join him.

He replied with a shrug and a smirk that startled her.

What's going on? She exploded. You're furious, is that it? What the hell does that shrug mean?

Olivier studied her; he looked confused, hostile.

No, he replied, it just means, bring on the day they invent those machines, that's all.

The children were watching them anxiously. Juliette's anger abated.

I'm sorry, she said. I really thought you were sulking.

After that she made quite an effort to dispel the awkward atmosphere. An effort, always, always her. Florence had told her: You can't make your relationship work all on your own.

And now Olivier was handing it over to her.

There are times like today, he said when they were alone later, when I feel there's so little complicity between us. We're in Italy, we're visiting these incredible places, and it's like you can't even see anything, like we can't share any of it.

She takes the injustice of this full in the face, tries to justify herself. Then some part of her rebels.

You know, I thought this affair really was over, and we were going away together to get to know each other again. I now see this vacation is just a test period for our relationship to be evaluated, our similarities and differences weighed up, and I'm being watched and compared. What grade did I get today then? Out of luck, our architectural compatibility is pretty much zero...I've lost all the points I earned with sex in the last few days.

Stop it, Juliette.

But what do I still have to prove? Of course it was better with her. I get the day-to-day stuff, the kids. I don't know if you realize this, but I won't be available indefinitely, waiting around for you to make your decision. The time will come when I call for an end, or I'll decide to stop loving you.

It's a vicious circle, he said. Can we get some sleep? We spend hours talking at night and then in the daytime we're exhausted, we drag ourselves around the place, weighed down by everything. I just had a terrible nightmare, I woke in tears, I dreamed I had to kill someone and Johann wanted to kill himself. It was horrible. Of course this has to stop.

Let's sleep, she said.

For a whole day and night they didn't talk about anything.

Olivier had brought Simone de Beauvoir's *The Woman Destroyed*, which V had given him. Juliette, who'd never read it, borrowed it from him one day on the beach and read it in one sitting, horrified. She'd expected a description of a passionate relationship. What she found, in the form of a personal diary, was the story of a death sentence, the descent into hell of an abandoned woman.

It was her own mother's story, thought Juliette.

Juliette didn't see anything of herself in this portrait of a conventional wife in the sixties, but that was just a detail. What was more disturbing was the fact that the mistress in the book played only a walk-on part with the husband playing a supporting role, and their love was seen only through the prism of the distress he was inflicting on the narrator. The novel closed with her coming home to a dark, empty apartment and ended with the words "I'm scared."

"Not much in common with us," Olivier had said with a smile and a shrug as he closed the book. Juliette was relieved to hear him say it. She saw confirmation of V's peculiar madness in this choice of book. Only a sick mind or one pervaded with hate could come up with the idea of giving a story like that to a lover in order to persuade him to leave his wife. She thought of that now infamous text again, "I wish she were dead," and felt very uncomfortable. She was struck, not for the first time, by the idea that V really meant her harm. It gave her the same feeling as when she was alone in a subway station or walking along a street at night and heard footsteps behind her. It was exaggerated, irrational, but the past had taught her that fear sometimes gave sound advice. A DANGER sign had lit up in her head. She tried to ignore it, but it kept on flashing.

# 25

A week had gone by. A relaxed, smiling, mischievous Olivier sat down under the arbor with a notebook.

I'm going to empty the bottle of Chianti and finish this letter.

How are you getting on?

I'm getting there. I'm planning to mail it tomorrow.

What does it say?

That it's over. Basically.

Are you going for long or short?

Kind of longish.

He frowned and looked at her inquiringly.

Do you think I should go for short?

She shrugged to mean she didn't know.

He went back to his notebook, thinking, pen poised. Juliette helped herself to a glass of Chianti too.

Gazing into the darkness, she suddenly said, When I think back to the phone conversation I had with her, this girl really is a kook.

He looked up, apparently stunned.

Why did you use that word?

What word? "Kook"?

Yes, "kook." That's one of her words, she says that. You never say kook.

Juliette sighed. She couldn't even use the words she wanted.

Of course I say kook. Everyone says kook.

Olivier pulled a face, unconvinced.

She didn't use that word on the phone to me, Juliette insisted, if that's what you're thinking.

If you say so.

How are you ending the letter?

Do you want to read it?

And he meant it: he was gesturing toward the notebook. She hesitated, caught out, then decided against inflicting the pain on herself. There were bound to be plenty of words in the letter that she'd find superfluous. But she really couldn't go correcting his breakup letter.

In their room later, she lay naked on the bed, staring up at the ceiling, and said:

There was trust. It wasn't easy, but there was trust.

You already said that, he retorted, but not aggressively. He sat down beside her and put a hand on her thigh.

And she notices, yet again, how he likes correcting her syntax, picking up on her repetitions, as if she were taking some sort of oral exam in front of him every day.

Maybe I did already say it, but it's still true. You lied to me.

You could see it like that. You could say I lied to you. You could also say I told you the truth after just three weeks precisely because I couldn't lie to you. Not the whole truth, the truth in stages, but still the truth.

True. You could see it like that.


They're right next to each other. Let's try to see it like that, she thinks. They make love.


When she woke the next morning, he seemed upset.

I dreamed you were angry with me and I was sad.

Suddenly struck by a revelation, she took him in her arms. Difficult though it was for her to take in, Olivier really didn't feel any guilt. He was probably aware deep down that he couldn't cope with it, so he was eliminating it before he was even aware of it, morphing it into hostility. Therefore any reproach on her part would only fuel further aggression instead of a sense of yearning or the expression of regret she kept hoping for. By writing his breakup letter, he was doing the most he possibly could. After all, he couldn't help his own lack of emotion.


He mailed the letter on the way to the beach.


Later, much later that same day, when they were lying alone in the darkness on the sun loungers on the terrace, he turned on his cell and found a text from V:

"Sending you a kiss from a sunny deserted beach."

Juliette made a huge effort not to show any feelings, but she found it difficult to take. Olivier noticed.

If you prefer, I don't have to tell you about it, it's not important.

She couldn't get over it. Was he still planning to lie to her by omission, to hide V's messages from her? Didn't he understand that the truth—the whole truth—between them was the only chance they had of finding a way out of this?

You see, she's not dead, she said. She's perfectly fine. She'll never let go of us.

Yes, she will. She sent that, thinking I'd read it in Paris. When she gets home to Paris, she'll have my letter.

Do you think it'll be enough? Tell me what you wrote again.

Olivier smiled ironically as if to say: You see, you should have read it.

It starts with: "There are lots of things to say, but the main thing is to work out how we got to that ridiculous scene."

Which one? Juliette interrupted. As far as I can see, there were several.

The scene on the day I left, me running away like that. I go on to talk about "it's over" and the difference between saying "it's impossible," "it has to stop," and "it's over," a difference I hadn't appreciated myself. It was you, and Tristan too, who pointed it out to me. And why I couldn't say it.

Why?

Yes, I explained why.

And why was it?

Because it felt like an insult to this unique thing we'd had together. And because I think I was waiting for her to be the one to say it.

Mmm. And then?

Then I went back over the last two weeks, over the fear I lived with—terrified of picking up the phone or going home—and the message from that moron (Tristan) that I pretended to take lightly but that freaked me out. I also said that I know—because she told me—that she's kept all my messages, that she's built up a whole case against me with every declaration I've ever made, which she considers binding commitments, so she can refer back to them and say: "When you say that, you can't" et cetera. And also that she was deleting other messages because there were some, not many, but there were some that said the opposite. She deleted all the ones that said: "This has to stop, it's too unbearable for Juliette."

Is that the argument you used? It's too unbearable for Juliette?

Isn't that true?

It wasn't only unbearable for me, was it? The fits of hysteria, the fainting in the street, the three-hour phone calls…try as I may, I can't see that it was *great* for you. Not for you or for her.

It was horrible, he said. Horrible. I can't imagine it starting over. What else did I tell her? That I now see that, of the two of us, I was the one who should have been sensible because she had nothing to lose. And at the end I said I've made arrangements so I won't be doing the Socialist Party summer rally, unless she lets me know I can go and everything will be fine, if she's come to her senses.

A pause, then he added: I'm hoping she's already gotten some way through the process since we left, that she's started her grieving and she'll understand.

The message she's just sent you doesn't point that way, Juliette replied skeptically. I'm worried that for now she doesn't think anything's changed.

Things have changed for me, we've had this vacation, we've gotten closer.

So I passed the test then, Juliette thought bitterly.

You look happy, she said. In your heart of hearts you're happy you've heard from her.

I'm happy she's not in a coma, yes. After we left last week, I was really scared. Having said that, I lied to her about the summer rally. It would really bother me not to go. But I said that so she couldn't think there was some implicit date there.
Apart from that, do you have any work "dates"?
No, he said, nothing major or unavoidable.

The next day they had their last evening under the arbor. The children were in bed. A relaxed Juliette poured herself a succession of glasses of wine on the terrace and, slightly under the influence, asked Olivier what he was referring to in his letter when he mentioned the declarations he'd made that V might hold against him. Olivier eyed her warily.

Things about love, he said.
What sort of things?

He didn't answer. They eyed each other defiantly for a moment, then Juliette spoke again.

I'll say them, and you can reply with a yes or a no. I love you? I've never been so happy?
Things about how exceptional the experience was, yes, but I've told you that.
Things about us? I want to leave my wife?
No.
What about us then?
I thought there were some things you didn't want to know.
But right now I'm asking you things I do want to know.
But I don't have to answer.

She fell silent. Actually, did she really want to know? But Olivier was talking again.

I told her things that wouldn't be nice for you to hear, for sure.
Such as?
I'm not going to tell you. But pretty much everything I told her about you wouldn't be nice to hear, I guess.

A pause. He laughs. She looks at him questioningly.

I can't help wondering what you imagine when I say "not nice to hear." I didn't say stuff like "she's old" or "she has a horrible figure," if that's what you're thinking.

She chokes on her drink and coughs.
Thank you.

I hope you can believe me, Olivier continues, I never envisaged leaving you. Maybe it did occur to me that, yes, some people get divorced, it does happen, but I never pictured it for me. I always knew there was something crazy about the whole thing. You know what Roland Barthes says in *A Lover's Discourse: Fragments*?

I'm sorry, she said, I haven't read Barthes.

Well, Barthes explains that that's what love is all about, saying those words. I knew I wouldn't have any sort of life with her, but instead I said those things.

Aha, she said doubtfully. Words or proof, we have to choose, is that it?

Sort of.

They'd come this far, so she decided to tell him what had been on her mind since the day before.

Can I ask you a question? Yesterday you said you could have not told me about her message. Could you really? Could you hide things from me still?

He didn't answer. She thought for a moment, then added:
I keep thinking about the time you spent with her *after* telling me. Did you make love to her between Aubigny and her housewarming?

She could feel his mounting irritation almost physically, as if she were inside his body.
I'm going to stop you right there, he said curtly, I don't have your chronological memory, there's no way I can remember.
You do realize, don't you, that you *swore* that what she'd said wasn't true when she called me at Galatea?
If you say so, you must be right, you remember stuff like that better than I do.
You swore it wasn't true when it actually was.
Of course, because I didn't want her to be the one to tell you.

His implacable logic. A lie justified and excused out of necessity.

But since we've been on vacation, I've been telling the truth.

She sighed.

Okay, I believe you, I have to believe you. But can you also understand that I'm likely to have my doubts sometimes, from now on?

Once again she noticed his complete inability to reassure her.

The following day they set off home to Paris.

# 26

Juliette had hardly set foot back inside Galatea Networks before a load of crap started piling up on her. While she'd been away, the Magellan project had got very behind, and the client had complained. She was called into the general manager's office to explain. Her commercial alter ego, who had also been summoned and was just as responsible as she was, swiftly exonerated himself and then stood impassively, arms crossed, watching her slide down the slippery slope he'd so carefully soaped for her. Juliette glanced surreptitiously at her watch as she submitted stoically to Chatel's criticism. Yolande was away on vacation, and the babysitter who was taking over for the summer wasn't available until Thursday. Juliette really had to leave at five to pick up her kids from the day-care center. After some shopping, bath time, and making the evening meal, she ended the day completely wired.

Olivier, on the other hand, came home from the newspaper in the best of moods. V had left a message for him: Everything was fine, she too had done some thinking during their two-week separation, she'd had his letter and she agreed, she wished him a nice summer and hoped they could continue to see each other as friends.

Juliette stared at Olivier in amazement. He was smiling.
I don't believe it, she said.
He instantly wiped the smile off his face and shrugged.
I'd have been amazed if you did.
Did you reply to her?
I sent a message wishing her a nice summer too. Like you, I thought maybe she'd change her mind and call me back in half an hour. But no, she sent me a text to say thank you. And that's all.
That's all.
Yes.
So?
What?
Problem solved, happy ending, roll the credits? Juliette sneered.
Anyone would think you weren't glad.

No, she wasn't glad, not at all. She felt on edge, disappointed, frustrated. Olivier was already talking about seeing V as a friend. She couldn't see how to stop him even though the thought of it panicked her. She'd been banking on another bout of hysteria, difficult scenes, angry screaming. The worst thing this girl could do to her was suddenly be all reasonable. Of course Olivier wouldn't countenance not seeing her just for his wife's sake. After all, Juliette herself went ahead and saw one or two of her exes from time to time.

I don't believe it, she said again. I don't see how you can switch from a relationship like that to a calm, serene friendship. Later maybe. Not just leading on from it like that, not without a clean break.

I don't know, Olivier said tartly. I probably don't know as much about stuff like this as you do. It feels doable to *me*.

He'd had lunch with Thierry, his editor, who, quite unprompted, had urged him to abandon his plan to go the Socialist Party summer rally at the end of August. Not so much because of his personal problems, Juliette realized, as because they needed an editorial manager in Paris at the time. Olivier had agreed but was obviously rather regretting it. Now that things were clear with V, he thought wistfully of how much he would have enjoyed being there. Any notion of what that would feel like for Juliette simply didn't occur to him, and when, halfway through a sentence, she carelessly dropped an "I can't ban you from going," he snapped back: Ban me?

She didn't say any more.

Juliette had a very difficult afternoon the next day. That morning she'd managed to deal with the most glaringly urgent problems and catch up on some of the backlog on the Magellan project. She was left with the Victoire file, the western front, as she now called it to avoid naming the girl. Since Tuscany, "Any news on the western front?" had been her way of asking Olivier how things stood with V. She could have chosen eastern or southern. Why the western? She had no idea. Westerly winds that bring rain, *All Quiet on the Western Front*...Since the day before, her heart had been fluttering anxiously at the thought that Olivier might start lying to her again. On their last evening in Tuscany, she'd said:

Promise me it won't all start again in Paris.

What exactly? he'd asked.

The lies, the half-truths, the omissions.

Detecting some form of criticism looming, Olivier had promptly turned cold.

It's funny. She says I've lied to her too.

She's right. The two aren't mutually exclusive.

Of course not. I can lie to both of you.

She hadn't secured any sort of reassurance from him.

She tried and failed to get hold of Olivier for several hours. He'd turned off his cell and wasn't answering his landline. She imagined the worst; her scale of "worst" had changed noticeably in the last few weeks and was in exact proportion to the amount of interaction between Olivier and V.

Olivier called Juliette back only after she'd left the office. He'd forgotten his cell phone at home. When she arrived home with the children, sure enough, there it was on the armchair in the hallway, switched off. She didn't think twice before turning it on. The screen said "3 missed calls" (probably hers), and the voice mail icon was showing (but then she'd left a message herself).

The little envelope icon for a new text was flashing.

She switched the cell off.

Sifting through her husband's cell phone wasn't at all compatible with the image she had of herself.

At least that was what she'd always felt until now.

Her image of herself must have seriously changed because this incompatibility suddenly didn't seem obvious at all.

The role of the dignified, irreproachable wife that she'd taken on in a long-lost past was just a front now, far removed from the pathetic creature consumed with jealousy that she'd become. She hated herself and hated V even more for bringing about this metamorphosis. She thought back to those two uncomfortable, anxious hours she'd spent this afternoon just because she couldn't contact Olivier and wondered whether that was now her lot in life.

The answer was yes, without a shadow of a doubt. Which made her feel acutely bitter. The way things were now, she thought, she might as well stop hiding her true colors and see her mediocrity through to its logical conclusion. She turned the cell back on, scrolled down to "Messages" on the menu and selected "Read." It was a small screen, showing only three messages. Three from Victoire, under her surname. There were probably more below, but Juliette didn't check.

She clicked on the first message, the most recent: "Thanks, me too. Kisses." The second: "Possible to stay friends? I'd like that." The third: "Sending you a kiss from a sunny deserted beach." That was the one Olivier had received in Tuscany the week before. Below these messages was another one, from an unknown number. She didn't open it, turned off the phone, and waited for Olivier to come home.

Everything okay? he asked brightly as he came in. Not great, it seems, he concluded when he saw her gloomy expression.

I had a horrible couple of hours this afternoon trying to contact you, she replied. It didn't put me in a fantastic mood. Then I turned on your cell phone and looked at your messages — it's scary, I never thought I'd come to that. You really should change your password.

Olivier made no comment; he didn't seem bothered. He told her he'd had no word from V, he'd just been out and about, no cause for concern, honestly. Nothing in the texts Juliette had seen contradicted what Olivier had told her the day before, but she no longer knew whether she could trust him.

The moment the children were in bed she put her arms around him and undressed him in the hall, then sat him down on a chair in the living room, straddled him, and, without a word, authoritatively drove his hardened penis inside her and made love to him violently, without tenderness, using him as she might a stranger picked up in a bar. Olivier didn't seem to notice and even appeared to like it, but she took no comfort from this. Their situation was hopeless, and physical love didn't solve anything.

Still quiet on the western front? she asked again the next day when Olivier came home.

He hesitated.

Pretty much, he replied. She came into reception at the paper to drop off a videotape, but it was—how can I put this?—outstanding business, he added quickly. A documentary we'd talked about and she'd promised to lend me.

Juliette nodded.

Any messages? No messages.

Just a tape? she asked thoughtfully. At reception? She didn't come up?

No, he replied, a little guarded. Anyway, she was heading back down south today.

Juliette didn't press the point any further at the time, but as she drank her coffee the following morning, she launched her offensive.

There is something strange, though, she said. How did you know she was leaving yesterday?

She messaged me telling me she was.

You told me yesterday you had no messages. Because you see, Juliette soldiered on without waiting for an answer, I don't really enjoy playing detective, but if it's over and you're talking every couple of hours and she's sending you three messages every day, I *am* going to end up having a problem with that.

There's no danger of that happening, he retorted curtly.

If Juliette had been a different person, perhaps she would have left it at that. But, being Juliette, she couldn't help juliet-tizing, and although she currently had the very distinct impression Olivier felt like killing her, she still didn't let it drop.

And wasn't there anything with the tape? Not the tiniest little note?

Olivier flew off the handle.

Yes, there was a letter. I don't even remember what it said, if that's what you want to know, you'll just have to read it.

He stormed out of the kitchen, came back with a piece of paper folded into four, and threw it on the table.

There, I was so bowled over by the letter that I don't even remember what it says. But you go ahead and read it, you're sure to remember it word for word in ten years' time.

She peered at the letter as if it were nuclear waste and didn't seem in the least tempted to get any closer to it.

I'm not going to read it. You tell me what it says.

Olivier hesitated for a moment, then picked up the letter, unfolded it, and read it quickly, his voice full of loathing.

"Having read your letter, I now don't have any choice… have to stop scaring you the way you say I do…heart still har-bors memories of incredibly intense times…hope that with time…establish a different connection…with love. Victoire"

(Miraculously meaningful name, thought Juliette. Thanks to its intimations of victory, the most insignificant letter or e-mail signed by her was transformed into a shriek of triumph.)

Happy now? he said, crumpling up the letter and throwing it in the trash.

I don't believe it, she replied stubbornly. She can't possibly accept a breakup like that. Either she's lying now or she was lying before.

The summer babysitter was starting work that day. Juliette had employed this perky, vitamin-enriched student during summer vacation for several years; the girl was a spiritual descendant of Mary Poppins and, although her name appeared as Julie on pay slips, she liked, for some obscure reason, to be called Zoé. She was more authoritarian and less affectionate than Yolande, but she had boundless energy, and the children adored her. At the end of the day, Juliette made the most of the freedom afforded by having Zoé at home and stayed on to have a drink with a coworker. When she arrived home, there was a nice smell of baking in the air. Johann and Emma were clean and fed and ready for bed, sitting on the carpet, laughing raucously at an improvised puppet show put on by the babysitter. The kitchen was impeccably clean and tidy, and waiting on the kitchen table were two huge slices of a cake that the children had made, one each for Juliette and Olivier. Juliette cast a casual eye over the trash can under the sink. Too late to retrieve V's letter. Zoé—she should have anticipated this—had changed the trash bag and taken the old one downstairs. Juliette briefly flirted with the idea of plumbing the depths of sordid behavior and going down into the yard to rummage through the garbage bin before the janitor took it out onto the sidewalk, and only just rejected the thought. It didn't matter, after all.

That evening Olivier admitted that after she'd left for work in the morning, he'd gone back up to the apartment to retrieve the letter from the trash.

You never know, I might need to remind her what she said sometime. Why are you laughing?

# 27

In the course of their interminable conversations in Tuscany, Olivier had explained to Juliette that one of the things that drew V to him was the idea of giving her son a family. She'd told him that Tom's father was using her health problems as grounds to try to gain custody.

You can imagine what that's like for her. If she and I lived together, it would give her an argument against that crackpot. She left him because he beat her up, apparently.

Olivier didn't miss the skeptical look in Juliette's eyes.

Rightly or wrongly she no longer gave any credit to anything V said. According to Olivier, the girl had had a pampered childhood, brought up by fawning, admiring parents. In Juliette's view she demonstrated all the symptoms of a horribly spoiled little girl.

Olivier reiterated the point.

No, seriously, I think the guy's a real dick. That's what Tristan said too.

I'm wary of people who have kids with dicks, Juliette replied without thinking, infuriated by V's extraordinary ability to portray herself as a victim every time.

It wasn't a very clever thing to say, in fact it was totally stupid, but Olivier had the good grace not to appear to have noticed.

Anyone can make a mistake, he replied. But I have to admit I've found myself thinking that if the guy beat her, it may well be because she was driving him crazy.

Then he added with a smile: We didn't land ourselves an easy one.

True, you picked a real nutcase, Juliette replied.

He immediately looked sulky.

Since reading *The Woman Destroyed*, Juliette had been disturbed to acknowledge a mounting feeling toward Victoire, a feeling she had to recognize as hate. She loathed what she herself was becoming because of this woman, loathed the violence building inside her. While still in Tuscany, on an evening when she'd had too much to drink, she'd told Olivier: The thing I can never forgive her for, the thing that makes me want to crush her head between two stones, is that she wanted to sleep with you next to my little boy. Had she really said "crush her head between two stones"? Yes, she probably had. Olivier had looked at her, horrified.

And yet Juliette knew that she should have resented Olivier and Olivier alone, that it was unfair of her to focus her anger on V, because what exactly did she hold against her? Certainly not her mental imbalance—Juliette wasn't really sure she was perfectly balanced herself, or to be more precise, she knew she had it in her to lose it in a major way; but she covered for herself well, and no one had noticed yet, which was all that mattered. Maybe it was the same for everyone: Each of us hides our own element of madness as best we can, only real excesses are punished, but as for everything else, our feelings are part of the secret of being who we are, our wildest thoughts and impulses, our sickest fantasies. So long as all that stayed securely fastened inside the internal straitjacket, it was no one else's business.

The problem was that Victoire's internal straitjacket, if she even had one, was made to a standard that left a lot to be desired.

Juliette couldn't cope with the way Victoire talked about her, the contempt she displayed for her. By what right did this girl judge her and the relationship she had with Olivier? In her day, Juliette herself had had a relationship with a married man, an affair that caused her much less suffering, or at least for a shorter time, than it did the couple she'd casually maimed. Florence, who had a similar liaison in her past, had recently told her: It's our turn to pay for what we did when we were twenty-five. It made Juliette think about her then lover's wife, made her want to apologize to her. She herself had no scar of any sort from that relationship, but what about the wife? And yet not even at the time, not even at the height of passion would Juliette ever have thought to say of her lover's wife: I wish she were dead. She would never have contemplated calling the woman at work or turning up at her apartment or doing one-tenth of the things V had inflicted on her.

What sort of trauma had V been through to justify behavior like this? Juliette had no idea, and worse, she really didn't care. Until she saw proof to the contrary, Juliette felt V was still responsible for her actions; the status of victim that she constantly claimed as her own didn't give her any special rights. The way she used and exploited her fragile state, whether real or simulated, to achieve her aims was simply offensive, and Juliette's anger went far beyond her personal suffering; it was a matter of ethics, it was the Woman in her who felt offended, the Woman who, aged twenty, had believed in the Sisterhood and that Women could and should be Strong and show Solidarity in the "warm yet simple, richly varied yet concise, eloquent yet sincere" world of Womanhood. Yeah, right. And Victoire called herself a feminist. It was enough to make you weep.

A few days after they returned from Italy, Olivier came home from work looking preoccupied.

A minor relapse on the western front, he said awkwardly.

Juliette was busy cooking. She stopped what she was doing but was careful not to make any sort of triumphant gesture, not to let slip anything that might possibly be construed to mean "I told you so," settling for casting a questioning look in her husband's direction.

She's in a bad way, having a terrible time with her son, her ex, she's down south. Apparently she's been beaten by her friend, you know, the one who worked at the business school.

Juliette opened her eyes wide, not believing her luck. This time it was clearly a delirious fabrication. Even Olivier didn't seem to be taking it seriously. He shot her a look that was both hangdog and conspiratorial, a smile playing on his lips. Juliette shook her head but made no comment. The relief she felt was tempered with fury.

And still it goes on, she thought. I mean, really, this is getting worse and worse, it's ridiculous what this girl can get her to do, poking around in texts not meant for her, fantasizing about a savage murder, and now this, worse than everything else, no, it really was outrageous to put her, Juliette, in this position, to make her doubt a woman's word when she says she's been physically abused, outrageous, but you know, in this instance, with the best will in the world, it's starting to be a bit much, this girl can't spend a week with a man without being hit, that's weird, it really is a bit weird, hard to believe, she's completely crazy, period, completely in la-la land, not that women don't get beaten up, of course they do, and a lot of them, Juliette's well aware of that, a lot more than people think, Juliette certainly knows that, although, now she comes to think of it, Juliette herself has never been beaten by a man, raped, yes, more than once, beaten, never, what's that all about? How strange.

Apart from that, what did she say?

Still the same thing, it's impossible, how can we go from what we had to this, you have no right, stuff like that.

And you?

I told her we're not starting all this again. She needs to refer back to my letter.

Refer back. Juliette likes the cool administrative tone of his chosen phrase. V can't have liked it.

Then we were cut off, I switched off my cell, I think I'm going to switch it off again, that's not a problem, is it?

A little later that evening Juliette sat on Olivier's lap and stroked his hair. He tried to hide it, but he was on edge.

It's a problem, he said. We know more or less how to handle it, we're going to handle it. But it's a problem.

Then he added: You're not surprised, you told me so.

No, Juliette wasn't surprised. She was a little worried and secretly relieved. This new outburst from V fit with what she'd anticipated. The nightmare of a reasonable V settling into their landscape was fading. When V was crazy, she was more predictable.

The following day Olivier came home from the news-paper late in the evening—the children were already in bed—in a state of panic. The drama had been building for several hours. V had come back to Paris and had laid siege to him at the paper. He'd waited until it was dark enough to sneak away through the parking lots. He'd been home only a few minutes when his cell phone rang. V was outside their apartment block with her son. Juliette felt her legs turn to cotton and her heart thump in her chest.

With her son? she asked incredulously.

Yes, Olivier confirmed. He looked appalled. We can't leave her out on the sidewalk with a three-year-old.

So?

She's coming up, said Olivier.

He looks at her anxiously.

Do you mind? Is that okay?

It's eleven o'clock, or thereabouts.

She nods slowly. Does she really have a choice? If she refuses, Olivier will go down. And anyway, let's get it over with.

She goes to check that the children are in a deep sleep and their door is properly closed.

This time it's happening, she thinks.

This is the final showdown, we're coming to the end of the story.

Confronted with the two of them, Olivier will have to be clear about what he wants.

Olivier goes over to the door. She follows him, glad she's tanned and wearing a dress, feeling pretty.

Before opening the door, he throws her one last look. Imploring, or something like that.

We're together on this. Don't be hard, okay?

She nods.

In every war, whether private or global, the network of alliances is key. She's become convinced that ever since they set off for Tuscany, Olivier has changed camps.

They're together.

It'll be fine.

# 28

She's in the lobby, teetering on very high heels, holding her little boy by the hand. Definitely a redhead, hard to get redder than that, her long, curly hair loose about her shoulders, but apart from that, Juliette thinks, unbelievably ordinary. Elegantly dressed, sure, but then—still in Juliette's opinion—kind of overdressed for a summer's evening. Not wanting to soften, Juliette has only glanced quickly at the child. Meanwhile Olivier is fussing over Tom, asking whether he's tired or thirsty and wondering out loud whether there's anything in the apartment for him to play with.

It might be best to settle him in front of a DVD in the living room, suggests Juliette, concentrating all her energy into suppressing the way she's shaking. Then we can go talk in the kitchen.

He glances questioningly at Victoire. She nods. She doesn't look all that crazy, not crazy at all even. In fact very self-possessed, very nicely brought up, from a good family. As she came in, she'd greeted Juliette with a tilt of her head, not smiling but polite, as if this was some run-of-the-mill courtesy call, as if she was just popping in for a cup of tea, as if it was quite normal to show up like this at your lover's house at eleven o'clock in the evening with a sleepy little boy clinging to your skirt. Her face is pale as the moon, but that's probably her natural coloring; either way it looks calm and bears no trace of tears. Juliette wonders whether Olivier's been taking her for a ride all this time. The woman standing before her bears no resemblance to the fury he was describing only minutes before, threatening to throw herself under a car or to collapse on the sidewalk. It wouldn't take much for Juliette to almost like her. She has to force herself to remember the messages Olivier played to her and the phone call she herself had had with V. Even her voice doesn't sound the same.

They go into the dimly lit living room, and on the way, Juliette smells her perfume, her unfamiliar, stranger's perfume, obviously something heady, something she's amazed Olivier liked. The only effect it has on her is its unfamiliarity. Olivier sits little Tom in an armchair, goes over to the DVD player, and knocks over a pile of DVDs in his agitation.

Put on *Little Brown Bear* for him, says Juliette.

Just then Olivier's cell phone rings.
Yes, she's here. Everything's fine.
It's Tristan, he tells V.
Fucking pain, she says.
Tristan has hung up.
He heard, Olivier says.

Juliette, as the point has already been made, puts friendship above everything else. The good impression V made on arrival is instantly swept aside.

Yep, thinks Juliette, she sure is unpleasant.

The three of them go to the kitchen.

Olivier sits V in Emma's little chair. Juliette positions herself at the other end of the table, and he stays standing halfway between them, leaning against the stove. V talks in a deep voice, addressing herself to him alone, ignoring Juliette, who sits watching her.

For a big showdown, the atmosphere is kind of genteel.
No hint, absolutely no hint of a boxing ring.
More like the Flushing Meadows finals, the crowd silent and attentive. Tense.

V is first to serve, not taking any risks, sending the balls long and easy. She's warming up.

She starts:
For three weeks now I've been trying just to blot this whole thing out, but it's not working. It's not possible. It won't sink in. Words really do have a meaning, they do mean something.

So far Juliette can't help agreeing with V. She suddenly thinks the girl makes perfect sense.

I never told you I wanted to leave my wife, Olivier replies.

Hello, the umpire's come up to the net. He's the one returning the shots.
He's not actually the umpire.
Actually, this is mixed doubles.
Except that she and Olivier are together while V is playing alone.

No. We didn't talk about her. We never talked about her. But do you remember when we talked about flings, you told me this wasn't a fling for you.

Maybe, I could have said that, yes, it's possible.

And the last few times we saw each other you seemed happy.

You mean when we had lunch, near the zoo, times like that? Come on, that was all under duress.

Maybe, but it was still—how can I put this—there was still love.

Yes, you're probably right, yes.

Olivier is very relaxed, focused, calmly returning each shot. Juliette doesn't have anything to do, she can stay on the baseline, letting her thoughts wander.

She smokes a cigarette.

Olivier glances at her from time to time, seeking her approval. She pretends not to notice.

Shouldn't have told her you loved her, thinks Juliette.
He's only getting what he deserves.

Saying "I love you," thinks Juliette, commits you to the long term, not like saying "I want you" or "It feels good being with you." V's right, saying "I love you" is an oath, it encompasses time and the whole person: "I love everything about you, I'll love you forever or at least for a long time." You can't say "I love you," and then five minutes later "I don't love you anymore," but fifteen years later, yes. What time span is implicit in the words "I love you"?
What sort of period are you signing up for when you say that?
How long is the lease?

V is stubbornly plowing on, reminding Olivier of the loving things he said to her, like a creditor producing his acknowledgment of debt. It's pathetic, clumsy, a terrible tactic, what's she hoping to achieve? Professions of love have a very limited time value, they're only valid in the moment, at the time they're said, or written, it's a very volatile currency, which experiences monumental crashes, the whole thing can collapse overnight, V can trundle out wheelbarrow loads of these words and spill them at Olivier's feet, but it's wasted effort, they're not worth anything anymore. How can she not see that?

In return, Olivier reminds V of all the declarations he made to the contrary, saying he wouldn't leave his wife, and it wasn't possible to love two people at once.

Basically, thinks Juliette, the main criticism you could level at Olivier isn't that he's full of contradictions, he's far from alone in that, but the fact that he throws them out at random without considering the effect they may have. In love, you owe the other person a minimum of coherence, you can't just dump all your feelings and paradoxes down in a heap like that in tiny little pieces, hoping they'll get their goddamn head around it, and single out the overall feeling, put all the pieces together so that it works and has some sort of meaning.

The match is going on forever. There's a click from the DVD player in the living room.

I think the DVD's finished, Juliette tells Olivier. Put *Roadrunner* on for him if you like.

Change ends.

Olivier goes into the living room to put on another DVD. Juliette and V stay alone in the kitchen, facing each other. V asks Juliette for a cigarette, and she obligingly hands her one, then V asks urbanely:

So, did you like Italy?

Juliette lets out a little laugh, looks heavenward with a shrug. Yes, it was nice, yes, she says.

The moment Olivier is back in the room, the rallying starts up again, but the mood is different. V gets more aggressive, she comes up to the net, her returns are snappier.

Why then? she asks.

Because, Olivier replies.

Because what?

Because I don't want a divorce.

That game seems to have been won. Glorying in it, Juliette tries out a service of her own from the back of the court. Big mistake.

And why don't you want a divorce? she asks.

Because I don't want all that unhappiness, Olivier replies, still talking to V. Because when I wake up in the morning and see Juliette, I don't feel the disgust I think you're supposed to feel if you want to leave someone.

Completely bombed. The service straight into the net. Humiliated, Juliette goes and picks up her ball.

Now that's a declaration, she says.

The match is over.

V may look haggard, but she's triumphant.

She gets up, goes over to Juliette, and, surprisingly, thrusts her hand at her.

Caught out, Juliette shakes it.

Like a passive victim, once again.

V bores her Norwegian murderess's eyes into Juliette's and says defiantly:

Either way, it'll start again.

Then she comes over all urbane again as she adds:

Do you mind if Olivier sees us out to the car?

Chilled to the bone, Juliette can hardly swallow, regrets shaking the offered hand.

She nods her head.

Thunderstruck.

When Olivier comes back up, she throws herself at him and screams: You can't say it, can you? You can't say you love me.

She pounds him with her fists, with all her strength. He tries to control her, pinning her arms as best he can. This time he succeeded, he succeeded in driving her crazy too.

Eventually she calms down, and he collapses into an armchair.

I'm so disappointed.

Disappointed with who?

With myself, myself, myself, he wails, now thumping his own chest. I thought that for once I'd done what needed doing.

Downstairs V had asked him: So don't you love me anymore?

He'd replied: It's over.

So she took that to mean you still love her, I imagine, says Juliette.

He puts his head in his hands.

So I had to tell her it's over, I told her it's over, now I have to tell her I don't love her anymore, next time I'll have to tell her I've never loved her, is that it?

# 29

What I still don't understand, said Juliette, is—

Olivier didn't let her finish.

If you could stop, he roared, if you could just stop starting all your sentences with "what I don't understand is," that really would be good.

Juliette looked at him in amazement. They'd stopped at a gas station on the freeway. She was standing next to him, laden with drinks and cookies she'd just bought in the store, while he filled the tank.

Why? she asked.

It's so aggressive, I feel so under attack, constantly required to give explanations.

Aggressive, she repeated, perplexed.

Yes, aggressive.

Reformulate my sentences and make sure I never start them with "I don't understand," she instructed herself inwardly as she climbed back into the car.

The second half of their vacation was starting. They were on the way to the Vendée region. Once they were back on the freeway, Juliette turned on the radio; it was news time.

"...in a coma. The actress Marie Trintignant has been admitted to a hospital in Vilnius, Lithuania, where she was staying for a film shoot. Her injuries are the result of a violent row with her partner, Bertrand Cantat, the singer from the band Noir Désir—"

Unbelievable, said Juliette.

What's going on, Mommy? Emma asked.
Shh.

Juliette listened attentively until the newsreader moved on to the next subject, then she changed the station several times, trying to find more information. But they were all saying the same thing. Nothing was known about the circumstances of the incident, only that the actress was in serious condition and that her partner had also been hospitalized and was being treated for shock. Juliette really liked Marie Trintignant; she was very susceptible to her charm, her kind of beauty. She felt peculiarly rattled by the news. Another station was playing a song by Noir Désir, most likely not a coincidence. Juliette took her finger off the dial on the radio, settled deeper into her seat and, gazing into the distance, succumbed to the music.

*I'm not afraid of the road,*
*Gotta see how it goes,*
*dip in your toes,*

*Meandering around the small of your back*
*It'll be fine, no turning back ...*

They reached Pornic in midafternoon. Juliette's father greeted them with a smile, on the doorstep of his oceanside house. Since he'd found himself a new partner—a new slave, Juliette thought—relations with his daughter had eased so much that after years of stalemate, she could now envision spending a few days at his place. Monique was the oil in the machine, and under her influence Jérôme even managed to pretend to take an interest in the children. He helped Olivier unload the luggage, grasping a suitcase in each hand to show just how fit he still was at seventy. As he took the bags, he told them that someone had called the previous evening and asked to speak to Olivier. Juliette instantly froze.

She wanted to know when you were getting here. But she didn't want to give her name or leave a message, he bellowed in his blaring voice—he was a little hard of hearing. He winked at his daughter. If I were you, Juliette, I'd be worried.

And he shot Olivier a smutty conspiratorial look. Juliette felt like biting him.

Olivier awkwardly mumbled something about work. He could feel the weight of Juliette's stare, heavy with resentment. Yes, he must have told V that Juliette's father had a house in Pornic and that they were going there for the second half of their vacation. It was before the last drama, at a time when he still thought he could maintain a normal relationship with her. V knew Juliette's maiden name and only had to look through the phone book.

He checked his cell phone again. Since Victoire had come to their apartment on Saturday evening, she'd tried to get hold of him several times on his cell but had left no messages. Right now he was panicking at the thought that she might call Jérôme's house again—or worse, turn up unannounced. For Juliette to be humiliated like that in front of her father, having to put up with his false concern and inappropriate remarks, would probably be more than she could bear. He decided to preempt this by calling Victoire first thing in the morning, praying to God she'd keep quiet until then.

That evening he lay in bed and watched Juliette undress. With her father there, Juliette had been on edge and clumsy all evening, like a cat on a hot tin roof. The little girl she'd once been was resurfacing in spite of herself. He suddenly found her touching.

You've got the body of a teenager, he said.

She smiled at him, surprised, and came to lie next to him naked. He automatically put his arm around her as he stared up at the ceiling, trying to spot the mosquito he could hear buzzing every now and then. It had settled in a corner of the room. As soon as Olivier saw it, he pulled away from Juliette's arms, apologizing, leaped to his feet, took off his T-shirt, and rolled it into a tight ball, which he launched quickly and accurately at the insect, squishing it dead. He studied the little splash of blood on the white ceiling with satisfaction, threw his T-shirt on the ground, and, standing there naked, turned toward Juliette, seeking her admiration.

With her head resting on her elbow and laughter in her eyes, she lay there watching him, her man, posing like a triumphant huntsman.

Good job, she said.

When she stepped out of the shower the following morning, she found Olivier had disappeared.

He's gone to the beach, Emma told her when she asked where he was.

Juliette's stomach constricted. She got angry with the children for no reason, then cut across the sandy little garden that lay between the house and the ocean, pushed open the wooden gate, and spotted Olivier striding backward and forward, frowning and silent, with his cell phone to his ear. It was still early, and the beach was almost empty in the mornings. She stood there watching him for a long time, waiting for him to notice her. When he finally realized she was there, he came a little closer to her. She sat down on the sand. He moved away again. She got up and started walking away; he followed her onto the path that connected the beach to the road but stopped a couple of yards behind her, not meeting her eyes. She sat on the low stone wall and listened as he said softly, "No, of course you mustn't do that." Seen from way up in the sky, their movements would have looked like some strange insect ritual. Juliette could picture V's face at the other end, and in her head she superimposed onto V's forehead the splash of blood that the mosquito had left on the ceiling the previous evening. She stood up and walked away toward the road with tears in her eyes. She was torn between going off on her own to dispel her frustration and anger with a good cry, and being reasonable, as usual. With some regret she decided, as usual, on the second option. She went back to her father's house to collect the children and took them with her to buy bread. Olivier's little conversation with V had been going on for nearly an hour now. They'd hardly left the house before they saw him, walking along the road and heading toward them, still on the phone. The children ran toward him, but he stopped them with a wave of the hand; she pulled them away, saying, "Leave Daddy, he's working, he'll join us later."

He did actually join them soon afterward, outside the newspaper booth.

Not having a clue how furious Juliette was, he talked to her gently, and her anger subsided.

She left me a text asking me to call her. I wanted to tell you, but you were in the shower. I was really scared she'd call your dad's house.

So what does she have to say for herself?

Nothing. She's crying.

And you, what did you say to her?

That I can't see what I can do about it. That I'm not in love with her anymore. She interrupted me right away, saying, It's fine, I got *that*. She acted like she knew that already, but actually I don't think it's pointless. Saying it, I mean.

Probably not, said Juliette.


They bought their papers and some bread, then sat on a café terrace on the beach where they could keep an eye on the children playing in the sand.


I told her you were the most important thing in my life, said Olivier.

All the tension Juliette had accumulated in the previous hour fell away. She turned aside to hide her face from Olivier.

You said that to her?

Yes, of course. I've already told her that.

And is it true?

Of course. Absolutely. There's nothing more important than you in my life. Nothing.

They sat in silence for a moment, listening to the sound of the waves. Then Juliette opened one of the newspapers. They all devoted several pages to the tragedy in Vilnius. Marie Trintignant was still fighting for her life. The Lithuanian doctors were saying there was no hope for her now. At her family's request, she was to be repatriated to Paris for a last-hope operation. Bertrand Cantat had tried to take his own life when he discovered the consequences of what still looked like a terrible accident—in the heat of the argument, he'd given Marie a furious shove. She'd lost her balance and hit her head on a radiator as she fell.

The row had taken place on the evening of July 26, the evening V had come to their apartment.

And are you really no longer in love? Juliette asked Olivier in their bedroom that evening.

No, he replied, sure of what he was saying, waiting to see her reaction. After a while he added, Are you disappointed?

She looked at him, not understanding. He was smiling.

Disappointed?

Do you think I'm fickle?

She shook her head slowly from left to right but didn't answer. Olivier would certainly always be a mystery to her.

Several days went by with no news of Victoire. Juliette started to think that this time she really had walked out of their lives.

You were right. You see, I do follow your advice, Olivier said. That's three times I've followed your advice: The first was when we went to Annecy, the second was when I told her "It's over," and the third was when I told her "I'm not in love anymore."

And is it the truth? Are you sure you're not still lying to me?

No, he said. It would be impossible. Even by omission. Anyways, every time I do, it lands right back in my face. I tell you everything now. Absolutely everything. I'd tell you about the tiniest text. The tiniest thing that happens between her and me from now on.

One evening when they've gone to bed early—Olivier is exhausted and wants to sleep—she reaches for him gently, they make love, and then she says:

I'm really sorry I stopped you from getting to sleep.

You never have much trouble stopping me from getting to sleep, he says.

She lies on her back, and as she often does after they've made love, she thinks about Victoire, she can't help herself, she thinks about how lucky she was, Olivier's hands on her, the loving things he said to her, that he'd never known anything like it. It would have driven Juliette crazy too.

I'd really like it too. I'd like you to tell me you've never known anything like it, she says, her eyes wide, staring blankly ahead.

He props himself on one elbow so he's facing her, forcing her to look at him, but unusually patient.

But I *haven't* ever known anything like this, he says. Anything that's even remotely like what I have with you, I keep telling you that.

She thinks he means it, is surprised that she's still weirdly unmoved by the words. Is it too late? She can't seem to shake off the sadness that's descended on her since this whole affair started, it feels like it's here for good.

# 30

The next day he gets a text from V and shows it to Juliette:

"Still hurting just as much. I'm having terrible dreams."

Then five minutes later:

"So how are you doing?"

Another the following day:

"Give me a sign of life when you can."

He then texts back, saying he doesn't wish to talk to her, but if he really must, he can manage it at about 10:00 p.m.

Juliette is fascinated by how cold he is, the words he uses: wish, refer back. This coldness comforts her, or at least reassures her, but it also hurts her because she always puts herself in the other woman's shoes. She imagines what V will feel when she reads the words, the brutality of them; she can't help it.

The reply comes a few minutes later: "Sending you soft, loving kisses."

Fighting this girl is like punching at water, there's no point, a few splashes, a few ripples, and the hole closes right over again. Olivier has often criticized Juliette for being hard, but this girl's just made of water, no substance, just tears, watch out for that. Water's deceptive.

Olivier looks at Juliette, trying to work out what's making her uncomfortable.

These messages don't change anything between us, do they? They're just inconvenient, like a flat tire.

A flat tire?

Yes, well, just an inconvenience, no worse than that.

Juliette thinks that if she were V, she wouldn't like being referred to as a flat tire. Or an inconvenience.

The following morning, two more messages. It's started again, it's clearly not going to stop. They go to the café on the beach and discuss whether it's better for Olivier to call V with Juliette there or not. In the end they go down onto the sand. He stays a few yards away; she can see him but, with the wind and the sea, can't hear what he's saying.

Well? she asks when he comes and sits down next to her half an hour later.

She broke down when I told her you knew about all her texts and all our phone calls, she asked me if I'd shown you the text she sent yesterday evening, I said yes, and she started screaming.

What was she screaming?

"No respect, Nazi, I am a human being," stuff like that.

The disturbing pleasure of suddenly finding you've taken on the role of tormentor. She remembers V's text: "The pair of you really make me puke."

Anything else?

She wants to know how I am, if I'm thinking of her, how things are between you and me.

And what did you tell her?

I told her things are fine, that I think we're over it, I told her we'd found this togetherness again, she asked me about you, in the end I got angry, I asked, Do you want to know how we make love, is that it?

How did it end?

She said she'd always love me. But I know that's a load of crap, she's saying that to wind me up because she knows it gets to me. I don't want her to end up a wreck, but when the summer's over, she'll fall in love with someone new, of course she will.

It gets to him.


So that was it, that was her strategy, thought Juliette, rolling with the punches, undying love, hunkering down and biding her time, endlessly patient, waiting for her moment, for the crack that was bound to appear between them, the one wrong step, the clash, an escape route for Olivier, a sword of Damocles for Juliette, when the hell was this going to end? She couldn't live in constant fear like this, it had to stop for goodness' sake.

And another message two days later: "Please can you call me? I miss you."

Juliette is in the supermarket, shopping for food; her stomach's been in knots all day. Unbearably presumptuous, she thinks. As if nothing's changed. I miss you. As if he hasn't told her it's over, as if they're going to see each other in a few days. Of course she misses him. And thank goodness she is missing him. About time V learned that when your heart's broken, you can't expect the perpetrator to comfort you. You get on with it on your own. You go cry in a corner, you send insulting letters, you deal with your shit yourself. A bit of dignity and humor and even pride, that all helps too, of course.

When she arrives back at the house, she finds Olivier in the bedroom.

Major relapse, he says.

I'm not surprised, she replies.

She called on an unknown number just as I was sending her a text to say I didn't think there was much point in us talking. I picked up.

And?

It started out pretty calmly. She told me about a dream she'd had: She was lost in our apartment, which was huge, she was terrified, it was horrible. I explained why I'm now telling you everything straight out, said I'd realized that every time I didn't tell you things right away—all through June and even after that—because I thought they weren't important and they were my little secrets, well, it always came out in the end, so that's the way we've decided to do things now. She listened.

Then it gradually got more heated. She said, "But couldn't you leave me a little space, a tiny little space in your life?" I told her no, and she deserved more than a little space in my life anyway, and we have to stop talking to each other and seeing each other until she really doesn't give a damn about me, so then she started screaming, saying she would do something stupid, the usual stuff. In the end I hung up, and I had a message from Tristan asking me to call him back. And my cell phone won't stop ringing. I'm scared she'll call the house here. I sneakily unplugged the landline. I hope your father won't notice.

Juliette thinks for a moment.
He's expecting a call from the plumber, she said.

They can't help smiling at the absurdity of it all, but it isn't funny, not in the least. Juliette sits down on the bed, with her head in her hands.
We'll never see the end of it.

He's beside her, putting his arm around her.
Why do you say that? Of course we'll see the end of it. I know this is going on too long, but I promise you we're getting somewhere. With each new outburst things are said, and I do think we're making progress.
He thinks for a moment.
I feel like calling Tristan, what do you think?
Whatever.

As soon as Olivier was out, Juliette looked through her things for the paperback copy of *The Woman Destroyed* that she'd kept on her the whole time since Tuscany, and she flicked through it quickly.

"But couldn't you leave me a tiny little space in your life?"

The sentence appeared on page 243.

But in de Beauvoir's books it was the narrator, the cheated wife, who said it.

Not the mistress.

This girl really is sick, thought Juliette, she's going completely off the rails, she's playing the wrong part, she's saying my lines, she's been playing the wrong part since the beginning, for God's sake, that's why she can't bear it when we go to the movies or the theater. In the book he only goes to shows with his mistress, she can tell something's not right, it's making her panic. And it's the same deal with their vacations. The phone calls. In the book the mistress ends up calling the guy at home, threatening suicide, he can't make up his mind, but in the end he goes, but oh no, not Olivier, failed again, tough luck, it won't work with us, that's not how our story goes, not mine anyway. She must be losing her fricking mind.

When Olivier returned about ten minutes later, he was all smiles. Juliette was about to light a cigarette even though it was only four in the afternoon, which was not at all typical.

You're not going to smoke at this time of day? he said, sitting down beside her.

I started smoking again on June first. I didn't touch a cigarette in Tuscany. My smoking rate is directly proportional to the frequency and intensity of the contact you have with her. So, Tristan?

He was pretty reassuring. He told me he thought we were over the worst of it. He thought I'd hung up on her, he just said not to do that, she couldn't stand it. I told him we'd talked for an hour, that's not what he'd been led to believe. He told me to think of her as crazy, and the breakup would take longer than a normal breakup. But he's known worse. I asked if he meant similar situations with other guys, or the early days of my relationship with her, he wasn't very specific, but I got the feeling he meant with other guys.

Juliette raised her eyebrows. When Olivier had thought of calling the psychiatrist handling V, Tristan had rushed to tell her Olivier wanted to have her committed. Right now *he* was the one saying she was crazy.

Yes, fine, sure, Olivier admitted, he is a bit shifty. But this time he was kind of okay, I promise. He said he was making the most of her being away to go on vacation himself, can you believe that? I can't imagine what the guy's family life is like.

Tough, said Juliette.

Of course he realizes it looks crazy. He said, "You have no idea how lonely she is. For her to resort to confiding in me, can you imagine…"

Juliette couldn't imagine it.

What that girl really needs is a good girlfriend, she said.

They were coming to the end of their stay. After dinner they went to make a reservation at the seaside restaurant for the next day; it would probably be their last night. Then they walked along by the ocean; it was hot, and there were people in the water.

When they got back, Olivier found a message from V: "Will you call me tomorrow?"

It's been a good vacation, he said as he took Juliette in his arms in bed. Hasn't it?

She laughed.

Yes.

We've found each other again, as a couple. Don't you think?

Yes. Well, it's more for you to say. It's more you who lost us as a couple.

It's not really that straightforward, and you know that.

I know, she replied.

It was their last day in Pornic. It was getting hotter and hotter, and they went for a swim early in the morning. They'd only just come out of the water and lain down on the beach when Olivier's cell rang.

It's ridiculous, he said, I turn my phone on, and bang, she's right there.

He pressed the right-hand button to reject the call. There was also a text asking him again to call her back.

The tone of her texts exasperated Juliette: "Would you mind..."; "Could you..."; "I'd like it if..." It was childish and submissive but also a little plaintive, needling even, and in so few words. Didn't she know how to be aggressive?

Toward the end of the afternoon other messages started coming in.

"Please call me. I'm stuck in the middle of nowhere near La Roche-sur-Yon."

She's a complete wack job, Juliette said, fuming.

Olivier couldn't get over it either.

That's for sure, he said.

First of all, what the hell is she doing in La Roche-sur-Yon?

I have no idea. She was supposed to be spending a few days at Île de Ré with one of her Socialist Party big shots.

And what's she expecting you to do? Go get her?

Almost certainly, Olivier said, laughing.

So, why didn't she call the prime minister? Or a tow truck?

She's traveling by train, I think. Of course the whole thing's bullshit, said Olivier. Her message yesterday was bad enough: "Will you call me tomorrow?" like nothing had changed, after the conversation we'd had that was really was bullshit. Is La Roche-sur-Yon on the way from La Rochelle to Pornic?

I think so. Pretty much. By train, I wouldn't know.

Actually, I'm imagining that she's on the way here and she's run out of gas. Is that possible?

Maybe, said Juliette. But why?

To see me, obviously. You know she does it to us every time we're about to leave somewhere. She wants to catch me before we go back to Paris, he said with a sigh.

When they returned from the restaurant that evening, Olivier checked his phone. He had nine missed calls. And a text in the same vein as the previous one. It seems she was still in La Roche-sur-Yon.

What the hell is all this about? Juliette exploded. And anyway, how can you end up in the middle of nowhere if you're traveling by train? If something goes wrong, the train company puts you on buses, don't they?

The last message was sent an hour and a half ago, said Olivier.

He was looking worried.

This is really freaky, he said. I'm terrified she'll show up any minute.

They put the children to bed, then went back to the living room.

You're not going to call her, are you? Juliette asked.

No, no, said Olivier. But what should I do if she shows up tonight? Take her somewhere?

Definitely not, said Juliette.

Get her to sleep here?

Stop it. If she shows up, we'll see. I'll handle it. We're not going to drive ourselves crazy before it's even happened.

They went to bed, lying naked against each other. It was so hot even a sheet was too much.

It's the end of the vacation, said Olivier.

We haven't made much progress since the beginning, Juliette said. It started with fear, and it's ending with fear.

It was still good, even so, said Olivier. Or maybe it was good because of that?

Juliette lay there deep in thought. Olivier was right. V's obstinate refusal to accept the breakup had created an undeniable, beneficial tension in their relationship. They formed a united front against her. Juliette wondered apprehensively what it would be like once they were back in Paris.

# 31

*Paris, August 11 (Agence France-Presse)—Paris has just set a new record with an overnight minimum temperature of 78° on Sunday night, the French Meteorological Office announced. This was the minimum temperature recorded by the Paris-Montsouris weather station and is the highest since records began in 1873.*

The temperature was comfortable in the offices of Galatea Networks, but it had been so hot over the weekend that the air conditioning had failed in the server room. The network had crashed, and now, on Monday morning, none of the computers was working. While the maintenance team dealt with the problem, the staff wandered idly from office to office and clustered around the coffee machine. In normal circumstances an incident like this would only have added to the engineers' usual stress, but so close to August 15 the atmosphere at Galatea was almost relaxed. Pissignac, in shirtsleeves and with no tie, handed Juliette a cappuccino and took the opportunity to tell her of his as yet unofficial appointment as marketing director. On a sudden impulse, Juliette touched his arm; Pissignac was startled, spilling some scalding coffee on his hand, and looked at her, terrified. She smiled. It was fascinating actually touching such a triumph of vanity and incompetence. Fascinating, but also mysterious. She congratulated him almost sincerely. She had no appetite for marketing, even less for power, and mostly felt pleased that she'd soon be rid of him. The moment she'd finished her cappuccino, she threw her cup in the trash and tried to call Olivier again.

Right up to the last minute they'd been afraid V would show up in Pornic. Overnight, Olivier had decided to forward all his calls to Juliette's cell (where did he get that idea from? Not her at any rate). As a result, her phone had started ringing from eight o'clock on the morning they were leaving, and it went on ringing uninterrupted until noon. The calls came from a variety of numbers, including V's usual cell phone.

You can pick up if you want, Olivier had said with a sly smile.

No thanks, Juliette had replied.

She was slightly horrified to imagine what V must feel when she kept getting her voice mail. Once again she was awed by Olivier's apparently inadvertent brutality toward V, which, retrospectively, mitigated the harsh way he'd treated her, Juliette, at the beginning of the affair.

Anxious to get away from Pornic, they'd left early and stopped on the way home to see some friends who lived near Le Mans. The farther they drove into the landmass, the more unbearable the heat became. Following their host's advice and the example he himself set, they tried to cool off by dipping into a nearby pond, but Juliette came straight back out, disgusted. The tepid, stagnant water left an oily residue on her skin, and she rushed to the shower, where she spent a long time rubbing herself with soap to try to get it off, but for several hours she felt like it was still clinging to her.

They'd arrived home exhausted, and as soon as they were in the apartment, there was a palpable tension between them again. V's calls had stopped, but neither Juliette nor Olivier was under any illusions: She would try to contact him the moment he was back at the newspaper.

I'm trapped there, he said. I can't get away from her.

But this really does have to stop, said Juliette. Even in terms of your career, if it goes on, people won't be able to take you seriously.

He'd started coming up with a strategy: sending V an e-mail to warn her that from now on, no conversation between them would last more than thirty seconds, which meant he could take her calls when he wasn't alone and could hang up immediately, using a panoply of rehearsed phrases that would appear perfectly banal to uninformed ears, things like "That's great, now let's do it."

So, at about 1:00 p.m. Juliette wanted to speak to Olivier. She called the paper and got his voice mail. She tried his cell phone, which was busy and diverted her to voice mail. On her second attempt fifteen minutes later, she started to feel creeping anxiety. At 2:00 p.m. she was on the brink of hysteria. She left Olivier a brief message: "Your phone's on voice mail, please call me back." Then half an hour later, in a strangled voice: "I don't understand how you can not call me back and leave me imagining God knows what."

And she was indeed imagining everything. An endless phone call with Île de Ré. Victoire turning up at the newspaper in person, maybe she'd even been there the night before outside their apartment, maybe Olivier had found her there when he went down to park the car. Which would explain why he'd been so weird all evening. Or maybe she was in the hospital somewhere, and he'd gone to see her. Or else ...

The phone rang while she was smoking a cigarette in the reception area, but the signal was poor, and Olivier was very obviously whispering. She vaguely heard that absolutely nothing had happened; then he hung up, saying he'd call her back soon from a line where he could talk properly.

At this point a very tanned Chatel appeared and invited her for a coffee in his office. Her phone rang when she was in the elevator; she apologized to her general manager and, without any further formalities, abandoned him there and went back down to the third floor. She still couldn't hear very well but grasped that Olivier had gone home to have lunch and hadn't realized his cell phone was off. He hadn't had any news, other than a parcel that had been mailed the day they'd left Paris and had arrived at the newspaper: a gift.

A notebook. An item of stationery. She heard the words "she already had" and "car" but gave up trying to understand what he was saying. She apologized, saying, It brings back too many horrible memories.

I understand, he said. But really, wait. I left you a message, did you listen to it?

No, she hadn't yet listened to it, but she did now once she'd hung up, as she walked up the stairs.

"Juliette, listen, I have a moment alone to tell you this clearly, my schedule from one minute to the next. I haven't heard anything at all, and it would be completely impossible, impossible, d'you get that, for anything to happen without my telling you. So stop. I understand how this can happen, but you're really losing it right now."

She immediately felt much better and climbed the last few stairs on the way to Chatel's office with a lighter step.

That evening she made Olivier explain the business about a present. It was a present for Emma, a little notebook with a padlock. Anyway, she already has one, doesn't she? I think I saw her playing with one in the car. Juliette listened in disbelief. The notebook with a padlock that I gave her for her birthday, yes. Hang on. She's buying a present for Emma?

Of course, because in her mind she and I are going to become a family, he replied lightly.

Seeing the expression on Juliette's face, he was quick to continue: I knew she'd sent me a present for Emma, she told me on the phone. But don't worry, I put it in a box I picked up from the post office, along with a sweater she gave me, and I'm going to send it all back to her. That's what I came home to do at lunchtime.

Juliette was slowly digesting the information.

And she posted it the day after she came here?

So it seems, he said rather irritably. Listen, it really doesn't matter.

Was there a note with it?

No.

And did you send a note?

Yes. I said: "I can't accept this gift for Emma. It's over, you know that."

Juliette stifled the wave of loathing that rose inside her every time this other woman came near her children, and they didn't mention the subject again all evening.

The night was even hotter than the one before, and she had trouble going to sleep. Olivier kept getting up too; they were lying naked, without a sheet, and with the doors and windows open.

The following day they went to bed early, and Juliette started leafing through an old copy of *Marie Claire* left at the end of the bed. She was half lying on her back, and every time she turned a page, the paper brushed pleasingly over her nipple.

Don't be grumpy, said Olivier, rolling toward her. You have an impeccable husband, okay children too, but most important a perfect husband. It's not a bad start, is it?

He kissed her stomach.

Stop it, you won't keep your promises. And this heat's gotten me all wound up already.

Really? he asked, starting to take an interest.

And he started stroking her with more conviction.

He made her come several times before penetrating her.

Then they went and sat together in a bathtub full of cold water. It was a couple thing, tender and intimate, something they never did. She suddenly felt good, relaxed. She made a few jokes.

You see, it's put me in a good mood, it doesn't take much.

The heat of their bodies didn't take long to warm the water by a couple of degrees.

After that she slept like a log.

# 32

Juliette continued to take a passionate interest in the Vilnius tragedy. She devoured the newspapers every morning. After her last-chance operation, Marie Trintignant had died in Paris. The autopsy showed how many times and how violently Cantat had struck her. In his statement, the singer had mentioned the actress's hysteria and claimed that she'd thrown herself at him first, screaming, "Go back to your wife," and he'd only tried to calm her. The victim's family had quite rightly been scandalized by this defense. Kristina Rady, the abandoned wife, had caught the first plane to Vilnius to support the man who was still her husband and the father of her children. There were photos of her very tenderly putting her hand on the presumed murderer's head as he emerged from court a broken man. Juliette felt that, on a different scale, this case had peculiar resonances with what she was going through, and she was amazed by the incredible coincidences: the hysterical mistress—or not; the flouted but loyal wife, who was also blond. What was more, the drama had happened on July 26, the evening Victoire had come to their apartment and Juliette had launched herself at Olivier, punching him furiously.

And so?

So nothing.

She restricted herself to stating the facts, drawing no conclusions, finding no signs or hidden meanings.

She was however disturbed by Cantat's accusations of hysteria against Marie Trintignant. After all, she knew about V's so-called hysteria only from what Olivier had told her. Perhaps he was painting a darker version of the situation in order to disguise his own weakness. Perhaps, thought Juliette, it was the men who drove the women mad.

Or the other way around.

Or both.

Perhaps it was love that drove people mad.

Or desire.

Or both.

Even the press was struggling to unravel the meaning of the Vilnius affair. The magazines were steering a course between passion—sublime passion, it was bound to be sublime—and deadly obsession; they were tying themselves in knots trying to explain how such wonderful love between two such pure souls could have ended in such a sordid, headline-grabbing event. A group of artists had paid dearly to buy a column in *Le Monde* to say that, in spite of everything, Cantat was a great guy. A psychoanalyst explained that no one is beyond the clutches of madness or a state of raptus, if you don't understand that, you've never been in love; a psychiatrist referred to femmes fatales who, even though they were victims, completely dominated their aggressors; meanwhile, following Gisèle Halimi's example, feminist groups howled that this was a chauvinist crime and made Marie the poster girl for the cause of Battered Women.

V, as chairwoman of SHE!, had stepped into the breach.

When Juliette found out from the press that V had taken part in a protest demonstration about violence against women, held on the place Colette, she knew that the vacations were over and that it wouldn't be long before Olivier had news of her again.

The anticipated phone call came one morning a few days later: a short conversation with Olivier. Victoire began by apologizing to him, he replied by asking her to stop calling him, she started to cry. Then yelled that no one had the right to treat a person like that. Whereas she really did have a right to talk to him. Are you going to do the same thing again and divert my calls to your wife?

This call was followed by another, which he rejected, but he then called her back. They had an equally short conversation this time, but it "went well," as he later reported to Juliette. Olivier told Victoire about how they'd left Pornic, how—because of her—he'd ended the vacation just as he'd started it, in a state of fear and on the run. She replied that she couldn't contemplate not seeing him again, not talking to him again. He objected that it was "unreasonable" to want to talk to someone who had absolutely no desire to talk to you. She conceded the point and ended the call by thanking him.

She'd told him that she'd missed her connection at La Roche-sur-Yon and all the hotels had been full.

I don't even know if it's true, Olivier added.

And even if it was true, Juliette said, you're not her husband or her father and you're no longer her lover. You're not her friend either. If being her friend means being Tristan, if it means scooping her up every time she collapses in the street, I couldn't take it.

I agree, he said. Maybe I should tell her that next time. That I'm the last person she should call when she has that kind of problem.

Not even the last, thought Juliette.

A few days later Juliette called Olivier to suggest they have lunch together.

Did you try to get me on my cell? he asked.

No, she hadn't tried. Why?

I've had several missed calls but no messages, he said.

Oh really, she said, how weird. Who on earth could that be?

She called him back in the afternoon: So, any news? No, he replied offhandedly, no news.

That evening, while he's washing his hands, he says: So, I had another phone call. We spoke for five minutes.

What did she want?

I don't know. It's just what you thought it would be, I think, her new strategy. Putting the relationship on a more normal footing.

And what else?

Nothing much, she's preparing for grad school, working hard. It was very mundane, there was no suggestion of seeing each other.

Basically you had a nice chat.

I didn't want to make a scene. If she's happy to call like that every couple of weeks, to be honest, I can't see the problem.

Juliette can see it, she can see the problem, but she doesn't say anything. She pulls a sulky face.

Watch it, he says, if it stops you from sleeping every time she calls, I'll be tempted not to tell you.

With that she feels completely deflated, flat as a pancake, bludgeoned.

A little later, he adds: And I reserve the right to choose when I tell you. When you called earlier, for example, she'd actually already called. But I was kind of in a meeting, I didn't want to talk about it.

So you told me "no news." But correct me if I'm wrong, the danger—well, the thing that could happen, the thing I think has already happened—the danger is that there could be something you don't tell me right away, then later there isn't the right moment, and it becomes impossible to say.

She doesn't get any sleep, thinking about this threat: I'll be tempted not to tell you. And that casual way he said "no news" on the phone, as if to remind her he's still perfectly capable of lying, would you like to see? Look, I'm doing it right now.

In the morning she's exhausted; she tries to hide it, a wasted effort. In the end she spits out: It's not her calling that's stopping me from sleeping, it's the fact you're still contemplating lying to me. Please be straight with me, Are you still telling me everything?

Of course I am. He leaves the house irritably.

She tried to call Florence but ended up getting Paul. Tell me what you think. Is it normal for her to be calling still and for them to be "chatting," is that normal, am I the one who's crazy? Tell me, you're a psychiatrist.

No, he said forcefully, I don't want to give you advice, I'd really rather not, but *no*, you're not crazy, *no*, they can't be friends, and this girl strikes me as seriously destructive.

Okay, thanks. I'm going to confront Olivier this evening. I just wanted to be sure.

She's waiting for him in the armchair in the hall. He comes home at 10:00 p.m., as planned.

Bang on time, she says.

What's the matter? he asks anxiously.

I'll tell you. Come, I've made you something to eat.

She takes him through to the kitchen, and he sits down to a plate of pasta.

I wanted to tell you I've been thinking about it all day, and first of all, I think it's disgusting after everything that's happened these last few weeks, for you to say, "If her calling bothers you, I'm going to start lying to you again." Not even "if you keep criticizing me" or "if you get angry," things I could just about keep under control, except that would actually stink too, now I come to think of it, but banning me from *feeling* or telling me I have to lie to you about how I'm feeling, that's outrageous. And like I said this morning, it's not her calling that stops me from sleeping, because incidentally, if that were the case, I wouldn't have slept all summer; it's you threatening me like that. Second of all—and I talked to Paul about this today to check that I'm not crazy, you can ask him what he thinks—I don't *want* you to keep on having these little chats with her, like you say, "if she calls me every couple of weeks like that, no problem," of course, and after a couple of months why not meet up as friends? It doesn't make any sense, last Friday you asked her to stop calling you, five days later she calls you and what you basically say to her is "Hey, it's good to hear from you" et cetera, so why wouldn't she do it again after that? It's like telling a kid he's not allowed on the table, and the next day he climbs on the table and you act like nothing happened, you stroke his hair and give him a kiss. So from my point of view, I couldn't care less if she has one of her outbursts, do you get that? Every time she has one I feel like we're getting somewhere, whereas now I suddenly feel we've gone back six weeks.

Obviously, she wasn't able to say this all in one go. On the third sentence he got to his feet, thumped the table, and yelled, You're pissing me off. Then he went off into his study with an "I'm not talking to you anymore," but she followed him and kept going. In the end he calmed down and said, I understand what you're saying deep down, but it's the way you say it I can't stand, it's so melodramatic, waiting for me in the hall, "I have something to tell you."

Yes, I know, she replies, you often criticize the way I say things, and my syntax, and I'm really sorry, but under the circumstances you might just overlook the occasional flaw in the presentation and listen to what I'm actually saying.

He collects himself.

I basically agree with you, he says. Only today I thought that if she called, I'd tell her that even conversations like the one we had yesterday aren't workable. You see, we're on the same page. But I have to admit I'm pissed at having yet another scene.

While she's at it, Juliette adds: As for putting off telling me the truth, I understand when you're in a meeting, but if you could avoid lying by saying "no news" and just tell me *something*, let me know you'll tell me later, personally I'd prefer that.

A few days later, as Juliette predicted, Victoire called Olivier again.

I declined the call, he said, then I sent her an e-mail telling her she shouldn't call me anymore, that even calls like the one the other day were a problem for us. She asked me what I meant by that "us." Of course I did it on purpose, so she could see we're together in all this now, you and me are together. She didn't like that, obviously. I e-mailed her again to say I'd call her back to explain it over the phone. Then I went to pick up the kids. I was rushing from one thing to another, so I texted her to say I'll call her tomorrow.

He looked at her, worried.

You okay?

She laughed halfheartedly, shrugged. I'm okay, yes, I can't really see what else you need to explain to her, but hey.

The next day, before leaving, she planted a little kiss on his lips and asked, When will you call her?

This morning, I think, after the editorial meeting.

Will you call me afterward?

If you like.

What sort of time will it be?

Midday or so.

At twelve-thirty Olivier called her.

Well?

A major scene. Like when we were at your dad's house. She cried and screamed, No one has the right to treat another person like that. I told her that the state she was in was proof enough this wasn't about just five minutes' chit-chat every couple of weeks. Then I had no battery left on my cell, I told her I'd like us to end the conversation, but that if she wanted to wait until my cell ran out of battery, we could. We were cut off.

How long did it go on?

I wasn't counting.

Approximately?

Fifteen minutes.

Hmm.

I've had three voice mails since.

Saying what?

The same thing, pretty much. As usual. Right, gotta go.

Okay. Bye, sweetheart.

That evening he told her V hadn't called back.

Uh-huh, Juliette grunted. Good, good. We'll see.

He added, I just want to tell you that now I not only don't feel anything for her, I don't even understand how I could have been attracted to her. When I think back over it, I can see just how violent the whole thing was.

Still nothing? Juliette asks the following evening.

Nothing at all.

He looks relaxed.

Do you think there's a possibility she won't call again?

I've no idea, he says. Yes, I think there is. It's the first time that after an argument like that, I haven't had any voice mails for twenty-four hours. Mind you, I did tell her that when she called and I saw her name on the screen, I felt pissed. I even thought of asking her—

He broke off.

What?

No, I won't do it, obviously. But I did think of it. I think she thinks that she and I still have secrets. I thought of asking her to e-mail you all the messages I wrote her. I know she's kept them, she sent me one yesterday. She asked me on the phone how I felt rereading my words.

And?

I told her it felt like...it had been a kind of madness.

Juliette thinks about this.

Did she send this e-mail before your phone call?

The day before. You know, I told you I wrote her first, and she'd replied et cetera. She sent one of my old e-mails as an attachment.

Oh yes, yes, yes.

Silence.

And what did this e-mail say?

I don't really remember, it doesn't matter.

"I love you, I've never felt like this, it was wonderful," stuff like that?

Stuff like that, yes. What difference does it make?

If she's going to send them to me, I'd better be prepared. Even if you haven't told her to do it, she might want to do it anyway. Either way, I think there's going to be some kind of closure, she can't just stop calling you like this. I hope there'll be a conclusive act. *I* need one.

There was her letter.

And that was a hell of a conclusive act. So conclusive that three days later she walked out of here, saying "Anyway, it'll start again." No, I'm thinking more something like sending me all her e-mails, something that will really stir up the shit between you and me.

Or dropping some bomb at work, he says thoughtfully. I have to admit I prefer the first option.

Juliette is secretly amazed that he seems so confident about how she would react in this first scenario, so sure she would cope with this like everything else.

A few days later she asks him, What did you say the other evening about how violent something was?

He doesn't understand, tenses visibly.

What do you mean, something violent? What are you talking about?

You said something, and I'm not sure I understood what you meant, so I'm asking again, that's all.

Violent, I don't know, yes, I must have said I was only now realizing that all this, which at first I thought was so lighthearted, how violent it's been. For her, when I see that she still wants to call me. For you, of course. And for me too.

That's not what it was, she says.

She trawls her memory, comes back on the attack five minutes later.

You said something that made me feel better, about how you now saw the whole affair, I thought you meant there was something violent about her, about your relationship.

I don't believe you, he says, exasperated. If you want to know how I view the whole thing now, why isn't that what you're asking me?

You told me you couldn't understand what attracted you to her, didn't you, something like that?

Yes, I said I couldn't understand how I could have been attracted to her.

There, that's what it was.

She suddenly feels all chirpy. He looks at her, dumbstruck.

I already told you that ten times.

No, you definitely did not, she says happily. You never said it before, and I wanted to be sure I understood properly. Sorry I'm making you go over some things you said, but you know I've had to listen to you I don't know how many times saying stuff like "It really was pretty special," et cetera.

Yes, but I could have had that feeling that it was pretty special with absolutely anybody. I needed to have that experience at that particular time, that's all.

She feels like saying he's going a bit overboard, "absolutely anybody" is too much. Let's say "almost anybody." Either way, she's feeling better, they can take the kids out on their scooters.

# 33

Days went by. The heat wave was over, so was the contract workers' strike. They were counting up the deaths in retirement homes. Bertrand Cantat was waiting for his trial in his Lithuanian prison. Nadine Trintignant was writing a book about her daughter in which she referred to him as "your murderer." Juliette was having more and more trouble tolerating her work at Galatea Networks. Since his recent appointment, Pissignac had adopted an infuriating swagger. He'd moved into his new office right next to Chatel's on the fifth floor and was more obnoxious than ever. She was surprised to find herself daydreaming about resigning, leaving Paris, and starting a new life somewhere else.

Olivier had no more news of Victoire.

Good, said Juliette. But still, I'd like an acknowledgment of receipt, something. She must be taking her grad school exams now. The written exams are this week.

Really? Olivier replied, surprised. You know more about it than I do.

On September 9 Victoire called Olivier when he was in a restaurant. He told her he couldn't talk, and she didn't call back. As a security measure, he sent her an e-mail shortly after that and copied Juliette in on it:

From: Olivier
To: Victoire
Cc: Juliette
Sent: Tuesday September 9 2003 21:34

Ref your call at about 3 pm today
Don't try to contact me again.
May I remind you of our last phone call:
You told me your thoughts and I listened. You mentioned violence, humiliation etc. but for my part, I've made a definitive decision not to have any further contact with you. There's no room for discussion.
Stop calling. I'm really very sorry to have to inflict those words on you again.

I don't know whether that e-mail was worth sending, Olivier said to Juliette that evening, I think she really gets it this time.

Juliette didn't react.

The next day he told her what the reply was.

Victoire said she was pleased with how she'd done on the entrance exams, and if everything went according to plan, she was off to Strasbourg for three years, which meant there would be no opportunities for her to see Olivier, so he needn't worry.

At the end she thanked him, without saying what for. She said "With love from."

I hate her, Juliette thought.

On July 3 the French president, Chirac, named the twenty members of the Commission Stasi with responsibility for considering the question of secularism in France. While the country waited for their conclusion, the debate about whether Islamic girls should be allowed to wear the veil in school calmed down, and V had to find another hobbyhorse to keep her media presence alive.

Poor Marie Trintignant, thought Juliette, it turned out to be her.

The Vilnius affair had shone a light on the issue of violence against women. Several television programs were devoted to the subject, and true to her strategy of using her status as the leader of a feminist group to raise her public profile and provide a springboard for her political career, V made sure she was invited all over the place.

She was talked about in the press and took part in a few TV panels.

Juliette stopped reading the papers or turning on the TV.

One day Olivier came home and said lightly, I don't know whether this comes under our transparency agreement, but there's a two-page spread about her in the paper this week. Thierry wrote the piece.

Juliette dissolved into tears. Olivier was astonished, irritated.

I can't help it if I cry, she said.

I thought we could joke about this, not that you'd pull a tantrum.

I'm not pulling a tantrum, I'm crying. I'd cry even if you weren't here, do you understand?

He did his best to comfort her.

I slept with the girl ten times, that's all, we can't torture ourselves over it for ten years.


Not long after that he found Juliette sobbing again. She was standing in the lobby of their building with a copy of *Le Monde* in her hand. He looked at her, horrified, and took her in his arms.

Honestly…If you knew how much I regret…when I see you like this.You mustn't be sad anymore.There really isn't anything to be sad about.The only thing that matters to me is us.

She could hardly catch her breath.

Tell me she doesn't mean anything to you, she spluttered.

But I already told you that a thousand times, without you asking. I couldn't give a damn about these articles.The other day I saw her on the Info Channel at work, I thought she looked kind of ugly, if you want to know, but well, I won't go on about it.

I think I'm depressed, she blurted.

No, come on, don't say that, what's happening to you, what's going on? he asked anxiously.

I don't know, I feel like crying all the time. When I think back over all this, I feel like our love's been damaged, trampled. I'm tired. I need to sleep, I'm not sleeping enough.

Well, sleep then, he said.

He sighed, put his face in his hands. I feel terrible.

I don't want you to feel terrible, she said. It'll pass. It just takes time.

She blew her nose and wiped her eyes.

I need to dig myself out of this sadness, she said. You know, maybe I really should take a lover myself. Or go back to see a shrink.


Olivier was worried, he confided in Paul.

Where do you stand with this girl? Paul asked.

It's over, Olivier replied. Totally over. I saw her on TV the other day and I even felt—how can I put this—a sort of hostility. It's all going on inside Juliette's head now.


But I get the feeling it's still going on big time inside your head, was Jean-Christophe's comment when Juliette reported this conversation to him as a conclusion to her account of the summer's events.

Jean-Christophe was back from a long vacation in Asia; he looked gorgeous and very tanned. And seemed happy. A new man in his life, most likely.

Juliette shrugged.

According to Paul, the process of de-idealizing love is a big step toward happiness.

Jean-Christophe thought for a moment, his eyes narrowed.

I kind of agree, he eventually replied. I've always thought passion was terribly overrated, given the energy/satisfaction ratio involved.

So I'm on the right track, Juliette concluded with a bitter little laugh. In my case, the de-idealization process is under way. It's even pretty far advanced.

On another day Juliette had lunch with Florence. She was tired; her eyes kept filling with tears. Florence had also seen Victoire on the Info Channel.

How did you know it was her?

Well, it said her name on the screen. Hey, she's really not that great. She looks older than she is.

You're sweet. Juliette smiled feebly.

I swear she does, she has more wrinkles than you do.

Florence had preoccupations of her own. At a friend's party they'd chanced across a female patient of Paul's. Feeling uncomfortable, Paul had kept away from the woman all evening but hadn't warned Flo in time to keep the two of them from getting into a conversation. Ever since, this patient had been carrying out an in-depth inquiry into Flo among their mutual friends. Flo had spotted her outside the children's school and suspected the woman was following her.

What's her pathology exactly, then? Juliette asked.

Florence shrugged.

Some standard-issue neurosis, she said. She's doing a complete transference thing, she hates me, that's all.

Florence smiled at Juliette.

You see, you're lucky. My situation's worse than yours. Paul doesn't have a choice, he can't stop her analysis. She has a hold on him.

This story made Juliette even more depressed. It was a sad state of affairs. We all were heading toward a world in which our therapeutic relationships were more solid and lasting, perhaps more necessary even, than those we had with the people we loved.

The very day the admissions results for grad school were announced, Juliette checked the Web site and had mixed feelings when she saw that, once again, Victoire had over-estimated herself. As an elected official and thanks to the increased age limit from which she'd benefited as a single mother, she had taken the supposedly easier entrance exams. And yet she still hadn't been offered a place. In all probability, this meant she would continue living in Paris. Juliette found she was back to longing for some conclusive act to demonstrate clearly that Victoire had broken up with Olivier, something that would allow her, Juliette, to move on at last.

She was no longer in any doubt about Olivier's determination or of his honesty toward her. Their relationship had changed since the beginning of the summer. There was a new gentleness between them, something akin to friendship. But they had different ideas about the reasons for this change. We made love, said Olivier. We talked, said Juliette. One evening they argued, as they used to in the old days, over a pointless issue, a nothing; then things calmed down, and the following day Olivier sent her an apologetic e-mail, which ended with these words: I love you.

Juliette imperceptibly started to feel better. She started thinking their marriage could last in this new unbalanced state.

One evening they went to the movies, and Juliette remembered the day she'd discovered Victoire existed.

Thank goodness she made such a scene the day we were meant to go to the movies, she said. Otherwise you would have gone to Rome together, and I'm sure now I would never have been able to forgive you. It would have been over between us.

Maybe deep down there was never any question of my going to Rome with her, he replied. Maybe it wasn't just by chance that I told you everything that day.

I want us to go to Rome at the end of April, she said. I want you to book a room at the Farnese to celebrate the thirteenth anniversary of when we met.

Or the end of May for the tenth anniversary of when we got back together.

No, she said, the tenth anniversary at the end of May can be in Paris. I'll take care of that.

The Farnese's expensive, said Olivier.

She looked at him.

But it's fine, he added very quickly. One night. After that we can go to Maria's.

Okay, Juliette replied, smiling.

Maria had finished her chemotherapy, the news was good, and she was keeping her morale up. Juliette admired her courage and had recently felt a strange surge of affection for her.

Back at home that evening, she goes to sleep in Olivier's arms. Do you love me?

Of course, he says, you're my love. Do you know that you're my love?

So do we still agree on this? Next year you'll ask me to marry you again.

And you'll accept or not.

And I'll accept or not.

They smile at each other.

I really did you a hell of a favor not throwing you out, she says. You'd have ended up with her, and I wouldn't give your relationship very long. In six months she'd have been saying, "If that's the way it is, go back to your wife," you'd be punching her in the face, it would be Vilnius all over again.

He stares at the ceiling, thinking out loud:

If she called back now, I know what I'd say to her. I'd say that I love my wife. She wouldn't believe me, but hey.

I thought you'd told her that. Already.

I did tell her that. But it wouldn't do any harm to say it again.

He's quick to add: Anyway, she probably won't give me another opportunity to.

They lie in silence for a while, then Juliette says:

If she ever did give you the opportunity, instead of saying "I love my wife," you could say "I love Juliette." It would be better. The person, not the role, you see. I'd like that better. If you could.

When you think back over it all, what do you think about? she asks him.

He considers this.

Mainly, I'm glad it's over, I think. Relieved. On the other hand, I can't really regret that it happened. I needed it so I could know where the two of us stood. Apart from that, I'm basically left with the sense of an ordeal that we came through together. Before, what I had with her, that's nothing.

Her letter. Do you still have it?

It must be around somewhere, yes.

I want you to destroy it. I don't want you to forget about it and for Emma or Johann to come across it one day.

He goes to find it, crumples it without even looking at it, and throws it in the trash.

She thinks it should have been burned.

But the following morning she's changed her mind and rummages through the trash after he's left for work.

She can't find it and starts to panic. Could he possibly have taken it out of the trash, again?

No. Thank God. Here it is. She opens it up carefully and stows it in the bottom of her bag.

Jean-Christophe said: Keep everything written.

You never know.

# 34

Even if she lived to be a hundred, Juliette thought she would never, never ever forget that moment. The horror of that moment. The cops showing up at their place in the early hours of the morning, leading Olivier away in front of his wide-eyed children—thank God he'd escaped handcuffs, but only just—and a horrified Juliette. His trip to the Thirteenth Arrondissement, flanked by police officers in an unmarked car, the sudden feeling he was an actor in a movie, some terrible B movie. Being in police custody.

It all had come to a head ten days before. Juliette had called Olivier at work to remind him that they were having dinner with Florence and Paul that night. She wasn't working that day and would plan to take the children over to their house as soon as they got out of school. She wanted to know what time he would finish and be able to join them. Olivier had completely forgotten this dinner. He looked at his watch, caught out. Four p.m., and he hadn't started writing the piece that the editorial department needed this evening. Luckily it was a very short article, under five hundred words. He reassured Juliette, promised he'd get to their friends' place by eight at the latest, and immersed himself in his work.

At seven he logged in to the paper's computerized editorial system, dragged his text into the window left for it, and heaved a sigh of relief. He turned off his computer, put away his things, said good-bye to his coworkers, went down the stairs four by four, and headed for the subway station.

At seven-thirty he was at Jaurès station. He decided to stop off at home to have a quick shower before going to Florence and Paul's. He whistled as he soaped himself in the lukewarm water. He was just coming out of the bathroom in his robe when someone rang the doorbell. Thinking Juliette had forgotten something and didn't have her key, he opened it unsuspectingly.

It was Victoire. She was standing on the doorstep shaking, her face distraught, as it had been in the darkest hours of her scenes during their short relationship. Before Olivier realized what was happening, she was in the apartment and had started wailing. Someone was coming down the stairs. Olivier quickly closed the door behind Victoire to stifle her cries, and she threw herself into his arms, sobbing. Panicking, he pushed her away, and as he did, his loosely fastened robe fell open. He retied the belt hastily and made an awkward attempt to soothe her, with a *Groundhog Day* feeling of reliving the same nightmare over and over. He wondered how this was possible, how did Victoire know he'd be at home? Perhaps she'd followed him. But it was most likely just a coincidence, she could just as easily have shown up when Juliette and the children were here. In her current state she was capable of anything. He was holding her by her arms, trying to keep her away from him, stopping her from clinging to him, and stammering, I don't understand, what's gotten into you? We said it was finished, I thought this time it was okay, you got it, we're not starting over. In return she was saying it was impossible, her life made no sense without him, she'd forgive him everything if he left his wife now and came to live with her, there was still time.

She's completely crazy, she's really out there, thought Olivier.

"Out there": That was exactly the expression.

She needed to get out there, out of his apartment and out of his life.

Just then Olivier's cell rang: Juliette's ring tone. Then the landline. His cell again. He was late; Juliette wanted to know where he was. He tried to be authoritative, raised his voice. That's enough, now, you can stop this performance. Anyway, I have to go, people are waiting for me. The thought of Juliette gave him strength, he remembered what he'd promised her and went on to say, I don't love you, do you get that, do you get that, yes or no? It's Juliette I love, Juliette, my wife. You and me, we're done.

Victoire tore away from him and looked at him with loathing. Your wife, she said scornfully. Is that her calling you now? Is it your little wifey whistling? Go on then, run, little doggy, run, what are you waiting for? Good God but he hated her, he watched her face distorted with anger, she looked like a hyena, how could he even have kissed her? Olivier's heart was beating furiously, pounding in his head; his eyes were clouding with red. He balled his fists. She kept going. You fucking used me, I hope it did you good, now you can show off at work, it's pathetic, pathetic, going around telling everyone you screwed me, you poor asshole, if you knew how much you make me sick with your shitty little life and your shitty little family. Standing on a side table in the hall was a framed photo of Juliette and him with the children. As Victoire said these words, she picked up the picture and hurled it to the ground with all her strength. The glass broke. Olivier was making a superhuman effort to control himself, he'd never struck a woman in his life, and he wasn't going to start today, but how could he get rid of her? The phone had stopped ringing. What if, wondering what was going on, Juliette was heading home? At the thought of her coming face-to-face with Victoire, he succumbed to panic. He snapped the front door open and, making use of the element of surprise, grasped Victoire by the arm, pushed her out onto the landing, and slammed the door behind her, then leaned against the doorframe, shaking, and listened.

Victoire had stopped screaming.

The silence lasted several seconds.

Then Olivier heard a dull thud, the sound of someone falling in the stairwell.

# 35

At the time he didn't understand what had happened. He hadn't wanted to contemplate Victoire's voluntarily throwing herself down the stairs. He'd convinced himself that in the state she was in, with her stupid high heels, she must have missed a step and tumbled down a few stairs on her backside. He'd hesitated before going to see whether she needed help, decided to wait awhile. He'd gone over to the window that looked onto the street, hoping to see her come out of the building. When he still hadn't seen her several minutes later, paralyzed with fear and still in his bathrobe, he'd made up his mind to go downstairs. She wasn't there either. He'd allowed himself to breathe again. She must have left even before he went to the window, which means it must have been very quick, she couldn't have been badly hurt.

He'd gone back up to the apartment, picked up the shards of glass from the photo frame, got dressed, joined Juliette at Florence and Paul's place, and told her the whole story.

In the ensuing two weeks he'd had no news of Victoire, but he kept an eye out for her name in the media, and when one of his coworkers said he'd seen her in a Socialist Party executives' meeting, he felt completely reassured. Until the day he was arrested, when he learned that after leaving his place that evening, Victoire had gone to a doctor to show him her bruises before accusing Olivier of physical violence in an official statement she made to the state prosecutor. Whom she happened to know personally. Olivier thought bitterly that he should probably count himself lucky she hadn't accused him of sexual assault while she was at it. It only needed someone to have seen him rushing downstairs after her in his bathrobe and it would have been an open-and-shut case.

Juliette had reeled under this blow too. But once she was over the initial shock, the fact that Victoire was pressing charges, with the backup of a medical certificate, had the paradoxical effect of producing an intense feeling of relief in her. If V had been pregnant, by what would now have been more than three months, there was no doubting that this fact would have been added to the file as an aggravating circumstance. The specter of a paternity suit being thrown at Olivier, a specter Juliette had tried to keep at arm's length all these weeks but had never entirely forgotten, was finally evaporating for good.

The very day after the arrest, she called the personal assault unit to ask for her own statement to be taken. The woman handling the file replied warmly, saying Juliette's call was timely because she'd been planning to contact her anyway. Olivier had been confident his good faith would convince the police, and hadn't felt he needed to appoint a lawyer. Before getting down to the precise allegations against him, which he'd obviously contested, he'd given a detailed account of what had happened in the last few months and had tried to explain Victoire's psychological problems. Unfortunately he'd deleted all her texts and e-mails, and had no material evidence of what he was saying. Besides, he was fully aware that the fact that the plaintiff was an elected representative, who counted several eminent figures in the political world among her contacts, and appeared to enjoy perfectly good mental health, did not plead in his favor. He'd then said that Victoire had been on sick leave for a year, a fact that could easily be verified. The woman he told this to had raised an eyebrow, apparently astonished; he felt sure that in her hearing a few days earlier, Victoire had failed to mention this detail. Olivier had given the police her psychiatrist's name and Tristan's number, explaining that the latter was a close friend of Victoire's and could confirm what he, Olivier, was saying. All in all, although deeply shaken, Olivier had emerged pretty confident—and free—from his spell in police custody, which had lasted several hours.

When Juliette came out of the unit's offices a few days later, she too felt reassured. The inspector had said she was about ready to end her inquiry; with Juliette's hearing, she felt the file would be closed and she'd be sending it to the public prosecutor.

Everything Juliette had told her, she'd confided kindly, matched her own conclusions, and although she couldn't second-guess the public prosecutor's decision, she led Juliette to understand the case would in all likelihood not be taken any further, particularly as Olivier had no prior record, and, anyway, there was nothing really serious about the bruising Victoire had sustained. Feeling a little calmer, Juliette had then said that in that case she was amazed by how quickly and brutally Olivier had been arrested. The inspector gave a fatalistic shrug, clearly meaning that had the plaintiff been just anyone, it surely wouldn't have been like that, but because she was an elected representative, the prosecutor expected the police to be especially diligent—a shame, thought Juliette, that this sort of diligence wasn't granted instead to Real Victims, who waited with fear in their bellies for their partners to come home and beat them up.

Despite his past lies, Juliette had never doubted Olivier's word for a moment. He'd sworn that there'd been a lapse of several seconds between his pushing Victoire onto the landing and the sound of her fall, and Juliette believed him when he said he was not responsible for that fall. She was sure that Victoire had staged it.

This was the conclusive act she'd been hoping for.

It was Victoire's Revenge.

Before asking Juliette to sign her statement, the inspector asked her to confirm that Olivier had never, never ever raised a hand against her, that he was incapable of physical violence, particularly toward a woman, and Juliette felt the shadow of Kristina Rady looming over her. Apart from the fact, she thought, that the Vilnius incident had had a tragic dimension, their story was still little more than a paltry settling of scores. At the last minute Juliette remembered Victoire's letter that she'd retrieved from the trash when she was at her most desperate, and she'd brought it to the unit to support her statement. The inspector had read it with interest and had taken a photocopy to put with the file. It was clear from the letter that Olivier was the one who was terrified. This probably didn't sit very well with the version of events Victoire had given the investigators—a version Olivier had not seen in detail—because Juliette got the feeling this letter was enough to tip the inspector's opinion definitively in their direction.

The hearing was over, Juliette had signed her statement, but the inspector didn't seem in any hurry to end the conversation. She was eyeing Juliette with curiosity.

Why didn't you register a complaint for harassment? she asked abruptly.

Juliette was taken aback.

Me?

From what you've told me, this woman harassed you on the phone, she followed you back to your apartment...there are laws against that.

Juliette didn't know how to reply. Complaints weren't her style, that was all. She remembered the day she'd told Olivier, "I warn you, next time she sets foot in our apartment I'll call the cops," and the look of hatred he'd flashed her.

She stammered.

It wasn't easy, my husband was in love with her...

The inspector nodded, unconvinced, and studied Juliette a little longer, apparently intrigued.

You must love him very much. Not many women would have put up with that.

Juliette's face went blank.

The inspector didn't probe any further but stood up, offered her a friendly handshake, and wished her luck. The prosecutor's decision, she said, wouldn't be made known for several months, but Juliette didn't need to worry too much.

Juliette walked out onto the rue du Château-des-Rentiers, feeling unsettled. She'd had this feeling several times in the last few months but never so forcefully as now. No one understood the way she'd reacted to Olivier's unfaithfulness and his lies and Victoire's aggression. Her behavior was incomprehensible. She felt humiliated by the inspector's compassion. She could feel tears welling in her eyes and at the same time a wave of rebellion rising inside her. She thought of her rape again. For in the same way people have a very clear idea of how women who've been raped behave, she thought, they also have a very clear idea of how a betrayed woman should behave, what she can and can't put up with, what she should and shouldn't accept, and in the name of women's dignity and integrity, the consensus was that it was their duty to be intransigent, that they were required to choose glorious solitude over flawed love. There was a very strong consensus on the subject; even Yolande had said it: Women mustn't put up with everything men throw at them. Well, tough, if that's what other people say. Juliette would bend, but she wouldn't break; she was the reed, she wouldn't be destroyed. It was her right to stand by her flawed love, her marital love, her shitty love, as V would have called it, even though Juliette knew that on the scale of different loves it was right at the bottom, way down at the bottom, at floor level, a pathetic thing, tiny, not like V's passion, which was something magnificent, infinitely superior in every way, and right at the top, way up at the top, off the scale, on a level with sublime passions, broken facial bones, and slanderous denouncements.

Two days before, she'd watched a television program about domestic abuse in which V was a contributor, and this time she hadn't switched it off, despite the bottomless feeling of disgust she felt seeing V parading as a mouthpiece for genuinely abused women. False victims, Juliette thought, are the worst enemies of real ones. For someone who was supposed to have been beaten up two weeks earlier, V looked in amazingly good shape, and Juliette had felt the same fascination as she had when Pissignac had been promoted to marketing director. People like him, and V, seemed to rise up inexorably. There was no doubting this girl had a great future ahead of her.

As for Juliette, she was no longer sure she'd be voting in the next elections.

A few days earlier she'd had a long conversation with Paul. When she asked him exactly what he thought V's psychological condition might be and how she managed to pursue her career like this despite her excesses, Paul shrugged. He didn't know V, so he couldn't hazard any sort of diagnosis, and anyway, he pointed out, psychoses weren't a rarity among political figures—that sort of conviction was very persuasive. Juliette was struck by his words: Paul had mentioned hysteria, which was associated with resolving the Oedipus complex and with idealizing the father; the absence of structuring frustrations, which is transformed into fantasies of omnipotence and a feeling that other people never measure up to you. To round it off, he talked about the eroticizing of suffering.

Becoming locked in a vision of the self as a victim in love, he added, means refusing to see the intrinsically conflictual nature of every relationship.

With that he stopped talking, a smile hovering on his lips, his eyes sparkling behind his round glasses. Juliette looked at him, wondering what he was getting at. Then he picked up a pen and drew a diagram of circular arrows on the tablecloth.

Couples, he explained, usually operate on the model of reciprocal constraints. It's the revolving door principle. The individuals seem to be going around in different directions, but the two movements actually have the same effect.

Which means? Juliette asked.

That each partner asks the other for something that, deep down, he or she doesn't believe is possible. For example, a woman who's been abandoned by someone will ask her new lover to love her but, as if she's afraid love is always followed by abandonment, she'll subconsciously do everything she can to drive him away.

Juliette wondered whether this little speech was aimed directly at her. She eyed Paul questioningly, but he just smiled. The first thing Olivier had done when they met was to leave her for Maria. Is that why she'd so quickly convinced herself he was the love of her life?

Refusing to be psychoanalyzed so summarily, she stared at the circle drawn on the tablecloth and replied with a precision typical of her engineer's mind.

In mechanical terms, your diagram here reminds me more of a bicycle wheel. So long as it's moving, you keep your balance thanks to kinetic energy. The minute you stop, you fall over.

Yes, that too, Paul agreed.

How about you and Florence, is everything okay? Juliette asked, on the counterattack.

Paul smiled, amused.

Florence was constantly making recriminations against him. Despite her own friendship with Florence, Juliette often wondered how he put up with her. She told him their relationship was a mystery to her.

Seen from the outside, he replied without batting an eyelid, all relationships are mysteries.

# 36

Tired of being viewed as a brute by his female coworkers, Olivier had asked to leave the political department. He was now looking after readers' letters and Internet forums. He could now work from home, spend more time with the kids, and ignore the rumors describing him as a thug that continued to circulate in the stiflingly small world of journalism.

Meanwhile Chatel had completely unexpectedly offered Juliette the position of technical director at Galatea, and she had moved into an office on the fifth floor, not far from Pissignac. In return, she'd had to relinquish her reduced workweek, but the work was fascinating, and Olivier was freer than he used to be, which was convenient.

A few months later, as predicted, V's charges were filed with no further action, and Juliette and Olivier were naturally relieved. Juliette remembered her conversation with the inspector, and without much conviction, she suggested Olivier himself should lodge a complaint against V for slandering him. Olivier's response was predictable and unequivocal:

There was no way he'd be "putting more coins in that slot," in his exact words. With the charges dropped, he felt he'd come out of it well, even though there was no doubt the whole business had done him wrong. Anyone who knew about it—and V made sure more and more people did—still had lingering suspicions. V fostered these suspicions as best she could and exploited them to help fund her business by complaining vociferously about the failings in the justice system concerning physical abuse toward women.

If you played that game, Juliette thought, you couldn't fail.

# 37

Franck walked Juliette all the way back to her apartment block. As they came out of the restaurant, he'd said several times, You look fabulous. He looked at her. You have a few gray hairs, you lost some weight, your short hair really suits you.

I'd like to see you again, he said outside the entrance to the building.

Easily done, she said. That's not complicated now.

Over lunch they'd talked about the present and about the time that had slipped by since they'd last seen each other—twenty years, at least.

And now he was suddenly telling her something about how he'd thought about her, every now and then, through all those years.

She leaned against a parked car and, keeping her eyes on the ground, replied: I have this memory…[she hesitated, then looked up at him]…How many times did we make love, once, twice, three times?

He swayed as if she'd hit him, was so visibly distressed that she was shaken too.

I have this memory…how can I put this…of your body…It was hard.

What she meant was the still vivid memory of his naked body under hers. He was, what, her third or fourth lover? His body under her, his muscles, his hard tongue in her mouth. His penis.

He laughed a little. Hard? I'm not sure I'm getting this.

He kept looking at her, his face distraught. We were too young. Especially me. I was convinced you were looking for something I couldn't give you.

If he kept looking at her like that, she was going to start crying.

You were so much more mature than I was, he said. I have to say you'd been thrown into life pretty brutally.

She didn't know what he meant, and thought suddenly about her abortion.

I don't know if you knew at the time, but I was pregnant. I had an abortion halfway through my oral exams.

His eyes were drinking in every inch of her.

Of course I knew. Don't you remember? You told me everything the first night.

Their first night? Juliette felt a black hole opening up before her and threw herself into his arms, hugging him.

They'd probably made love much more than two or three times. She was afraid she'd hurt him.

I was in love, though. I do remember that.

He shrugged.

We were so young.

He was still staring at her, still looking emotional.

He said her name.

She felt her longing explode deep inside her like a bullet fired at point-blank range. She hadn't felt that for years. The intensity, the brutality of desire. She pulled away from him, caught Yolande's eye as she walked past them on the sidewalk. Oh my God, if one of the neighbors saw her.


On their second lunch they kissed in the car. He was perfect, said exactly what had to be said: What's happening to us? What's going on? Look at me, tell me, why did you call me? You tell me you've been faithful for ten years. What's going on?


So she told him the story, as briefly as possible.


When she finished, she added: I don't want to use you.

You haven't changed, he said. You're the most incredible mixture. I thought you were gorgeous. And you're still beautiful. I've always thought you were incredibly intelligent, brilliant.

How could someone cheat on a woman like you? he asked.

I get the feeling you're ready to do something stupid, he said. Don't do something stupid. Think of your kids.

It's weird, he said, it's nothing like holding someone new in your arms, a stranger.

I want you, she said.

I want you, he said.

It's that wanting that's really missing, she said, not the pleasure. Don't you think?

They both went their separate ways for a few days' vacation with their families. They had a couple of hasty conversations but, never sure they were truly alone, they were tense and abrupt.

It is incredible, though, she said. I've just realized how incredible it is.

You've only just realized, he replied. I realized right away. But you're responsible for all this, aren't you?

She loves his voice. So familiar she can't believe it's possible, I must have known someone recently with the same sort of voice. She can't think of anyone.

Her name spoken by that voice, the look in his eye that goes with it, makes her shudder.

I'm still pretty shaken up after the other day, he said.

Me too, she replied.

Three days without speaking to each other. She can't stop thinking about him. She fantasizes, that she's making love to him or, better still, that she's sitting next to him in the car and making love to him without touching him, in words.

If they made love to each other for real, it would probably all be over.

She thinks about Olivier too, obviously, about how much she'll hurt him, about the hell they've just been through that she definitely doesn't want to experience again.

She can't help herself. She's been drawn in.

A two-minute conversation the day she gets home. She's left a message, waits three hours for him to call back, and it already hurts.

She needs to stop now. If this is about understanding what Olivier experienced, she's there. She knows. But it's impossible to stop now. The wheels have been set in motion, and they're powering away in the dark.

He calls her, she asks if the weekend went well. He says, Yes…well…three days without talking to you does kind of feel like a long time, though.

She doesn't say anything.

They're seeing each other tomorrow evening.

**NELLY ALARD** is an actress and screenwriter who lives in Paris. Her first novel, *Le crieur de nuit*, received the 2010 Roger Nimier Prize as well as the 2011 Grand Prix National Lions de Littérature and the Simone and Cino Del Duca Foundation Prize for the Support of Literature. In 2013 she was awarded the Prix Interallié for *Couple Mechanics*, the first woman to win the award in more than twenty years.

**ADRIANA HUNTER** studied French and Drama at the University of London. She has translated more than fifty books, including Hervé Le Tellier's *Eléctrico W*, winner of the French-American Foundation's 2013 Translation Prize in Fiction. She won the 2011 Scott Moncrieff Prize, and her work has been short-listed twice for the Independent Foreign Fiction Prize. She lives in Norfolk, England.